About the Author

Virginia Moffatt was born in London, one of eight children, several of whom are writers. Her eldest brother has written a theology book, one sister is a poet, a second a translator and her twin is a successful author.

Virginia has always been a writer, but only began taking it seriously in 2004. Since then she has published *Rapture and What Comes After* (flash fiction, Gumbo Press, 2014) and *Echo Hall* (novel, Unbound, 2017). She also writes non-fiction. She blogs at 'A Room of My Own' where she publishes flash fiction, short essays, and reflections about writing and reading.

After working in social care for thirty years, she has held a variety of jobs and is currently employed as a procurement and contracts manager in a multi-academy school.

Virginia is married to Chris Cole, director of Drone Wars UK. Two of their children are now at university, the third lives with them at their home in Oxford.

The Wave

Virginia Moffatt

OneMoreChapter

A division of HarperCollins*Publishers*
www.harpercollins.co.uk

One More Chapter an imprint of
HarperCollins*Publishers*
1 London Bridge Street
London SE1 9GF

www.harpercollins.co.uk

A Paperback Original 2019

First published in Great Britain in ebook format by
One More Chapter 2019
1

A catalogue record for this book is
available from the British Library

ISBN: 978-0-00-834074-2

This novel is entirely a work of fiction.

This novel is entirely a work of fiction.
The names, characters and incidents portrayed in it are
the work of the author's imagination. Any resemblance to
actual persons, living or dead, events or localities is
entirely coincidental.

Typeset in Minion by Palimpsest Book Production Ltd,
Falkirk, Stirlingshire

Printed and bound by CPI Group (UK) Ltd, Croydon, CR0 4YY

In loving memory of Pip O'Neill, and my parents,
Ann and Joseph Moffatt, who taught me
how to face the wave.

'Death closes all: but something ere the end,
Some work of noble note may yet be done'
                              Alfred, Lord Tennyson, *Ulysses*

The Divine Office (Liturgy of the Hours)

'the recitation of certain Christian prayers at fixed hours according to the discipline of the Roman Catholic Church' before the second Vatican Council (1962-1965)

Vespers Evening Prayer 'At the lighting of the lamps' 6.00 p.m.
Compline Night Prayer before retiring 9.00 p.m.
Matins During the night or Midnight
Lauds Dawn Prayer 3.00 a.m.
Prime Early Morning Prayer 6.00 a.m. (the first hour)

Twitter

MattRedwood@VolcanowatchersUK 21 s They were wrong about the Cumbre Vieja volcano on La Palma. If you're in Cornwall don't even stop to pack. Get out NOW.

BBC Breaking 12.20 p.m.

. . . *Downing Street confirms the Prime Minister has cut his bank holiday weekend short and will be making a statement at 12.30 p.m.*

Facebook
Poppy Armstrong

30 August 12.45 p.m.

I am going to die tomorrow.

Sorry to be so melodramatic, but if you've seen the news, you'll know it is true. It took a while to sink in, didn't it? The idea that, only yesterday the geologists at

Las Palma were so sure the seismic activity they were observing was nothing unusual they didn't even raise an alert. The revelation that if it hadn't been for a bored intern noticing that the tiny tremors were building to a huge unexpected one, we'd have been carrying on with life as normal. The knowledge that it took so long for that intern to persuade her superiors that they were about to witness a massive volcanic collapse, there are now less than twelve hours before half the mountain falls into the sea, raising megatsunamis that will hit the American, UK, Irish and African coasts by eight o'clock tomorrow morning. So that I and thousands of others will be killed by the time most of you are getting out of bed. The how, when and why of our deaths making headlines around the globe, before it has even happened.

I'm still trying to think of it as a blessing of sorts. After all, it's more than most people get – victims of car crashes receive no such warning; the terminally ill can't know the exact point their disease will overwhelm them; the elderly face a slow decline. I'm lucky, really, to know the precise instant my life will end. It provides me with this one, tiny consolation: knowing how much time I have left means I get to plan how to spend each moment. And I mean to make the most of every last second.

Because . . . for me, the information has come too late. The authorities have managed to evacuate some hospitals, and it seems that local dignitaries can't be allowed to drown, but they say there is no time to execute a rescue plan for the rest of us. We will have to make our own way, by road, rail or boat: three million people attempting to leave this narrow peninsula simultaneously. Already, it is a less than edifying sight. The roads are too narrow, the station too crowded, the boats available in insufficient numbers. I do not want to spend my last hours like this, frantic, rushing, out of control, in a race I have no chance of winning.

Perhaps I am wrong, but I have weighed the odds, and finding them stacked so heavily against me, I have made my choice. If this is the remaining time allotted to me, I will spend it doing what *I* want. The sun is shining, the surf is up. It's a perfect day for the beach. There's no point keeping the shop open, so I will pack a bag, bring my tent, and pitch it down at Dowetha Cove, my favourite place in the whole world. If this is to my last day, my last night, I want to spend it doing everything I love: swimming, surfing, lying out among the stars. I want to make the most of the time left to me.

Perhaps there are some people out there who feel the same. If so, it would be good to have company.

Join me, won't you?

Like Share Comment

25 Likes 10 Shares

15 other comments

Alice Evans Roads not too bad at the moment. I wish you'd come with us, Poppy, but sending you lots of love x

20 mins

Jill Hough Poppy, I just don't know what to say. Thoughts are with you.

10 mins

Andrew Evans Saw the news couldn't believe it. Are you really stuck? Useless, I know, but sending love.
Yan Martin We've not met but I've made the same calculation. See you on the beach.

20 seconds

VESPERS

Poppy

I stand at the top car park, gazing down on the beach below. If I needed any confirmation the news is not a hoax, the silence and emptiness provide it. On a sunny August Bank Holiday, with an offshore wind, the sea should be full of surfers and screaming children diving through the waves. The sand should be crammed with family groups, couples sunning their bodies side by side, pensioners in their fold-up chairs. Everywhere should be movement: parents struggling down the slope with bags and beach balls, their offspring running ahead, shouting in anticipation of the joys to come, people in wetsuits striding towards the water, surfboards under their arms. But the beach is vacant, the air free of all human noise, the only sound the screeching gulls and the ruffle of the wind in the bushes behind. It is as if the world has ended already and left me, a sole survivor, to survey the remains. Normally, the sight of an empty shoreline would fill me with joy – the knowledge that these waves are for me alone – but not today. Today, I find myself unable to move, either to the car to collect my belongings, or to the beach below. Instead, I stand by the sea wall, staring at the yellow sunlight glistening on the blue-green waves, listening to the birds whose calls rise and fall with my every breath . . .

Years ago, when I was little, I used to stand at this spot, on the last day of the holidays, not daring to go down. Every step forwards was an admission that it was nearly all over, that there was nothing to look forward to but the long journey home and school the week after next. Every year, Mum, perhaps, sensing my emotions, and who knows, maybe even sharing them, would tap me on the shoulder, 'Come on, I'll race you,' she'd say, knowing that my desire to win overtook every other feeling. Standing here, I'm overwhelmed by a wave of longing for her, wishing she was here, issuing me with such a challenge again. A useless desire at the best of times – she has been gone so long, I sometimes struggle to remember her face and voice – but today it seems more pointless than ever. What could she do, if she were here? What can *anyone* do?

A glance at my watch is a reminder how quickly the minutes are passing. The sun is still high in the sky, but it is moving inexorably towards the west; the surf is at its best now, but that will pass. I need to get down there if I am going to make the most of it. And really I should make the most of, and stick to my plan, otherwise I might as well have gone with the others in the van. I have to be decisive. I return the car, grab my rucksack, tent and surfboard and walk towards the slope. I will have to come back later for the furniture and refreshments, but it's still awkward carrying so much stuff. I stagger down the stone path, which gradually gives way to sand, first a light dusting and then my feet are sinking among the hot grains. It is a struggle to stay upright with all the equipment I am carrying, but I force myself forward, sliding down the incline until I reach the firmer sand just above the high tide mark where it is a relief to put everything down. As I am sorting out the pop-up tent, a memory surfaces – another day, another pop-up tent, another beach – Seren and I preparing for our first surfing adventure. 'It's not as good as Dowetha,' I'd said, 'but it will do.' I had had every intention of bringing her to Dowetha one day, before every-thing went wrong between us. I never will now.

Once I have set up camp, I realize I am happy to be alone for once. I appreciate the freedom of undressing with no one watching, the fact that there is no one in my way as I run to the shore. No one to jockey with for the best position in the water. No one to block me as I throw myself into the ocean, drenching myself in the spray and foam. The sea has been waiting for me; I gasp at the cold, as it welcomes me into the rise and fall of its chilly waters.

When I have acclimatized to the shock, I paddle out to the breaker zone, watching for the swell coming from the horizon. I position my board, wait for the right moment, and then stand upright to ride the wave. Soon I am lost in the act of riding through water and foam, warmed by the sun, cooled by the wind, repeated over and over again.

I am so absorbed that, at first, I don't notice the man on the surfboard. It is only when he has paddled to the breaker zone a few yards away from me that I spot him. He is tall, white, with a mass of curly hair. He nods hello and I acknowledge him with a raised arm. I don't like to talk when I'm surfing. I prefer the silent communication of lying in wait together, rising to hit the crest at the perfect moment, sweeping towards the beach at speed until the foam peters out into tiny bubbles, where we can jump off and head back to our starting point. Over and over again, we follow the waves in the same pattern. Occasionally, I give my companion a smile after a particular good ride, but in the main we are both focussed on the line between the area where the surf forms and the beach. Our world is reduced to this one short journey from sea to shore, over and over again until I have lost count of how many waves we've ridden, how long we've been in the water.

At last, the chill of the sea begins to penetrate my wetsuit, my shoulders start to ache, and so I shout, 'Last one?' He nods, and we ready ourselves for the next swell. This time, as we mount our boards, the wind builds up and it is harder to stay steady. I crouch down low to avoid toppling off, glancing behind to see a mountainous wave racing towards us. I time it perfectly, catching the crest and pulling myself up. I stand triumphant on its back, enjoying the thrill of the rush to the shore, before I notice something is wrong. The other surfer is not with me, and when I look back I can see his surfboard floating on the water. There is no sign of him. In a panic, I paddle towards it as fast I can, though it's a struggle in the stronger current and the increased swell. Spray breaks over my head, salt water fills my mouth, causing me to retch. Ahead of me I can see a head bobbing up and down, arms flapping; then he sinks below the surface, a few feet from his surf board. My arms are hurting with the effort, my body exhausted with the battering of the waves, but I cannot abandon him. I cannot. The knowledge that I cannot abandon him, gives me a spurt of energy, shooting me forwards to the spot where I saw him go under. I dive down, eyes smarting, searching for his body in the blur of blue, green and yellow. I can't see him, and now my lungs are gasping, so I swim to the surface, gulping huge breaths of air. I am about to dive again, when to my relief his head comes back up again. I race towards him, grabbing his torso before he can sink again, holding tight as a large wave rolls over our heads. He is heavy, gasping for breath; it is a struggle to keep hold of him, particularly in these strong currents. His board is still bobbing to the side; his leg has caught on the leash and it is too tight to disentangle out here. I tell him to lie back and he relaxes into my body – which makes it easier to keep hold of him as I backstroke towards the board. As we arrive, he has the sense to grab it and I can push him up. Soon he is lying on top, red faced, worn out from the effort to survive; for a brief second I wonder whether it was worth it, for either of us. Then practicalities intervene: we are cold, tired, we need to get back to land.

Thankfully, once he is a chance to recover his face begins to lose its purple flush; he is able to raise himself to a paddling position. I give him a push in the right direction, before striking out for my own board. I mount it and follow in his wake as he begins to paddle, first tentatively, then with more strength and purpose. At last we reach the shallows, where we slip off, wavelets splashing around our feet. He staggers to the edge of the beach, trailing the surfboard behind him, before sitting in the wet sand. The cord has tightened with the struggle; it takes both of us to loosen it, and wrest the rope off. He is left with an indented mark all the way around his ankle which he rubs ruefully.

'Thanks. Thought I was going to drown for a minute ...' He grins, 'Ironic, considering.'

'Considering.' I return his grin. 'I'm Poppy.'

'I know. I saw your post. Yan.'

'You're the one who replied? I thought you might be joking.'

'It's like you said ...There's no point hanging around, we might as well make the most of what's left.'

I am so happy that someone read my post that I smile broadly, immediately regretting it when his returning smile is accompanied by a look I find all too familiar. My 'puppies' look', Seren used to call it, in honour of a long chain of men whose crushes developed within minutes of meeting me. I never quite understood it as I never intended to give them any encouragement. Seren thought it was a combination of having big breasts and smiling too much. Perhaps she was right, but I'd discovered by then that people trusted me when I smiled, and being penniless and parentless, I'd always had more need than she for allies. Back then it was easy enough to deter the puppies with a casual kiss for her and an arm around her shoulder. I have long since lost that defence, and somehow I always find words fail me. I am left with deflection, so I suggest we go back to my car for the rest of the gear. Thankfully, he is happy to agree, and by the time we reach the car park, the doe eyes have gone. Which is a relief. Because now he is here, it is a physical reminder to me that I haven't imagined this whole thing. There really are only a few hours left. The knowledge is terrifying enough without any of the complications unwanted attention can bring. What I need tonight, is a friend, someone who can help me make it through the dark. Watching Yan lift the furniture out of the car as he chats away cheerfully, I think he might be able to do that, which is a comfort, because comfort is what we both need.

Yan

*P*oppy . . . *Poppy* . . . *Poppy* . . . A name to march by. A vision of pale beauty on Facebook – slim hips, round breasts, long black hair - that is going a long way to helping me fight off the fear. It's a fantasy I know, but given I've had the shockingly awful misfortune to be trapped here by the floods, I deserve a little luck, don't I? *Poppy* . . . *Poppy* . . . *Poppy* . . . I walk through the shrubland to the beat of such thoughts. There's a breeze up, but the sun is strong, and with a tent and food supplies on my back, the journey is tougher than I'd expected. I haven't been this way for ages, and have forgotten how the land rises and falls, the bushes overhang, their roots throwing obstacles in my path. I stumble frequently. Today is made even worse by the waterlogged soil, which has created bog after bog for me to navigate. Normally the sight of the sea ahead – greeny-blue water glinting in the sunshine – would be enough to motivate me, but today it has lost its allure. It's not just the thought of the destructive powers that will be unleashed tomorrow – I am thirsty, sweating; my legs ache, my boots are clogged with mud. I can't help feeling that by the time I arrive at Dowetha I'll be too tired to appreciate it.

At the stile onto the cliff path, I stop for a break, relieved to remove my burdensome rucksack and hurl it to the ground. I find a bottle of water and a bar of chocolate, plonk myself on my coat to protect me from the damp earth. I sit with my back against the wall, gazing back at the cow field I have just crossed and the standing stones in the distance. I'm hoping that by not looking at the sea, I can quell the panic, and pretend for a short while at least this is an ordinary hike, on an ordinary day, and nothing much is about to happen. I fail miserably. As soon as I stop, the full force of the last few hours sweeps over me like a tidal wave. My mind races through the events of the day, over and over again, leaving me no room to escape . . .

The news trickled out slowly at first. A twitter rumour followed by a rash of speculation on Facebook. Followed by a breaking news line on the BBC. By the time the first full article was up, their website crashed. Last time that happened was 9/11. Remember that? I was sitting at a computer at York, horrified by the suffering of people thousands of miles away. Today, as my screen filled up with a dizzying array of facts and figures, images, analysis, infographics, it dawned on me that this time the rest of the world would be the appalled bystanders, while I was here, right in the thick of one of the danger zones. And being on peninsula meant this particular danger zone would be more dangerous than most. I'm a statistician; it didn't take long to make the calculation, to realize there was no hope of getting out of here alive. They were too many people, trying to leave by too narrow an exit. We didn't have a chance. With the whole of the South East and Welsh coastlines expecting a battering, the government made it clear evacuation efforts would have to be focussed further north. There would be no use relying on the Dunkirk spirit to come to our aid. It's not that people wouldn't want to help, but anyone with a boat would be too busy getting themselves to safety, they wouldn't have time to come down here and rescue us. There was some talk about organising plans, but most commentators agreed that there weren't enough airstrips, and with the airlines arguing about airspace, the unions about staffing, and the Transport Secretary being too paralysed with doubt or fear to intervene, the wrangling got nowhere. It was clear to me we were on our own. There would be no way out.

I'm not sure how long I sat at my desk, considering my options. Should I cadge a lift from James in the vain hope that we could outrun the water? Hide under the duvet, with a bottle of whisky for company? Pills before bed, so I'd never wake up? None seemed appealing. It was only when I turned to Facebook that I found what seemed to me the obvious solution. The minute I read Poppy's post, my mind was made up. Making the most of the time left sounded better than sitting in traffic or drinking myself into a stupor. And she was hot, the kind of woman I wouldn't normally have a chance with. But in these circumstances? Anything might happen. So I gathered my belongings together, swimming trunks, warm clothes for the night-time, kagoul just in case, camping equipment, sleeping bag, tent, food and threw them in a backpack, and because I hate leaving a book unfinished, my partly-read copy of *The Humans*.

I was just emptying the fridge when there was a knock at the door. It was James, bag over his shoulder, keys in hand, road map at the ready. Oh, James. Ever the optimist. I tried to explain to him he was wasting his time but he wasn't having any of it. He was desperate to persuade me to join him but I was equally adamant. Story of our friendship. Him half-full, me half-empty. Always leads to arguments in the pub and then days of mutual sulks till one or other of us tries to put it right. Today we took great pains not to go into our usual combative mode. When it was clear we couldn't agree, we had a rather awkward goodbye on the doorstep and went our separate ways. It was so odd, that goodbye on the doorstep. Five years of propping up the bar, putting the world to rights, and now we'll never see each other again . . .

. . . Never see each other again. The reality of that hits me like a wave of cold water. I managed to keep the dread at bay while I was walking, but now I've stopped for a bit, it is rising in my stomach again. I push it back down again as I get to my feet. I should keep moving, live moment, by moment. There is simply no point thinking about the future I don't have. It doesn't change anything. I hoist my pack back on my shoulders. The straps chafe; it feels heavier than before, but the rest and food has done me good. As I walk, my thoughts return to Poppy; I imagine her falling off the board, enabling me to come to her rescue. In her gratitude she opens up her wetsuit, and lets me rub my face in her breasts, and more besides . . .

Poppy . . . Poppy . . . Poppy . . . I walk to the beat of her name, thinking only of the ground in front of me, till I reach Dowetha. I dump my luggage at the clubhouse where I keep my surfing gear. I grab a wetsuit, and force my thighs through the constrictive material. Jeez, I've got fat. Working from home has confined me too my desk for too long. I catch a glimpse of myself in the mirror, wincing at the beer belly that indicates too many nights in the pub, too few in the water. *God, I need to lose weight*, an absurd and pointless anxiety now. I pick up my board and leave my gear behind. There is no need to lock the doors behind me – who will come here today but me?

As I turn towards the slope, it suddenly occurs to me that the message was fake, that I have turned up here full of ridiculous hopes that are about to be dashed. That all I've done is tire myself out with a long walk to reach a deserted beach and the prospects of facing my death alone. It is a relief to reach the top of the slope and see signs of her presence. A small blue tent pitched above the high tide mark, towels and a blanket spread out beside it. And there she is in the water: a slim figure, striding the waves till they crash on the shore. It is all the signal I need to run down to the water's edge, ploughing through the waves with my board. I am careful not to come too close, I don't want to crowd her. She is so focussed, she doesn't notice me at first; it is not until I reach the surf zone that she acknowledges me with a wave and a smile. What a smile. It drives away every fear. I no longer care about anything other than the bliss of surfing alongside her. Waiting in unison for the swell, positioning the board, crouching, standing, riding the wave, till it takes us back to the beach. Then striking back out to sea for more. Again and again and again. We do not speak, we do not need words, already we are intimate. I could stay like this for ever.

That's until the cold begins to seep through my wetsuit as the waves begin to strengthen in intensity. Ploughing back to the breaker zone begins to be an effort. Pride won't let me stop till she does, and I am grateful when, at last, she shouts this should be the last one. I ready myself for the coming wave, rising at its approach, and then . . . disaster. The surf is stronger than I anticipated, I turn too sharply and slip off the board, my foot tangling in the rope. Suddenly, I am dragged under the water, eyes stinging with the salt, a rush of blue, green and yellow, a deafening gurgle of sea pounding my ears. I try to force myself upwards, emerging to gasp a breath before another wave knocks me down again. My lungs begin to hurt with the pressure, my eyes to tingle, my head to pound, as I flail up and down through the foam. Fuck, this is what is like to drown. As I slide down again, it crosses my mind that I might as well let it happen now. If I survive this, I am only delaying the inevitable. Why bother fighting it for the sake of a few more hours? But even as I have the thought, something inside refuses to give in to it. I push myself up through the water, and suddenly there she is. Her arms are round me pulling me through the waves. It wasn't quite the way I planned it, but I love this sensation, lying back safe, cradled, as she transports me to my board, pushes me up, and helps me get back to the shore.

Once out of the water, and after we have disentangled the rope, I am able to sit back and catch my breath. I rub my ankle, red from the pressure of the rope, and thank her. 'Thought I was going to drown for a minute . . .' I grin as the thought occurs to me, 'Ironic, considering.' She grins back. When we introduce ourselves and I explain her Facebook post brought me, her smile is even warmer; I melt. I can't stop myself from giving her a dopy smile in return. Luckily she decides she needs to change, giving me the excuse to return to the surf hut and do the same. By the time we meet at her car to collect the rest of her gear, I have composed myself enough to ensure I don't make an absolute tit of myself.

Half an hour later, we are sitting back at our tents, with a cup of tea and two large slices of Madeira cake. She has taken off her wetsuit, and is now dressed in shorts, a loose cotton shirt and a bikini top that is low cut enough to give a good view of her breasts. I look away quickly, hoping she hasn't noticed me ogle them, though her arch smile suggests I haven't been as discreet as I'd wished. I resolve to rein it in. I need to take this easy if I'm to have any success

'So what now?' I say as I finish the last gulp of tea.

'Fancy a swim?'

'Always wait at least half an hour in case of cramp.'

'Says who?'

'My mother,' I say, laughing 'Fuck knows if it's true. It's just what she always said. Which reminds me.' 'I suppose I'd better call her . . .'

'. . . but you don't know what to say?'

'Nope. How about you?'

'My parents died a long time ago.'

'Sorry.'

'Don't be. Are you close to your mum?'

'Not especially. She lives in Poland now. She's a bit of a recluse.' To be honest, I don't know if she'll even have seen the news. It's been at least six weeks since we've spoken, so how can I ring her now and tell her I'm going to die tomorrow? I could add that our relationship, always a tricky one, had got worse after Karo's death, but that's way too intimate for someone I've just met. I take a different tack.

'What do mums know anyway? Let's risk cramp.'

The wind has died down, but the current is still strong. Without our wetsuits the water is gaspingly cold, though once we start moving around we soon warm up. We race each other across the bay, dive and tumble, splash and jump the waves as if we are ten years old. It is exhilarating till the exertion of the surfing catches up with us and we decide, simultaneously, to head back to our camp. We dry ourselves off before flopping onto the towels. Poppy starts spraying suntan lotion.

'Do my back and shoulders, will you?' she says sitting up. Her skin is soft to the touch; I rub the lotion quickly and pull on a shirt before she can return the favour. I dive back on the towel and pick up my book; the last thing I need now is an embarrassing arousal. Particularly when she is lying so close to me. I wish I could reach out and touch her, confident that she'd respond in kind but she has given no indication that such advances would be welcome and I don't want to push my luck. I force myself to focus on the page.

Soon, my eyes are crossing and before long I am asleep. I am walking in a forest with Karo and Mum, who is a few yards ahead of us. Karo and I are getting tired, we ask Mum to slow down, but she quickens her pace. *Mum,* we cry, *slow Down, Wait for us.* She doesn't seem to hear us, and so we raise our voices louder. She stops this time, turns round and looks at us. *But Karo, Yan, you can't follow me. You're dead. Why didn't you tell me you were going to die?* I wake with a start. My eyes are full of tears, and to my embarrassment I have dribbled on the towel. I can hear voices above my head. I wipe my eyes and mouth discreetly and sit up. We have a visitor, a white woman in her sixties, who is sitting beside Poppy, talking quietly.

'This is Margaret,' says Poppy. 'She was in her car, but she needed some fresh air. Margaret, meet Yan.'

'I'm not sure if it's sensible,' Margaret's voice is shaking, 'I should be on the road, really, but the traffic . . .' I exchange a glance with Poppy, not sure whether I should feel glad or sad to be proved right. Margaret takes a deep breath and carries on, 'It was so hot and there were so many cars – I just had to get out . . .'

'Looks like you need to rest for a bit,' says Poppy. 'Why not stop and have a drink, then check traffic in a while. If things are better, you can get going, but if not, you can stay as long as you like.'

I know it is churlish, Poppy is right to be so sympathetic and, after all, this is what she promised she would do. Still, I can't help resenting this stranger interrupting our little idyll. I am not sure I want to share Poppy with anyone.

'This is so kind of you.' Margaret accepts a proffered cup of tea.

'Don't mention it,' says Poppy. 'The more the merrier, wouldn't you say Yan?'

'Of course.' I am forced into my very best polite smile. I even let her know she can use the surf club if she needs to recharge her phone. But, although I take the tea Poppy offers, and join them on the chairs, I don't join in the conversation; I pretend to read my book instead. It's not Margaret's fault – she seems pleasant enough – it's just that she's shattered the intimacy Poppy and I have been building up. And now there are three of us, the atmosphere isn't quite the same.

I can see it is going to be a very long night.

Margaret

I am in the middle of ironing when I hear the news. I'm still trying to work out what I think about the end of a play that I've just heard and at first I'm not really paying attention. It is only the mention of La Palma that makes me take notice. All at once, I am back in that horrible room sifting through paper after paper, trying to make rational decisions about which organisations to save and which to cut. Every decision was a bad one, but at the time some options were more palatable than others. La Palma was one of many such arguments. David tried to persuade us we needed the early warning unit because one day something bad would happen. He used the example of Cumbre Vieja to illustrate his point, providing graphic detail of how monitoring seismic activity could prepare us for its possible collapse, enabling us to evacuate. His projections even identified Cornwall as a high risk area. But Andrew was equally persuasive the other way, arguing that we couldn't afford the luxury of spending money worrying about things that might never come to pass. Now it seems that that David was right: the decision we made was the worst of all and I am caught in the middle of it. Shocked, I drop the iron on my favourite shirt. It sizzles, marking the material with a permanent burn as I pull it away. I curse and then it occurs to me that a ruined shirt might be the least of my worries.

The funny thing is that, once I've convinced myself that the choice we made eight years ago has nothing to do with what is happening now, my first thought isn't escape, or whether I might drown. It isn't even Hellie. My first thought is that I should ring Kath. Ring Kath? That's a joke. We haven't spoken for years. She'd hardly appreciate a phone call from me now and where would I start? I switch the iron off, put the shirt to one side and sit down by the window, considering my options. The sun is high in the sky, its beams glinting on the blue water in the bay in front of me. It doesn't seem possible that this time tomorrow it will be gone. I stand there for far too long, pondering what to do: a balance between driving long distance with my dodgy knees or scrambling for a place on the train. Even getting to the station will take some effort. Hellie always said I'd regret living this far out of town but up until now I've always told her she worries too much, citing the freedom of walking into open countryside from my front door. Today, for the first time I have to admit maybe she was right.

Hellie . . . Thinking of Hellie makes up my mind. I have to get to her as quickly as I can, and judging by the pictures on my TV screen I'll have no chance of making my way through the crowds at the station. Knees or no knees it looks like the car is my only option. I send her a reassuring text and begin to get ready to leave. Despite the urgency, once I've made the decision, I just cannot make myself hurry. A sense of disbelief washes over me. I still can't quite take in the thought that I am leaving my home for good, that by this time tomorrow the house will be gone and with it all the possessions I can't take with me. I find myself paralysed with indecision about what to take and what leave behind. Some things are obvious: Grandma's recipe book, my wedding photos and Hellie's baby pictures. Others less so. I want to bring the painting of Venice that hangs in the living room. Richard and I bought it on honeymoon – it's had pride of place in all our houses since – but it's heavy and takes up a lot of space. I'd love to keep the family Bible. It's been with us since 1842, with every generation meticulously recorded since then. With regret, I decide to leave it: it is just too bulky. I spend far too long trying to choose what stays and what comes with me. In the end, I store the Bible, the painting and a couple of other precious items in a cupboard upstairs, wrapped in plastic, in the vain hope that this will protect them from the sea. It seems criminal to leave such things behind, but I just can't manage them. It's going to be hard enough that I'm going to have to camp in Hellie's tiny flat for a while without me filling it with clutter. So, in addition to the personal items, I just take a couple of suitcases of clothes, a handful of my favourite novels, and a few CDs.

I am just about to leave when I remember Minnie, my nearest neighbour. She has no family and I can't imagine the carer has been in today. Who's going to look after her? I'll have to bring her with me. I drive along the lane, park in the drive by her cottage and walk up the garden path. There is no answer to my knock, which is not unusual. Minnie often naps during the day, leaving a spare key under the mat for the rare visitor. I have been telling her for ages it's not sensible in this day and age, but today I am glad she does so.

I call out a greeting as I enter. There is an answering shout from the back room where I find Minnie sitting in a chair, looking out to sea. The TV is on low and there is a remote control on her lap.

'Is it true?' she says. 'What they're saying on the news?'

'Yes, I'm just about to leave.'

'I thought it might be a hoax – like Orson Welles, perhaps.'

'Sadly not ' I sit next to her and take her hand. 'Come with me.'

'Where?'

'We have to get to higher ground. We have to go now if we're to have a chance.'

'I don't know, dear.' Minnie shakes her head. 'I don't think I can leave this house.' Her clock strikes one o'clock. I try to ignore the panic that it invokes and concentrate all my efforts on her.

'You'll drown if you stay here.'

'But this is my home, dear. I have nowhere else I could go.'

'You could stay with me and Hellie.'

'Your daughter? She won't want an old woman like me around. She's got a little one to look after.'

'We'd manage.'

'I think I'd prefer to stay here. In my own bed. With any luck I'll sleep right through it.'

Why does she have to be so stubborn? I blank out the ticking clock and offer to make her a cup of tea, hoping that perhaps she just needs a little more time. Hellie calls while I am in the kitchen. 'Mum, where are you? Are you on the road yet?'

'At Minnie's. I'm trying to persuade her to leave.'

'You need to get going; they say the roads are jammed already.'

'I will.'

'Please get out of there.'

'As soon as I can.' There is a wail from the end of line.

'I must go. Toby needs me. Call me when you're on the road.' She hangs up.

With renewed urgency, I return to the sitting room, only to find that Minnie has fallen asleep. Her mouth is open, her head droops forward on her lap. She often does this, drifting in and out of wakefulness for short intervals. I have to leave, but I can't just abandon her. I put the cup on the coffee table and wait, watching the rise and fall of her chest. It is just like sitting with Grandma, in the days before her final illness. I was in my twenties, then, a time when old age seemed remote and unreal. Forty years have passed since and though I still have the energy and health of the well-off retiree, a life like Minnie's can't too far away. Perhaps she is right. Perhaps it would be best to sit and wait for the wave to take us away rather than escape to battle through years that will only weaken my body into helplessness. I shake my head. What am I thinking? I've only been retired a couple of years. There is so much I want to do still.

'Margaret? Are you still here?' Minnie suddenly raises her head, 'You must be going, dear.'

'Not without you.'

'It's all right, dear. I'm too old to start a new life. I'd rather stay here.'

'But . . .'

'I'll be asleep, anyway. I never get up before eight. Much the best way.' She waves away further protest. 'Don't worry about me. I'll be fine. I've got Misty to look after me.' Right on cue, the grey cat enters the room, meanders across towards his mistress and sits on her lap, purring contentedly. 'You see? I have everything I need right here. You have a daughter and grandchild to live for. *Go.*'

I hate to do it, but Minnie is insistent, and she's right – I do have more to live for. I head out to the car, drive off down the lane and onto the road to Penzance. At first all is well. I speed along, hopeful that the reports of traffic jams were exaggerated. Even so, the sight of the vivid green grass, the bright blue sky and the sea sparkling in the distance is filled with menace. As if, underneath the surface of the water, there is a malevolent being that will bring the sea to life and destroy me. I feel sick and anxious, a mood not improved when I hit a queue of cars four miles from Penzance.

The traffic moves slowly. I inch forward and now the traffic reports are of solid jams further ahead. By three o'clock I have just reached the outskirts of Penzance. This is a nightmare, made worse by my engine beginning to steam. In my hurry, I forgot to check the water levels. Something else Hellie is always nagging me about – this car has a propensity for overheating if stuck in traffic too long. I switch off the engine to cool it down – the cars ahead aren't moving, anyway – and try to think. I glance down at the map. They say Dartmoor is safe, but that's still over eighty miles away. I've driven four miles in two hours. At this rate, I'm never going to make it. That can't be right. It can't be possible that I won't get out of this alive, that I'll not get to see Hellie and her family ever again. I pull out my map to see if I can find an alternative route. But the radio announcer is reporting pile ups at Bodmin and Redruth and gridlock on every road going north. There are no alternatives, this is my only way out.

I put my head on the steering wheel and howl. I've had long and happy life; in a previous era sixty-seven would have been considered a good innings, but I'm not ready to die yet. I still have too much to do. I am booked on a tour of Greece and Italy in the summer. I have signed up for a Masters in Theology in the Autumn. Hellie is pregnant. It cannot be possible that I will miss out on all that. But . . . there are too many cars, the road is too packed. If we don't get a move on, nobody in this jam is going to make it. None of us. By tomorrow morning we might have reached Truro – and it won't be far enough. Even if we could outrun the wave, the constant rain this summer means that the water table is so high the whole county will be awash with water. A line from the Bible comes to me: 'The water prevailed more and more upon the earth, so that all the high mountains everywhere under the heavens were covered.' So God, you gave Noah fair warning – why not us? And don't tell me a wild theory about a possible volcanic collapse was a divine message. Not on the basis of that flimsy evidence. Why didn't you give us more? Why didn't you allow us enough time to build ourselves an ark? Why are we left behind to drown?

I cannot stand any more news, so I switch to the CD player. Immediately the sound of French monks singing Vespers in plain chant calms me.

Glory be to the Father, and to the Son, and to the Holy Spirit:
As it was in the beginning, is now, and ever shall be, world without end.
Amen.

I stare at the crowded road ahead. It may be my only chance of escape but I'm beginning to believe it's no chance at all. I am hot and tired and I can't stay in this car for much longer: I need some air. I passed the turn to Dowetha Cove a mile or so back. Perhaps if I go down to the sea, spend a bit of time by the water's edge, the fresh air will revive and renew me. Perhaps by then the traffic will have died down and I can try again. I am not giving up yet, I tell myself, I am just taking a breather. I turn the car round, passing the long queue of drivers heading towards Penzance. Ahead of me flecks of golden sunlight light up the blue sea, calming my spirits. I text Hellie, *traffic slow, but on my way*. I don't want to worry her yet. I just need to get out of the car for a bit, breathe some sea air and then I can be on my way again.

James

I hate it when Yan is right. He's always so smug about it. Even in these circumstances, if we meet again, I bet he'll be smug. Because he always is. It's infuriating.

I was so sure he was wrong three hours ago when I turned up on his doorstep, telling him we had to go, NOW. He just replied in a maddeningly patient voice that due to the number of cars on the road, the average speed of traffic, bottlenecks and likelihood of crashes we wouldn't be going anywhere. He smiled like a patronising professor, putting me right on the glaring errors of my pathetic dissertation and was totally immune to my increasingly panicked pleas that he leave with me. I couldn't understand how he could stand there, so resigned to the fate I was certain we would be able to escape. I know he's always had a fatalistic streak, but this deliberate refusal to move seemed stupid beyond belief. Though I begged and begged, he wouldn't budge. In the end, I had to give up on him and go it alone. I hated leaving him, but if he was going to be such a stubborn bastard there wasn't much I could do about it.

I was still sure once I was on the open road. Though it was busy, the traffic kept moving initially, while sunshine, green fields and glittering sea lifted my spirits. Poor Yan I thought, as I raced towards Penzance. Poor Yan. I put the radio on, singing along to Uptown Funk to push my fears away, as I pretended that this was just an ordinary summer's day and I was heading north to see friends. It worked for a while, but my optimism was short-lived. The road stayed clear for only a few miles. As signs to Penzance began to appear, suddenly cars were coming from every direction. Red brake lights flashed up in front of me. Drivers beeped their horns, yelling obscenities at each other as I found myself at the end of a long queue of traffic and came to a grinding halt. I wound the window down, pushed my seat back, grabbed a sandwich and told myself it was a small setback. It wasn't time to panic yet. I switched on the radio to hear the tune that has tormented for too many months . . .

> *Never Leave Me, Never Leave Me*
> *Believe me when I say to you.*
> *Love me, darling, love me, darling,*
> *Cos I'll never, ever be leaving you.*

Lisa's first big hit as she transitioned from dreamy ballad singer to techno pop artist, the song that told me that she was gone for good. The song she wrote for the man she said had broken her heart, that she dropped from our set because, she said, she didn't need to think of him any more. The minute I heard her new version, the version she had released without telling me – same lyrics, same basic melody, but surrounded by a thudding beat and a swirl of technical effects – I knew it was the goodbye she hadn't got round to saying to my face.

Oh Lisa . . . It had been weeks since I'd allowed myself to think of her. Having wallowed in a miasma of self-pity for the six months that followed her departure, I had been trying to put her behind me. I'd almost been successful, too. It was only when I caught a news article, or heard her on the radio like this, that the familiar sickness returned, the longing for the woman I could no longer have.

Lisa, Lisa, Lisa . . . I loved the way her red hair fell in front of her face and she had to flick it aside. I loved her talent and the force of her ambition that drove her to make the most of her gifts. I loved the way she could single me out in a room with a look that said I was hers, she was mine. The whole time we were together, she made everything right. I thought she was all I ever needed, which made her absence, when it came, so unbearable. And even after all these months, hearing her voice was painful. It made me wonder whether she had seen the news, whether she was thinking of me at all. Whether somewhere her stomach was lurching like mine as she realized that I was in danger. I took out my phone. Despite my attempts to eradicate her from my life, I'd not managed to delete her number yet. I'd stopped the late night calls pleading for her return, but I hadn't quite had the strength to let her go all together. I scrolled through my contacts to find her smiling face, the last picture I took, one day on the beach just before she left. I pressed dial – and then stopped immediately. What was I thinking? There was nothing she could do to help and I shouldn't ask. Even if she did respond, it would only be out of pity. I don't need pity now. Actually, thinking about it, pity would be the worst. I put the phone away, relieved to see the car ahead was moving forward. I followed suit. We crawled around the outskirts of Penzance as I raised the clutch, pressed the accelerator, shifted forwards and stopped. *Clutch, accelerator, stop, clutch, accelerator, stop, clutch, accelerator, stop.* I tried not to think about how long this was taking, but instead that every move forward was taking me out of the danger zone.

Even so, I was beginning to doubt myself, so I was pleased by the distraction of the sight of a young black woman at the junction to the A30. She was standing by her backpack and, although all the cars were going past, she had the confidence of someone who knows they will get picked up soon. I pulled over.

'Want a lift?'

'Please.' I climbed out, put her backpack in the boot and opened the front for her.

'Thanks,' she said, kicking of her shoes. 'I wasn't sure if anyone would stop. Everyone's a bit . . .'

'I always stop for hitchhikers,' I said. Now I could see her face more clearly, she looked familiar, but I couldn't place her and I didn't want to say anything for fear of sounding creepy, 'I'm James, by the way.'

'Nikki. You haven't got anything to drink have you? I'm gasping.' I handed her some water. 'How come you're hitching?'

'Couldn't get a train.' She looked out of the window. 'Beautiful day, isn't it?'

'Yes.'

'After all that rain. Lovely to have the good weather again.'

'Yes.' Clearly she wasn't keen to talk about our situation. I took her lead. Tried to pretend we were just a couple of people who had just met, travelling together for a while. It was better than giving into the gnawing anxiety that Yan was right, that we wouldn't get out of here alive. 'So what do you do then?'

'Right now? I'm a waitress in a chippy in Penzance.'

That's where I'd seen her before. 'I was in there the other week. You probably don't remember . . .' She stared at my face a moment, 'Yes,' she says, 'I do. You wanted a saveloy and we'd run out so you had to wait. The wanker behind you was less patient, and kept shouting at me to hurry up, even though I couldn't cook them any faster. You told him to shut up, which was nice of you, given how big he was.'

'I wouldn't have done it after hours,' I said, grinning. 'But 6.00 p.m. in daylight, with loads of people around? I'm very brave in those sort of situations.'

'Well, anyway, I appreciated it.' Nikki smiled back, filling me with a sense of joy that I hadn't felt in a long time. It was crazy considering the fact we had just met, but somehow it seemed as if we'd always known each other.

'It's just a summer job,' she said. 'I've just finished a Masters in French Language and Literature. My parents are in Lagos with my brother and sister, so I offered to look after their house, while I sort out what next. How about you?'

'I work in an antiques shop in St Ives.'

'That's unusual.'

'For someone my age? I would have thought that a few years back when I was working in the City. But the job bored me, and I wanted to make music. So I jacked it in to come down here to play on the folk scene. The shop was supposed to be a stopgap, but I got hooked on the smell of old furniture and the music thing didn't work out, and here I am . . .'

'That's cool.' Phew, unlike Lisa she didn't think it a dead-end job that made me dull. The conversation flowed for the next hour, enabling us both to pretend we haven't noticed how long it has taken us to reach our current location. There's been a white van in front of us for ages, blocking the view, but the road has dipped and now we can see over it to the long line of cars stretched ahead. They are barely moving. I have been driving for three hours and travelled eight miles. At this rate, we have no chance of reaching safety in time.

'Shit,' said Nikki. 'That doesn't look good.'

'No.'

The Wave

She looks away. I have a feeling she might be about to cry and not want me to see. I am close to tears myself. I was so sure Yan was wrong and I was right, but now, as I sit here and weigh up our chances, I have lost that sense of certainty. I switch on the radio to hear the news that every road north is blocked, a fact confirmed by my satnav, which is helpfully stating that the current estimated time of arrival will be eighteen hours. Eighteen hours? That's three hours too late. We sit, staring at the road ahead, unsure what to do. It seems impossible that we could die tomorrow. We are too young, there is too much we haven't done. Keeping moving is our only chance of surviving. The hopeful side of me wants to keep moving. Wants to pretend that the satnav is broken, the traffic reports are exaggerated. But I can hear Yan's voice in my head, 'You'll get as far as Falmouth before the wave sweeps you off the face of the earth.' Despite his tendency to over-dramatize, I'm reluctantly beginning to concede his point . . .

And it's terrifying. I am twenty-nine years old. I don't want to die tomorrow. I should have years ahead of me. Years to achieve all the goals that seem to have eluded me. I had such grand plans when I left my corporate hell hole and moved down here. I was going to record an album, live the life of a simple artist. I've managed none of it. I enjoy my job but all I've got to show for the last few years is the hours I've put in to pay my rent. And when Lisa came into my life, all my ambitions became subsumed by hers. What a waste.

'I was thinking,' says Nikki softly, 'that woman on Facebook might be right . . .'

'The one at Dowetha Cove?'

'I saw the post while I was standing there. I didn't want to believe her, but I've seen the station, and . . .'

'My friend Yan is already there.'

Ahead of us, the white van moves forward but it is belching smoke and is forced to pull over to the side of the road. As we pass, I see the driver standing looking grimly at the steaming, overheated engine. I think about offering a lift, but almost immediately we come to a halt again. I look at the map, my watch, the tachometer. I look at the queue of traffic ahead that's going nowhere. It is hot in the car and the sandwiches are getting stale. I gaze at the blue sky and the glowing yellow sun. At this time of day the sea will still be warm and I wouldn't mind a swim. I think if I spend another hour in this car, I am likely to go mad. Nikki looks at me and nods, even though I haven't said anything.

The road ahead is blocked, but the south road isn't much better. Despite Nikki's news about the station, it seems as if some still think there might be trains and are travelling in the opposite direction. Either way, we aren't getting anywhere in a hurry. Weighing up the odds, I come to a decision. If it's a choice between sitting here for hours waiting for the inevitable, or sitting on the beach . . . I rev the engine, indicate, turn out of the traffic queue, point the car in the opposite direction, and take the road south.

Nikki

The sun streaming through the curtains wakes me, but it takes a while for me to come to my senses. I feel hot, my body sluggish. What time is it? I only turned over for a quick doze at nine, thinking the street noises would wake me, but I'd forgotten I switched rooms last night after being freaked out by noises in the graveyard. The back bedroom is much quieter and so I have slept on undisturbed. Shit, it's nearly one o'clock. I'll have to get a move on if I am going to make my train.

As I draw the curtains I remember I promised Mum and Dad that I would mow the lawn. They'll be pretty pissed when they get back – they're so proud of their English country garden, it makes them feel like true Brits. They'll be mad as hell when they see the tangle of brambles smothering their rose bushes and the grass almost as high, but I couldn't help it. I've been doing lates all week and just haven't had the energy. I will scribble them a note and hopefully they'll ask my brother, Ifechi or Ginika, my sister to do it and will be over it by the time I'm back.

I take my scarf off, rub my hair with pomegranate oil and comb it through, tying it in a pony-tail to keep it off my neck. I'm hot and sticky and still smell of chip fat. There's no time to shower; instead, I have a quick wash, moisturize and hope the coconut oil masks the smell. I throw on blue shorts and a lilac T-shirt, stuff clothes and beauty products in my bag and rush downstairs. I'm hungry, but there's no time to eat either, so I grab an apple and a packet of crisps. I'll just have to hope the train's buffet is well stocked.

I am out of the house and down the alley in no time. There is no one much about; they're probably all at the beach. I speed right at the corner, then left. It is only as I'm approaching the Longboat Inn that I notice something is wrong. The road ahead is jammed with cars in both directions and the station is densely packed with people, all the way through the car park round to the harbour. The queue spills out into the road and stretches back alongside the railway tracks down to the pub. What is going on? I fight my way through the crowd and join the end of the line. My train is in the station, but I can see it is already full; I doubt I'll even get on the next one. I find a place behind two middle-aged white men. One is hunched, with a worried expression on his face, the other rocks back and forwards besides him. I take off my backpack and place it on the ground.

'What's up?'

'Eh?' The worried man is about to respond, when the

other one, starts saying and over again, 'The wave, the wave, the wave,' as he rocks. My neighbour turns to him in soothing tones, 'It's OK, Paul. We're getting on the train and we'll be fine.'

'Will we, Peter? Will we, will we?'

'Of course. Why don't you get your DS out and play a bit of Pokemon?' Paul acquiesces. He pulls the DS from his pocket. It has an instant calming effect; he sits down on a suitcase and is soon absorbed in his game. The worried-looking man turns back to me. 'My brother. Gets a bit anxious. He's autistic, you see. What did you say?'

'What's happening?'

'Haven't you seen the news?' I shake my head. He shows me the headlines on his phone. A volcano collapse, a megat-sunami, and the whole of Cornwall under water. I can't take it in. It explains the crowds, but it just doesn't seem possible looking at the calm, sparkling sea. I scroll through my phone to find the story is everywhere. My inbox is full of messages. *Nikki it's Stef, are you OK? Niks it's Max, ring me. Nikki darling it's Mum, where are you?* Even my little sister Ginika has texted, though I note wryly Ifechi hasn't bothered. There are too many to respond to, and I don't know what to say anyway. But I reply to Mum telling her I'm waiting for a train, and send Ginika a message to say I'm having an adventure. After that I sink to the ground, my legs shaking. If only I hadn't been so tired last night. If only I'd stuck to my original plan and travelled through the night after work. I'd be with Alice in Manchester, glad of my lucky escape. That last-minute decision to have a lie-in has come at quite a cost.

'Are you all right?' Peter says as the train pulls out of the station. I'd have hoped it might mean the queue would move forward but it doesn't shift.

'What do you think?'

'Sorry, stupid question. But it's too early to panic. It's only an hour and a half to Plymouth. They're bound to lay on extra trains, aren't they?'

He's being kind and I can see he is trying to reassure himself as much as anything; but I'm not so sure. They have struggled with staffing on this line lately, and what if there isn't enough rolling stock? I have too many questions, and I am so hungry and thirsty I can't think. I open the pack of crisps, wishing I had brought a drink. I daren't go into the shop in case I lose my place. The sun is hot and I feel dizzy. I close my eyes. There is something of the heat, the stink of petrol, the beeping horns that reminds my first trip to Lagos when I was eight. I was such a pampered child! What a fuss I'd made about everything, the crowded streets, the dust, the lack of amenities in my grandparents' house. It was a wonder, Dad would say in later years, that they hadn't packed me on the first flight home.

The sound of an engine makes me open my eyes as a sleek red train comes into view. The crowd cheers as it arrives at the station until they spot the number of carriages. Only six! They should be laying on twice that many. There are shouts from the passengers on the platform who rush forward as the railway guards try and keep control. Gradually the train fills and the queue moves forward. By the time it is ready to depart, we have moved a few hundred yards further up. It's not far, but it *is* progress. I eat the apple slowly. With any luck, I'll be away by six. The train leaves. Hopefully the next one will be along soon. But nothing comes and there is no information when I check the website. I try to calm my nerves by listening to Rihanna, try to imagine this is all over and I'm out of the danger zone heading to Manchester. It works for a while, but then I sense the mood of the crowd change. I take off my headphones and catch the tail end of an announcement over the tannoy. I cannot make out the words, but ahead of us there are angry murmurs that quickly become shouts. The rumour passes along the line until it reaches us. *Trains are needed for evacuation of the northern coasts. There will be no trains from Penzance after four thirty.*

Two more trains. That means only two more trains. Everyone is making the same calculation and suddenly the patience of the queue is exhausted. People rush forward from every angle, jumping in the road between cars to get ahead of their neighbours. Everyone is yelling and ahead of me I can see a couple of fights breaking out. Peter pulls his brother to one side, clearly intending to wait it out, but I can't see any point in staying here. I jump to my feet, pushing against the throng surging forward, fighting my way down the road until, at last, I am clear. Now what? Hitch a lift? It seems the only option left. I walk up to the junction for the A30. The road ahead is filled with traffic. My heart sinks; this looks as bad as the trains. The cars are moving slowly, but none seems inclined to stop. I check my phone; I'm thirsty. I really wish I'd brought a drink with me. To distract myself, I scroll through Facebook, looking for some signs of hope that people are getting out. But all I find is a post that is being shared widely. A woman called Poppy inviting people down to Dowetha Cove because she thinks we can't get away. It seems defeatist, but then, looking at the road ahead, maybe she has a point.

This is ridiculous. I can't believe escape isn't possible, that someone won't stop for me. Right on cue a car pulls up and the driver sticks out his head. He is older than me; I notice dark wavy hair, kind eyes. Not another beautiful white boy. I swore off them after Patrick. But then he smiles at me and, despite myself, I smile right back.

'I'm James,' he says as I slip into the passenger seat.

'Nikki.' I kick off my shoes and somehow, white boy or not, I feel immediately at ease. He offers water when I ask and is interested in me and interesting to listen to. If I don't think too much, I can continue to pretend this is just an ordinary summer afternoon. That I have just met a man who might be worth a bit of time and effort. I've always been quite good at telling stories, and this one is a reassuring one. I am happy, I am safe. Good times lie ahead.

Handsome white boy is as good as I am at keeping it

light and the hour passes swiftly, particularly once I discover he was the one to send a prize arsehole packing the other week. Even so I can't help noticing we're not moving as fast as we'd like. Every time there is a break in the conversation, I try not to glance at my phone which is full of news of bad traffic. I try not to think about how slowly we are travelling or how long it will take us to get anywhere. It is when we reach the top of the hill that I cannot stop pretending. The traffic is almost stationary for miles ahead. The radio and James's satnav confirm it. We cannot get out.

I turn away from him. Despite our instant camaraderie, I don't feel able to show him my feelings yet. I gaze out of the window again at the sea, the beautiful, calm, perilous sea. The sea that will kill us tomorrow. How can that be possible? All my plans, my dreams of living in Paris, of working as an interpreter for the UN, gone in a flash. And my family. What can I say to my parents? To Ifechi and Ginika? Being a teenager is hard enough. How can I do this to them? I think again about that post on Facebook, the thought that if there's no escape, spending time with others, having fun, might be better than sitting in a hot car going nowhere.

It turns out that James knows about the woman on the beach too; his friend Yan is already there. The thought hangs in the air that we might turn back and join them but we don't say anything, and when the van in front pulls off, James drives on as if we are going to continue. But shortly after he stops. We look at each other, though we don't say a word, we both know what the other is thinking. James indicates right and turns the car around to join the last stragglers driving to Penzance in search of a train. As we pass the cars driving north, I can see the astonishment on the passengers' faces. I'm astonished, too, but the die is cast. I was dead before I even woke up this morning. This is the only option left to me now and I am going to take it.

Harry

Harry Edwards. Survivor.

That's me.

Always have been, always will be.

There's no fucking way a stupid volcano is going to stop me now.

The whole world might have heard the news and panicked, but the minute I found out, I started thinking, as I always do in a crisis.. While everyone else was running scared, I started planning ways to escape. Even though I had a hunch this was a hoax, I wasn't taking any chances. Watching the pundits on the telly with their charts and CGI images declaring the end to be nigh, I couldn't help remembering how the same serious people told us Trump would never win and Brexit would never happen. Tonight, when that volcano doesn't collapse, I'm convinced they'll all look very stupid. But it's better to be safe than sorry, isn't it? So, I weighed up the options and came up with the perfect answer. The road was the obvious choice, but also the stupid one. With so many holidaymakers trying to get along the same narrow route, I knew it would get clogged in no time. And the railway wouldn't be much better. I knew this was a situation that required an intelligent solution and I found one. I bought myself a boat. I discovered a bloke online who has a holiday cottage in Penzance and a motor cruiser in the harbour. Now Shelley and I are heading into town while all the sheeple are travelling in the opposite direction. I felt smug at first, seeing them all going nowhere fast, knowing we had our way out, but I should have factored all the idiots going into Penzance to try the train. We've been stuck in traffic for an hour now, a delay we could do without. I'm trying not to let it bother me. We're still moving faster than the cars going in the opposite direction, and once we're on the water there'll be no stopping us. But I could do without the sun pounding through the front windows; even with the side ones down, the Maserati is hot and sticky. The only thing I have against this car is the lack of air conditioning.

'Are you sure it's going to be OK?' Shelley says for the third time as we crawl past the supermarket by the roundabout.

'Of course it is. I said I'd sort it and I've sorted it. And you know the best part, babe?'

'What?'

'We've got ourselves a brand-new boat. When all the fuss has died down we can moor it down somewhere on the south coast and spend weekends out on the water. You'd like that, wouldn't you?'

'That would be lovely.' Shelley's voice doesn't have quite as much enthusiasm as it should have, doesn't have quite as much faith in me as I'd like. She used to always trust my judgement, but lately she's been questioning my decisions a lot more. Perhaps it's inevitable, now we're living together. But I could do without it right now. Right now it would be nice if she showed a little faith. After all, I'm doing this as much for her as for me.

The road towards the harbour is even more jam-packed than the A30, cars are stuck in both directions, horns beeping, drivers shouting. I look at my watch. Three thirty. I said to the bloke in London we'd be here by three. I text him to say we're nearly there. The cars ahead are maybe going nowhere, but it's not far.

'Come on, we're walking.' I pull up in a lay-by.

'I've got my heels on.'

'It's less than a mile. Grab your bags.' I take out my suitcase from the boot and pull up the handle. Shelley has brought two huge holdalls which she places on each shoulder, like ballast balloons. She follows obediently as I make for the harbour. The journey is more complicated than I had anticipated. The road is crowded with people waiting for the train or trying to get to the harbour and it is a struggle to make our way through. Cars beep incessantly and, as we approach the car park, we can see a closely packed throng reaching all the way to the quayside and along to the main docks. The crowd is thinner on our side of the road, but it's still an effort to push our way against the tide of people heading for the station. The mood is unpleasant; there are shouts and scuffles and across the way I can see a couple of big blokes sizing up for a fight. I want to get to the boat as soon as possible, but every few minutes I'm stopped by Shelley wailing for me to slow down, pleading for help with her bags

'I did suggest one bag only,' I say when she catches up.

'I need them both.'

I want to suggest that she dumps one but she has a face that suggests tears are imminent and an argument will only slow us down. There's nothing for it but to take one of hers and keep moving forward. It is hard work, harder as we arrive at the quay, where we are pressed in on every side, with some people heading in the direction of the station, others towards the harbour in the hope that the one ferry will return and rescue them. I push a path through the wall of bodies, conscious that all it would take would be for one trip and we'd be trampled on. At last we make it through to the quayside where I sit down in the wall to catch my breath. Shelley throws her bag down with relief, and then gazes past me towards the quayside. 'Is there enough water?'

I turn round. The tide is going out. Already the mooring chains are half exposed to show their green seaweed and barnacle coverings. The waves lap against an edge of dirty brown sand which is filled with small wading birds searching for food. It should be just about deep enough to depart but then I realize something else. There isn't a single yacht or speedboat left. Not one. All that remains are a few battered rowing boats that wouldn't make it further than the harbour wall. Where is my boat? Where is my fucking boat? Even though the evidence is in front of me, I still can't accept it. I walk over to mooring nineteen where Bob the fisherman was supposed to meet me. There is nobody there, and the mooring chain leads nowhere.

'Was it definitely here?' says Shelley. 'Not round the corner?'

'Don't be stupid, Shells. This is where they keep the private boats. The docks are for commercial vessels.'

'Perhaps he moved it.'

'Shit,' I say. 'Shit, shit, shit, shit, shit.' A seagull flies overhead, depositing it's droppings on my shoulder as it passes. Shelley laughs.

'It's not funny!' I'm furious, but she cannot stop giggling, until I shout at her, 'Shut the fuck up, will you?'

'It was just the timing.' She gets a tissue out of her bag and removes the worst of the gloopy mess off my T-shirt. It leaves behind a white smeary stain. I ring the owner, no answer. I send him a text. No answer. Then another, which finally gets a response. *Sorry – boat's been sold. Bob waited till three thirty but had to leave; he sold it to someone else. Hope you can find another.*

What about my refund, arsehole? I text back, but he doesn't reply. Fucker probably thinks I'm done for, and he might as well pocket my £500. He doesn't know what's coming for him. When I get back to London, as I definitely will, I'll take him to the cleaners. No one gets the better of Harry Edwards, no one.

'What are we going to do?' Oh, Shelley. Why are you so young? You're beautiful and sweet but not much good in a crisis. 'Give me a moment to think.' I look around the harbour. There are thousands of people between here and the station still thinking they might get a space on a train, or a ferry. I can't see it myself, there are too many of us. There is no point hanging about here.

'What are we going to do?' wails Shelley again.

'Ssh, I'm thinking.'

I check the news. The roads are as clogged as I thought they would be. There's also no point attempting to travel north. Clearly not worth taking a risk on the internet again, but surely not every boat will have gone? Surely, in some little cove somewhere, someone keeps a boat for their occasional trips to Cornwall. Some lucky bastard who decided not to come down this weekend will have left us a means of escape that's just waiting for us to collect it. All we have to do is explore the bays between here and St Ives. Surely there will be something for us somewhere . . .?

'We'll look for another one,' I say.

'Where?'

'In a mooring somewhere. Come on, Shells.'

'Alison's just texted, asking if we're OK.'

Alison is Shelley's big sister. She's not my biggest fan, nor I, hers. She thinks I'm not good enough for Shells; it will give me great pleasure to remind her in future that without me her sister would have drowned. 'Tell her we're fine, we've got a plan,' I say. Thinking of sisters, I am reminded of mine. Should I text Val, let her know what's going on? Don't be stupid Harry. She doesn't even know we're here. Why worry her? Best to let her know when we're safe out the other side, when I can brag about my brilliant survival skills.

We force our way back through the swell of people, a deeply unpleasant experience. Sweaty bodies push against us, the smell of panic and fear. I can feel Shelley stumbling in my wake, but I can't hold her in this crowd, we both have to make our way through, until, eventually, we pass the station and are back on the road again.

It takes half an hour to reach the car, place our bags back in the boot and set off again. We crawl back along the way we've walked, but once we're past the quay the road is clear and I'm back in control. We're not like the hopeless hordes in Penzance, heading nowhere. We've got a plan and it's a good one.

We start at Mousehole, but it's just like Penzance. A handful of rowing boats are left in the quay. I consider whether it's worth trying one of them, but they just don't look seaworthy enough and I'm definitely not a strong enough rower. I look at the lifeboat station, but that too is gone; according to Twitter they've taken a load of people up north to safety. Shame we didn't get here sooner. Still, I refuse to be deterred. There's plenty of places along the coast; I'm sure we'll find something. It's just a matter of persistence, that's all. We climb back into the car and drive on.

The third bay reveals nothing, either. Shit. I don't say anything to Shelley, but my heart sinks, and for the first time I experience a flutter of doubt. I'm getting tired and hungry. I wish I'd told her to pack some food, though to be honest she really should have thought of it. After all, I've been doing everything else. We drive on. I am trying not feel a bit sorry for myself, when I spot a sign for Dowetha and my spirits rise again. Surely, this time we'll find something? I put my foot on the accelerator and speed in the direction of the beach.

Shelley

Harry is everything to me.

It's been that way for years. I adore him.

I'd do anything for him, follow him anywhere . . .

And yet, lately, I have found myself asking myself whether any of this is true any more. Harry's been my life for so long that I've never questioned him until lately. In the beginning, he seemed so thoughtful and sensitive. I was his special girl, his fair lady, his queen. He always checked how I was and made sure no harm would come to me. Yet today, when I'm frightened, really, really, frightened, it's like he hasn't even noticed. I know he's trying to get us out of here, and maybe he's right that a boat is the answer. But it wouldn't hurt to ask me how I'm feeling, surely? He's not even asked my opinion, just assumed he knows best. When I do try and say anything, he just sighs and speaks over me. It's infuriating, insulting and upsetting all at once. But I still stagger after him in my five-inch stilettos, holiday bags balanced on shoulders, because, after all, what else can I do?

The trouble is Harry is always so sure he is right – there's never any room for doubt. I suppose that's what attracted me to him in the first place – that sense of certainty. I love Dad, of course I do, but he's got this annoying habit of always seeing the other point of view, always weighing up one side against the other. Which was a bit wearing for a teenager looking for definitive answers. I think that's why Harry's absolute conviction was so attractive. Here was someone who knew exactly what he was doing, what he thought about everything. A real man, who understood what was what. The fact that he had money and was prepared to share it just added to the allure.

I wasn't even supposed to be in the bar that night. I'd only gone because Liv reckoned we could get in if we had fake ID and I was trying to prove her wrong – and because I'd just had a row with Dad about my lack of GCSE revision. It was unusual for me to be so daring, to pretend to be at Liv's when we were outside the nightclub hoping our false documents would get us inside. I was astonished that they did and even more so that it was so easy to pretend to be eighteen with all the men at the bar slavering over us, all eager to buy us a drink. Harry was the one who stood out, though. Tall white, muscular, he had something about him – a toughness, a sense he got what he wanted – that I found instantly appealing. Even the age difference didn't bother me – it made him seem trustworthy. He offered us cocktails and treated us like grown-ups. It was so nice to be taken seriously for once; Dad and Alison always treated me like a kid. I lapped it up.

He invited us both back and we drank prosecco and ate canapés on his balcony. He talked about his hotel business, all the celebrities he'd had stay. It all seemed so glamorous and exciting. Liv was worried he might be a creep, but he didn't try it on, and when I said it was time we went, he ordered a cab for us, kissed me on the cheek. So, of course, I gave him my number. I didn't really expect him to call because nothing like that ever happened to me. But he did, and he took me to a posh restaurant and told me he thought I was beautiful and asked me out. I had to confess about my age, then, and he was perfectly lovely about it. He said he thought that I was very mature for my age – he'd assumed I was twenty at least. For the first time in years I felt that I really mattered. It wasn't that Alison and Dad didn't love me, or I, them, but they were so close after Mum died that sometimes I felt a bit shut out. Harry said I was the centre of his universe and for a long while that held true and he was everything I needed.

But lately, it's all felt a bit wrong. Ever since I moved in, it's begun to feel like he's taken me for granted, that I'm not as important as I once was, that other things – work, mates, TV – come higher on his list. Take this holiday, for example. He's promised me a holiday for ever. He's had business trips to Rome and Paris, looking into setting up there, but he's never taken me, even though I begged him. He said I'd only be bored, as he would be working, but one of these days we'd do it properly, do New York, maybe.

But that's never happened. We only came down here because he was meeting some potential investors in Penzance. He said that Cornwall was much nicer than New York anyway and we'd avoid jetlag. He only had a few work meetings, he said, and after they were done we could go to the beach. But the meetings lasted all day and in the evening he went drinking, leaving me to mooch around the cottage on my own.

It hasn't all been bad. The cottage was pretty enough, it was rather like the house in Yorkshire, where we lived in before Mum died. So even though I was a bit lonely, I felt quite at home. I watched my way through lots of box sets, and once or twice I got the bus into town to have a spa. On the second day, I found that the cupboard door in the back sitting room actually led into a small music room. There was a piano and piles of sheet music, including a bunch of folk songs that I used to sing with Dad. It had been years since I'd sung them, but since there wasn't anything else to do, I thought I might as well give it a go. Though my voice was a rusty at first, the old tunes soon came back, reminding me of happier times – Dad and I performing for Alison and Mum in the days before her illness, when we were a proper family. I'd forgotten how much I loved singing with him, and how content the four of us were just to be together. We never seemed to hang out like that after her death, I think we all missed her too much.

But even rediscovering music couldn't make up for the

fact that I was alone for most of the week. And there was no way I could tell Harry about it – he'd only have laughed. Folk music is so not his thing. So as the week went on we just got further and further apart until last night, when I begged him to spend some time with me. He was clearly feeling a bit bad, because he said sorry and promised that today we'd do something together, Land's End, sit on the beach, cream tea. My kind of day. Perhaps his negotiations had really completed, or perhaps he just he simply wanted sex. Whatever the reason, he seemed genuinely apologetic that he'd neglected me, promised today would be perfect and we had dinner on the terrace. Afterwards, when we made love out in the garden, among the glow-worms, he called me his special girl, his lady, his queen. He was as sweet and as kind as he was right at the beginning and I slept well and woke full of hope that we'd just been going through a bad patch and today would put us back on the right track.

I was so happy this morning as we had a leisurely breakfast and began to get ready for our trip. It was only when we were about to leave that we heard the horrible news. Ever since, Harry has been obsessed with finding a boat. It's a good thing, of course it's a good thing, if it ensures our survival, but I can't help feeling that he has set himself an impossible task. I don't want to think what that might mean, and I haven't expressed the thought out loud, but what are the chances, really? Was it any surprise that all the boats in Penzance had gone? That the person on the internet sold the boat to someone else? Hasn't Harry been saying for years it's a dog-eat-dog world? Why would it be any different for him? I understand his fury at being let down, but it's astonishing that he didn't see it coming, really. So, when a bird shat on him, I couldn't help laughing out loud. I suppose it wasn't kind of me, but, honestly, it's the only funny thing to have happened today. Because when I let the thought in, that Harry might be wrong, that there might not be a boat to find, I am left with the inescapable conclusion that I'm about to die because my boyfriend was too mean to take me to New York. It isn't fair. I am way too young. I haven't even begun to live.

We've been trailing through the bays ever since that lost boat of Penzance. The treacherous thought that Harry is wrong has grown with every failure to discover an alternative. And the unfairness of it, the absolute bitter unfairness of it, keeps sweeping over me. I am twenty years old. All I have done with my life is meet Harry and work as a nanny for two years. I will never go to America, never go to Paris where I always fantasized that Harry might propose, never work out what my life could be about. I'll die without have amounted to anything very much.

All this is running through my head, and Harry still hasn't asked me, hasn't even stopped to wonder why I am veering from tears to anger so quickly. Apart for a snarky query as to whether I've got women's problems, he is oblivious to my feelings. He is too focussed on his personal mission, fulfilling his own personal myth that he will be the hero to save the day. I want to believe in him, but I've been teetering on the brink of disbelief since Penzance, and if there's nothing at the next cove, I really don't think I can go on any more. If he would only stop for a moment, talk to me, give me a hug, tell me that it will be all right, that he's with me and he'll take care of me right to the very end. Perhaps, if he did that, I might be prepared to stick with it. But he seems incapable of doing anything other than drive to the next bay and the next.

So here we are, parking the car at the top of another beach. To my surprise, we are not the only ones there. An old Ford Fiesta, a hatchback and a mini that has seen better days are already here.

'Aye, aye,' says Harry, 'We might be on to something – others might have had the same idea.' I'd like to think he is right, but before we are halfway down the path, I can see there is no hope here. The beach is too shallow for a jetty and there's no sign of any boats. What I do see, however, is a small group of people gathered by a tent, and a campfire. When Harry spots them, he stops, probably thinking there's no point continuing. But I am curious, so I walk on. I wonder who they are and what they are doing here, looking so relaxed and carefree, considering the circumstances. It crosses my mind that they don't realize what is happening, that we should warn them.

'Where are you going?' asks Harry.

'To check if they are OK.'

'We need to keep moving.'

'I'm tired. I want to rest for a bit. And they might have food.' I think at first that he's going to leave, but after a moment he follows behind. Perhaps he's curious, too. Or hungry, more like.

My stilettos are useless in the soft sand, so I discard them at the top of the beach and swing them in my hand. The sand between my toes is warm, reminding me of childhood holidays, happier days. It's a long time since I've walked barefoot in the sand. I'd forgotten how I always enjoyed this sensation. I reach the group – a couple of men and women in their twenties and thirties and an older woman in her sixties. She shouldn't fit in, but she looks relaxed, sitting in a chair, swigging coke from a bottle, her feet spread out in the sand. Perhaps she's someone's mother.

'What are you doing here?' I ask as I reach them.

The man with curly hair says, 'We've worked out we can't get away. So we've decided to sit it out. Enjoy the time we have left.'

'Join us,' says the young black woman. 'We've plenty of food and wine.' Harry rolls his eyes, I can see him thinking *bunch of hippies*, but I'm intrigued.

'We can stay, can't we, Harry?' He looks like he's about to walk off, but he nods. 'For a while.'

I sit down on the blanket, introduce myself and take the offered glass of wine. For the first time in six hours I breathe deeply. I sip the wine and look at the sea. Tomorrow, if we don't make it out, it will consume us, but at this moment the beach, in the pink and blue light at the end of the day, seems to be the most beautiful place in the world.

Facebook Messenger
To: Seren Lovelace

6.30 p.m.

Have you seen this Facebook page everyone's talking about? People gathered on Dowetha Beach. The hair's different but that's Penny, isn't it? Andy.

To: Andy Jones

God. I think you're right. S.

BBC Breaking News 6.45 p.m.

. . . Downing Street confirms that the Natural Disaster Early Warning Unit, cancelled due to government funding cuts could have identified the problem sooner. Senior volcanologist claims lives will be lost because of it. More to follow . . .

Virginia Moffatt

Facebook
Dowetha Live

30 August 6.50 p.m.

Image: Group selfie, four women, three men, sitting round a campfire.

Welcome to Dowetha Live.

We're down in Cornwall and we don't think we can get out in time. So we're staying here, to enjoy the time we have left.

It's beautiful on this beach. We're going to share photos and thoughts as the night goes on. But we know it won't be easy. We could do with some help, so please leave encouraging thoughts below.

Word of warning. Trolls not welcome. Your comments will be deleted and you will be blocked.

Like 20 Share 10

Sue Hastings. I can't even . . . Wow. You're amazingly brave. Sending love and thoughts.

Alec Howes. Hope you find friendship and comfort tonight. Solidarity.

2 mins

Salaam Mosque. The community of the Salaam Mosque will be praying for you throughout our daily prayers. We are with you in your sadness and fear. Inshallah you shall find hope and generosity in these last hours. Love and Peace. x

10 mins

The Wave

Facebook
Poppy Armstrong

30 August 7.00 p.m.

It is six hours since I last posted. Six hours! I am overwhelmed by the warmth of your messages, and for your concern for me. Thank you. I'm afraid I cannot answer everyone so please accept this general post instead. The most important thing to tell you is that I am no longer alone. There are several of us now. Some came by chance, looking for sea air. Some in response to my message. Some because they have run out of places to go. And despite what is to come, Dowetha has served up its best for us today. Strong winds, and bright sunshine, made for a perfect surf this afternoon, followed by an invigorating swim. The air has stilled since and now the water is calm. The sun is setting, sending us red beams across the water, a final reminder of the beauty of our days, before the onset of darkness. Pale blue lingers in the sky – soon it will be replaced by blackness of night as the stars rise to shine on us for the last time

It is still hard to imagine it as we've sipped our beer or wine and nibbling salt and vinegar crisps, waiting for food to cook on the barbecue. Hard to face the fact of our deaths when we feel so alive in the warm glow of day's end. Hard to realize this is the last time any of us will listen to the soft splash of the waves on the shore – the sound of the

Virginia Moffatt

sea moving back and forth, back and forth. Today has been like any of the other summer days I have spent here, surfing, swimming, sunbathing. It's been just another summer day except for the knowledge that a volcano 2,000 miles way is about to collapse. That our fates were decided by cracks that appeared in its surface long before most of us were even born.

We have had our fair share of complaints sitting here, about the unfairness of it all. *If* the scientists had not made such a terrible mistake, *if* we hadn't moved here to escape the smoggy dangerous city, *if* only we'd gone to visit friends as we'd planned . . . *If, if, if* . . . we'd be watching on TV like the rest of the horrified nation, instead of sitting here, with the cooling sand slipping between our toes, as the mournful gulls circle above us.

We keep wondering whether we were wrong to stay. Perhaps some on the road will make it in time. But those who tried, report sitting in solid traffic as cheese sandwiches congealed and engines over-heated. They carried on until the point at which it was clear they would not be moving any further; turned round and ended up here, lured by the open air, sea, the promise of company.

I suppose we could still go home. Bolt the door, draw the curtains, and hide under the duvet. We could spend the time watching box sets of *Star Trek* or *Friends*, *The Sopranos* or *House*, Anything that helped

74

us while away the time and pretend our world is not about to end.

And the wave will come for us wherever we are, and whatever we are doing. So I am glad we are here to face it. Tomorrow morning, nine hours after the collapse of Cumbre Vieja, the sea will draw in its waters with the deepest of breaths. It will retreat far down the ocean bed, revealing the inhabitants of the sea bed – bass, cockles, mussels, crabs and snails – exposed for a moment to the air. And we will know, then, that the wave is coming for us. A thousand feet of water racing towards us, condemning us to death.

It is still hard to imagine it, sitting here on this perfect summer night, the sun departed, the first stars beginning to light the darkening sky, that tomorrow this will all be gone. *We* will all be gone. So we try not to. Instead we will sit by the campfire, telling each other the stories of our lives. Hands held in the darkness. Offering comfort in the face of what is to come.

The night will pass slowly. Watch with us if you can. When morning comes, we will be gone

Like Share Comment

30 likes 22 shares

Five other comments

Jake Marsden Silly bitch. You should have left. You deserve to drown

Alice Evans It's very slow now. We're hoping it will improve when we hit the dual carriageway. Singing silly songs to keep our spirits up . Glad you are not alone x

10 mins

Beverley Lewis Oh Poppy, you amaze as always. Will text you, perhaps we could chat?

3 mins

Finn Matthews. Lots of love, and ignore the trolls

2 min

COMPLINE

Poppy

The first wave of nausea hits me when I finish my post. I have managed, so far, not to think too much about tomorrow, but as I watch the red sun moving towards the horizon it occurs to me that this will be my last sunset. I am suddenly very aware of the thump of my heart, a heart that beats faster the more I think about it. Below me, I can see the glow of the campfire, and hear the murmur of voices above the swish, swish, swish of the waves, the squawks of sea birds. I should feel peaceful sitting here watching Venus rise in the pale blue sky, surrounded by the warmth that still lingers now the wind has died down. On an ordinary evening I would be feeling calm, happy, relaxed.

But this is not an ordinary evening. Now I am alone, I am hit with the full force of that. Nothing is typical tonight. My chest tightens and my breathing quickens. I try to focus on the sound of the waves, the rhythm of the water moving in and out. But it only serves to remind me of the wave that is to come. Breathe deep, I tell myself, breathe deep, but all I do is gulp the air so fast I cannot breathe. My vision blurs. I gasp and I gasp and I gasp – I am drowning in my fear. I cannot make it stop. The sickness builds up inside me until, all of a sudden, I cannot hold it in. I turn around in time to throw up in the bin behind me.

Throwing up helps. I breathe a little deeper, and then deeper still. Presently, I find I am able to stand up. My legs are shaking, but they are strong enough to take me to the clubhouse toilets where I wash my face and rinse my mouth. I gaze at myself in the mirror. I don't look too bad, considering . . . I don't let myself finish the sentence. I need to compose myself before I go back to the others. I don't want them to see me reduced like this. I invited them so I wouldn't be alone tonight, but now they are here I find myself wanting to be the person who holds it all together. I am not quite sure why. Perhaps I want to be seen as strong, because generally I am not. Or perhaps I am just seeking redemption. My reflection stares back at me, as it reasserts the deceptive mask of calm, the face that says all is well. It's been a while since I've had to use this trick; I'm a little unsettled by how easy the habit re-establishes itself. I check myself in the mirror again. I look fine. It is time to go back.

At the top of the slope, I slip off my shoes. The path still retains the heat of the day. But when I cross to the sand, though the surface is warm, the granules are cool underneath. It's a pleasant feeling, and one I won't experience for much longer, so I take my time, making the most of it. The smell of smoke and sausages draws me back to the campfire where Yan has been busy in my absence.

'Grub up,' he calls and we obediently form a queue for food. I take a plate and plonk myself down by Nikki. Yan sits down next to me. We seem to have got through one bottle of wine already, so James opens another one, passing it round the group. I pour myself a glass and swill a mouthful of Rioja in my mouth, glad I bought the good wine with me. For a while, everyone is too busy eating and drinking to speak much, which gives the chance to observe them discreetly. I've decided already that Yan is all right. More than all right. He's mucked in, cooked and worked hard to make everyone feel welcome. It's just a shame that I wasn't imagining his interest earlier; he keeps giving me sideways glances when he thinks I'm not looking. It's just as well it's not just the two of us; it should make it easier, to avoid any moment that might signal intimacy, but it's a nuisance. Why does life have to be so complicated even now?

Our most recent arrivals, Shelley and Harry, are sitting slightly apart from the main body of the group. I'm taking that in the way I'm sure Harry intends. He has made no bones about the fact he thinks we're stupid to be sitting here, not trying to escape. I get the sense that she might be thinking otherwise, but she seems content to let him do all the talking, which makes me respect her less. Why are some women so content to walk in a man's shadow? I've never understood that. Still, it doesn't endear her to me. I move on.

Margaret. Now Margaret is a different sort of woman completely. Though she was flustered on arrival, after a cup of tea and a chat, she soon settled in. Watching her, as she sits with food on her lap, a plastic mug in her hand, she retains the authoritative air of the former civil servant, the person you can trust in a crisis. As if to confirm my thoughts, here she is offering to get some more tents from home later. She smiles at me and I immediately feel a rush of warmth towards her.

James and Nikki complete the circle. They are sitting quite close to each other. He is whispering something in her ear and she is grinning. They've only known each other a few hours, but there seems to be something between them. Do people really fall for each other that quickly? Or is it just the situation we find ourselves in? Whatever the reason, it makes me feel happy, right at this moment, that I've been the means of bringing them together. Of bringing us all together. I have a momentary rise of panic when I think what that means. I push it firmly back in its box. I am determined I will not let fear ruin this evening.

'Fuck,' says Yan, interrupting my thoughts.

'What?'

'The BBC is saying that a few years ago the government cancelled the National Disaster Early Warning Unit. They're saying that it could have saved us...'

Fuck indeed.

'That's assuming it would have worked,' says Margaret.

'Of course it would have worked,' says Harry sharply.

He glowers at Margaret who blushes for some reason. Time to change the subject.

'Let's play a get-to-know-you game,' I say with my best hostess voice. 'How about we share our favourite memory?'

Harry rolls his eyes, but to my surprise is the first one to contribute. 'That's easy . . .' Shelley gazes at him, with a smile that suggests she knows what he is going to say. The smile tightens into a thin grimace when he adds 'Losing my virginity to Aileen Cooper. I was fifteen, she was seventeen. I was the envy of the class . . .' He turns to her, not appearing to see the tears in her eyes, 'What about you, Shells?'

'Five years old, walking in the park with my Mum, feeding the ducks. I used to love doing that.'

'Mine's with my grandmother ,' says Margaret. 'Being in her kitchen while she cooked bread. Feeling warm, safe, loved.' Shelley nods, and moves closer towards her.

'Riding the surf on Bondi Beach. That was some fortnight,' says Yan.

'I always wanted to do that one,' I say, realising with a jolt that I'll never have the chance now. 'For me it's probably seeing the Niagra Falls for the first time. It was winter, the water was half frozen in weird shapes, and I had the whole place to myself. I went back years later in the summer when they were roaring and you could take the boat to the bottom and get splashed by the spray, but it wasn't quite the same.'

'Wish it was cold enough to freeze the sea tomorrow,'

says James. We laugh, even Harry. 'My best moment? Getting a first. I'd worked so hard, and I was so proud. The day I got the email . . . well, nothing's quite topped that since.'

'My family,' says Nikki, her voice soft, and close to tears. 'Being with my parents and siblings. Any time, anywhere, any place.'

'Well, that was all very heartwarming,' says Harry. 'How about your worst moment?'

My heart sinks. There is no way I can share my worst moment. Not just because it is so awful I try never to think of it, but if I told them what I'd done, they'd hate me for sure. As Harry regales us with a story about a lost deal, I rack my brains to come up with an alternative. 'So that's my worst moment – apart from right now, of course.'

'Harry!' says Shelley. 'That's an awful thing to say, when everyone is being so kind.' Harry doesn't apologize, but prods her for an answer. She gazes into the fire, pulling at a strand of hair, then says, 'Mum dying was awful, but at least were all together with it, flunking maths GCSE for the third time was somehow worse, because it was just me on my own. Dad had stopped being cross by then, he was just so disappointed. I couldn't bear his disappointment.'

'Falling out with my cousin,' says Margaret.

I'm still trying to think of an answer, when Yan steps in. 'The day my dad left . . .' He shakes his head, 'Even today, it's hard to talk about . . . What about you, Poppy?'

'My parents dying.' It's not entirely untrue. That was a

terrible day. And, in a funny sort of way, it's partly responsible for where I ended up. But it's not my worst day ever,
not by a long chalk.'

Everyone nods. Yan and I have managed to gain the
sympathies of the whole group.

'Nowhere as bad, but getting lost when I was four, was
pretty dreadful,' James says, 'I thought my parents would
never come.'

'Similar,' says Nikki, 'Only I was eight and we had just
arrived in Nigeria, so it felt even scarier.'

'Touché,' says James, squeezing her arm. I raise an
eyebrow at Yan, *that was quick,* and then wish I hadn't,
there is far too much suggestion in his returning glance.
I'm grateful to Margaret for offering me an escape.

'I think I'd better go and get my tents before it's too late,'
says Margaret.

'Want some help?' Yan asks.

'That would be kind.' Yan jumps up and I'm relieved.
That's one less thing to worry about for a while.

'All the more wine for the rest of us,' I say as they depart
up the beach and the conversation turns to favourite
comedy shows. We all agree *Friends* was great, but too
many repeats may just have killed it. Nikki thinks it's a
bit problematic these days, but I think that's just political
correctness. James likes *Big Bang Theory,* Nikki, *Episodes,*
though maybe it's not a comedy in the purest sense. I love
Catastrophe and am devastated that Carrie Fisher died
after she'd shot the last episode. We all loved *Fleabag.* James

likes all the old classics like *Porridge* and *Open All Hours*. Though reprising the last two has been a mistake. He concludes that *Dinnerladies* is genius and what the world really needs is a new *Gavin and Stacey*.

There is a lull in the conversation. James picks up his guitar and begins to sing a song that sounds vaguely familiar, Ed Sheeran I think. He has a pleasant voice and he plays well. It is almost possible to imagine, listening to him that tonight will be no different from any other beach night: good food, wine, good company before bed, and waking up to sunshine and the promise of another fine day in the morning. The song ends and he begins another. '21 Guns' by Green Day. Of all the songs he could have chosen, he has to pick Seren's favourite. I wish he hadn't. I don't want to spend these hours thinking back on my mistakes, the apology I never gave and never will now. I sip my wine, watching the fire as stick by stick ignites, blazes orange, crumbles and fades to white ash at the base of the flames, reminding me how quickly time is passing. There is so little left to me there is no point dwelling on the past. I lied and lied and left her in ruins, but it was a long time ago. I can't change what I did, and there's nothing I can do that could make a difference now. I stand up to put more kindling on the fire. Sparks fly as I lay it in the centre of the flame and the branches burn brightly for a while, lifting my spirits. But it is not long before the light flickers as they begin to crumble and fade, with the same inevitability as all the rest.

Yan

The burgers are sizzling on the barbecue. In front of me, the sea burns in the light of the setting sun. Red sky at night, shepherd's delight. Tomorrow will be glorious. A day for swimming, surfing and sunbathing – except it won't. I'm not going to make it past eight o'clock . . . The thought stops me in my tracks. I've spent all afternoon trying to avoid the truth and now it staring right back at me. This sunset will be my last.

It doesn't seem possible.

Smoke stings my eyes, accompanied by an acrid smell. Shit. The food is burning. I salvage the sausages, but the burgers are black. That'll teach me to wallow in self-pity. I shove them into a plastic bag and grab some more from the cold box. Good job Poppy brought so much with her.

'Everything all right?' calls Margaret.

'Fine.' I've got over my resentment that she has deprived me of sharing this night with Poppy alone. I've had to because after she came, who should pitch up but James? And with a beautiful woman in tow, which put paid to any supercilious triumph I might have felt at being proved right. I really don't know how he does it. First Lisa, now Nikki. Why can't I have luck like that? My mood wasn't much improved by Harry and Shelley's arrival. Another gorgeous woman, but this one with a man twice her age. I decided immediately that he was a total arsehole. He had to be. He certainly put a dampener on the campfire conversation – it's clear he thinks we're idiots – so I volunteered to make supper to keep out of his way. I was doing quite well until I let a thought about tomorrow creep in. I won't let that happen again. I turn the burgers and keep my mind focussed on the task in hand.

Soon the meat is cooked and I have a queue of people ready to eat. Poppy is last. I'd like to think she did that on purpose so she could sit next to me, but I'm fairly sure that's not true. She was probably just being a polite hostess, making sure the guests had eaten first. Still, I take comfort from her warm thank you for the food, which gives me the illusion that I'm her co-host. I watch her discreetly when she isn't looking; please God, if you exist – which I really doubt – but if you do, please give me this last morsel of comfort. If James can find himself a woman today, surely I can too?

The sun is nearly gone; it hovers on the horizon, glowing orange and red, the evening star shining brightly beside it. It is still warm, the air calm, the ebb and flow of the waves hushing us. It's a perfect end to the day. To . . . my last day. I bite into the burger, trying not to think that this is my last supper. It doesn't seem real. I realize that I haven't called Mum yet. I check my phone. It's nearly eight o'clock and Warsaw is an hour ahead. She'll be getting ready for bed. If I call her now it will only make her anxious. I shouldn't do that, it wouldn't be fair. Besides, she wasn't any help when Karo died, why would that be any different tonight? Wouldn't it serve her right if I don't speak to her ever again? If she hears on the news and has to deal with it all by herself, like I had to? No, that's too cruel. I have to speak to her, it wouldn't be fair. I stare at her number. I won't phone now – it's too late. Probably best to call first thing, keep it simple, say goodbye and leave it at that. It's not as if she needs me anyway. Not when she has her church group, her Father Piotr, and the dogs to keep her busy.

I am about to put my phone away, when a news alert flashes up. Fuck. The government cut the early warning unit that might just have saved our lives. Fuck. Fuck. Fuck. I realize I must have said that last one out loud, because Poppy asks how I am. Stupid idiot, I should have kept this to myself. Now I've silenced everyone completely. It's bad enough that we are here. But the thought that we might have avoided it . . .? No one looks at each other, we're all thinking the same thing I expect. No one knows what to say. And then, thank God, Poppy suggests a getting-to-know-you game. What a hero. She must be feeling as awful as the rest of us but here she is pulling us together, helping us through the fear. The least I can do is take her lead sharing my memories of Bondi Beach. God, I loved it there, it was one of my best times ever. Why didn't I stay ? I could have applied for citizenship eventually – if I'd only stayed, I be watching all this from my TV.

Don't think about it. There's no point thinking about it, or about the government cuts that got us here. If I listen carefully to the others, I can stop myself focussing on the negative. It's easy enough till Harry speaks. I was right, he *is* an arsehole. He shares a story from his sleazeball past and doesn't even notice how much it upsets Shelley. I'm not surprised, then, that he shifts the game to get us to talk about our worst moments. I'm with Shelley: isn't it bad enough we're here? What's the point of thinking about our bad days now? Nonetheless, tonight has a bit of a Truth or Dare vibe about it, and so I tell them the truth and talk about the day Dad left. I don't go into too much detail, just how he walked out mid-row saying, sorry kids but he couldn't take it anymore. I don't explain why he couldn't take it or how Mum retreated into her room and stayed there for days, leaving me and Karo to fend for ourselves. I've never told anyone any of that I'm not going to start tonight, I pass the question to Poppy instead.

She talks about the death of her parents in a car crash. It is not surprising, given what she's said earlier, but for some reason, I've got the impression she's not telling the truth. That she's come up with a stock answer because the real one is worse. Though I can't imagine what would be worse then losing your parents at such a young age. I must try and ask her later, hopefully, we're building enough trust between us that she'd be willing to share. James and Nikki both tell similar stories; they smile and he touches her. Jammy bastard. Noticing it, Poppy raises her eyes at me and I raise mine back. That's hopeful, isn't it? If she's willing to share a silent commentary with me, maybe she'll be willing to give me a chance. Maybe I'll strike lucky, too. But before I can follow up, Margaret says she needs to get the tents. Stupidly, in my attempt to impress Poppy, I said I'd help earlier. So I have no option but to follow her to her car.

'How far is it?' I say as I clamber into the passenger seat.

'Three miles. Shouldn't take long at this time of night, with the roads this empty.' I gaze out of the window. The last vestiges of light are being squeezed from the horizon behind, but above the high green hedges, all is blackness. Normally, I like driving at night-time, finding something soothing about moving through the darkness, the road ahead illuminated by the headlights, the occasional flash of another car. But not tonight. Tonight, the hedges press in menacingly, the lack of traffic increases the sense of isolation, the feeling that danger is close and I cannot prevent it.

'Here we are,' she says as we turn into a narrow lane. 'That's my house on the right, but first do you mind if we call in on my friend Minnie first, see if she's OK?'

'Of course.' We continue up the lane till we reach a privet hedge and row of poplar trees, behind which there is a small cottage. The lights are off, but we can hear music.

'She must have fallen asleep with the CD player on,' says Margaret as she picks up the key from under the mat and opens the door 'Min?' There is no answer, but a cat meowing. She switches on the hall light. I follow her through to the sitting room at the back of the house. The old woman is sitting in an upright chair, looking out towards the sea. The moon has risen, catching the light of the setting sun from the other side of the world; it hangs like a golden globe above the ocean, it's beams picking out the grooves on her face, and . . . something is wrong. The cat is pawing at her feet and yet she is making no response. The angle of her body is odd. Her limbs aren't relaxed, as they would be if she was sleeping, they are stiff, awkward. Her eyes are open. Margaret turns on the light, and now I can see the woman's skin is leached of any colour, smooth and waxy, like a mannequin.

'Oh!' Margaret's cry is as piteous as the cat's.

'Is she . . .?' She nods as she sits down, looking at her friend.

'I'm sorry.'

'Would you mind . . .?' Margaret tries to gather herself together. 'Only I think the cat might need feeding. The food's in the kitchen – on the right.'

I have never seen a dead body before. The undertaker suggested it with Karo but I couldn't bear to. The sight of the old woman gives me the creeps. I am only too happy to be given a practical task to take me away from the room, the corpse, the pale skin, the blank eyes. I find the cat food in a cupboard, open the tin and bang it. The cat comes running and is soon munching on the chunks of meat. I open another one and leave it in a bowl besides the first. I have no idea how much food a cat might eat in eight hours, but it seems cruel for the animal to be hungry. I fill up the water bowl to the brim and reluctantly return to the room. Margaret has placed a blanket over her friend, closed her eyes and is now sitting beside her, holding her hand. She is praying.

'The Lord grant you a quiet night and a perfect end,' she concludes, before leaning over and kissing the old woman's head. 'Come on,' she says.

We return to the car in silence and drive back to Margaret's house. It is only when we enter that she says, 'Before we do anything, do you mind if we have a drink? There's a bottle of white wine left in the fridge.' I nod, and follow her from the kitchen to the patio in the back garden overlooking the sea. We sit gazing over the view that was Minnie's last, drinking the wine.

'Are you all right?' I say. 'That must have been quite a shock.'

'Yes . . . no . . . I'm not sure.' Margaret twists her glass, her voice shakes. 'The thing is, when I saw her earlier, she said she'd like to go like that, fall asleep looking at the sea. But I thought she meant she'd just not get up tomorrow. I didn't realize she'd take pills. I should have stayed with her.'

'Perhaps she wanted to be alone'

'I wish I'd been there to hold her hand.'

93

'You came back.'

'Yes.'

'What was that prayer you were saying? It sounded vaguely familiar.'

'Compline. Night prayer. Prayers the monks say. It's a good one for the end of the day, the end of a life. A reflection on events, a hope for a better time to come.'

'Not much hope in our situation.'

'True. Though that doesn't make prayer is useless.'

'Doesn't make it useful!'

'That's a matter of opinion.'

'I gave up on it all a long time ago. My mum's Catholic but . . . let's say she didn't give God a good image.'

Margaret's phone bleeps 'Do you mind? That's my daughter. We agreed to Skype.'

'Why don't you show me the loft and I can be getting the tents while you do?'

She points me in the right direction and disappears to the sitting room where I can hear the murmur of voices. I pull down the loft ladder, clamber up, turn the light on, and search for the tents. They are buried in the corner behind a couple of dusty suitcases and camping equipment. I gather them up and throw them down the hatch and climb down after them. Margaret is still talking when I put the ladder away and so I load them in the car and sit in the front seat, waiting for her.

She arrives shortly after. Despite the upset of the evening, and the probably difficult Skype call with her daughter, she doesn't appear to be as flustered as she was when they first met. In fact, she doesn't seem to be worried at all. How can she be so composed?

'Can I ask you something?' I say as she drives down the lane. 'Are you scared?'

'Petrified.'

'You don't look it.'

'Looks can deceive. I'm terrified.' She turns the wheel as we approach a bend. 'I'm angry, too. I have no right to be, I know. I'm older than all of you. I've had a good life, a happy one, mainly. I've loved and been loved, I've had a child a grandchild, and another on the way. I've achieved most of my ambitions. But I'm not ready to go yet. Not like this, so quickly. My last years in the civil service – they were tough. I spent years delivering cuts I didn't believe in, and I vowed that when I retired, I'd make up for it. I've hardly had time to get started. I've not had time to say goodbye to the people I love and I've got unfinished business with some. All I've got is tonight and that's it. It's cruel.'

'Yes—'

'But you know what? As my mother would have said, "There's no use crying over spilt milk." None at all.' She switches on her CD player – monks singing the words she just prayed with Minnie, '*The Lord grant us a quiet night and a perfect end.*'

The music is soothing, the sentiment well-intentioned, but as we drive back through the darkness, I feel anything but comforted.

Margaret

It takes me less than half an hour on the beach to decide that I am going to stay. It is not just that the company is congenial – Poppy and Yan could not have been more welcoming. But it is clear, when Nikki and James turn up, that the traffic situation isn't improving, which is confirmed when I check the BBC. There are mass evacuations from every affected coastline in the world, but everyone agrees, the road jams are worst in Cornwall. By six o'clock all the reports are saying no one south of St Austell can be sure of reaching the safety zone, confirming once and for all that we never stood a chance. Poppy and Yan had the right idea from the beginning. So now I have made my decision, I feel more peaceful. It is far better to spend my time here enjoying the scenery, eating, drinking and being merry. If this is my last day on earth, and it looks like it will be, it is better to be in company, than cursing, alone, in my car.

It is only Hellie that is bothering me. Of course, I'm scared but I can see a benefit in going like this. At least I will be spared the gradual encroachment of old age, the deterioration of mind and body, the indignity of needing help with bodily functions. At least I won't be a burden to my daughter in an age of dwindling public resources. It's not the same for Hellie. She still needs me. For advice with the new baby, help with Toby, just for my presence in the world. Richard's dead. My brother Andrew is dead. Hellie has no other family but me. Well, no family she's in touch with. It would be different if Kath and I were still speaking – at least she'd have a kind of substitute – but I can't imagine Kath being too receptive to that idea if I try to contact her now.

I have all this in mind when I call Hellie to let her know my decision. Though I intend to be rational, so as not to upset her, that quickly proves impossible. I can tell when she answers the phone that she is anxious and things don't get much better from there.

'Where are you?' she says. 'Are you making progress?'

'Have you seen the news, love? The traffic is going nowhere.'

'What are you saying?'

'I'm sorry . . .'

'No, Mum . . . no!' her voice is almost a whisper. 'You must be able to get out. Just keep moving and you'll be fine.'

'I'm afraid I won't.' She is silent, and then I can hear that she is crying. 'I'm sorry,' I say, as if that can help matters.

'Where are you, then?' Hellie tries and fails to keep the wobble out of her voice.

'Dowetha Cove. I've met some people. They're nice. I'm going to camp with them tonight.'

'You? Camping? I thought you hated it.'

'Only when it's raining.'

'It was always raining.' This is better, keeping it light.

'Anglesey, when we thought the wind would blow us away.'

'Dartmoor, when the car got stuck in the mud.'

'Oh gosh, yes.' I giggle, remembering how I revved and revved only to sink deeper and deeper, till a neighbouring camper rescued us with a tow rope. 'Don't forget Wye Valley when we flooded.'

'I thought we were going to drown.' The laughter leaves her voice. 'Oh, Mum . . .'

'Is Ed home?' I try to revert to motherly briskness.

'He's just walked in.'

'Good. You'd better tell him what's happening. I've promised I'll go and get some tents, so I'll Skype later. Say around eight thirty?'

She agrees and I hang up.

I wish I had a sister, or Hellie did. I wish she had someone other than Ed to turn to. It's not that he isn't lovely and kind; I just think she is going to need more help than that. If only Kath and I hadn't argued. If only we hadn't been so stubborn. If only we'd proved better grown-ups than our fathers. But we weren't. Our row in 2010 was as stupid as theirs in 1959 and 1985 and just as irrevocable. Both of us too proud to be the one to admit we were in the wrong, to make the first move to put it right. Oh Kath! After all these years, I miss you still. I wish we were still friends. It would make all of this a little bit easier.

Still. There's no point worrying about what you can't have, as my mother used to say. A mantra I repeated to Hellie time and time again after Richard died, when money was tight and I couldn't afford a treat. Enjoy what you have, I'd always add, it's more than most. I should really live by my own words, shouldn't I? I stand for a moment, staring out over the beach. It is a spectacular evening. The air is still warm and the red sun is hanging above the horizon, its reflection distorted by the ripples of the sea. I watch the flurry of activity beneath me, as the campfire is being set up and Yan is sorting out the barbecue. Despite the fear I feel, the sight fills me with joy. I stride back to the camp, offer to help with the cooking. Yan is happy doing it on his own, so I enjoy teasing him from the sidelines about his inability to cut an avocado properly and the fact that he burns one lot of burgers to a crisp. He seems to appreciate it and teases me back with affection.

The feeling of warmth and laughter stays throughout dinner, till Yan shatters it. Damn. I've begun to feel a connection with these people, particularly with him. Why does he have to be the one to break the news about the volcano project? I can see in his eyes how much the news devastates him. Everybody is immediately quiet with the shock of it. I am, too. I had no idea this would get out.

There is an empty space into which I could speak. *Should* speak. Explain my part in it. It's not exactly my fault, but . . . I open my mouth; nothing comes, and then Poppy distracts us with a question and the moment is gone. The conversation lasts long enough for everyone to forget, I hope for good, and long enough for me to remember I promised to get tents.

I'm glad Yan comes with me. It is getting dark now and I hate driving in the dark. Particularly now the anxieties are crowding back in. It is good to have company. It is steadying. Though I haven't had a drink, the stress of the day has made me a little lightheaded. Having Yan besides helps me concentrate. I like this thoughtful young man who is doing his best to take care of me. 'This must be what it is like to have a son,' I say out loud.

'How come you didn't?' he asks as we drive through the darkening lanes.

'We wanted one. We would have. But . . . Richard, my husband, died in a train accident.'

'I'm sorry.' He is very kind. It crosses my mind that perhaps now is a good chance, to tell him about my job. How I came to be part of the team that cancelled that damned unit. He'd probably understand. Probably. But then I think of his face when he saw the news and his comments about funding cuts and I don't know where to start. Instead, I tell him about Richard,

'It was a long time ago . . . Poor Hellie. She was four at the time. Too young to really make sense of it. Because it was such a major news story, she's grown up with her father's death being very public. And here I am doing this to her again. On a bigger scale.'

'Hardly your fault.'

'True . . . Yet this is what she has to face.'

We reach my lane. Yan is amenable to visiting Minnie first, so I drive straight to her house which is in darkness, a CD is playing at the highest volume. Minnie is very deaf these days. It's just as well she has no neighbours or she'd be for ever getting complaints.

It is only when I enter the living room that I realize something is wrong. I've seen enough dead bodies to understand why Minnie is so stiff. 'Min!' I cry and then see the empty bottle of pills on the table. Suddenly all my calm feelings evaporate. I shouldn't have left her. When she said she wanted to sleep, I thought she meant she would have an early night. I didn't think she was going to do this. I shouldn't have left her. I didn't get away, anyway, and if I'd been with her, I could have stopped her. We could have comforted each other till the end. Yan hovers at the edge of the room. Seeing how nervous he is, I send him to the kitchen to feed the cat. I am glad of the chance to be alone with Minnie. I close the eyes that are staring out to sea, find a blanket to cover her up and take her hand. She shouldn't have been alone. I shouldn't have left her alone. I am crying as I recite the 'Our Father', followed by a 'Glory Be' but by the time I conclude with the last words of Compline, I am almost in control. 'The Lord grant you a quiet night and a perfect end.' At least Minnie's end has been peaceful, on her own terms, and I don't have to worry about her any more.

After I've kissed her goodbye, I take Yan to my house where a shared glass of wine helps restore my equilibrium. He's sensitive enough to offer to go in the loft, allowing me time to call Hellie. She appears on my monitor, her face red and blotchy. She has clearly been crying but now we are able to talk, she is making a huge effort. She tells me the latest news about Toby, who is sleeping, and Ed, who pops back in to say hello. How much time do we have? As long as we want. Ed will wait, Yan will wait. It's not as if we have to rush back to the beach. Yet we are both conscious as never before, that no matter how long the call is, it won't be long enough. There is so much we could say, yet none of it seems important or worthwhile. In the end, we resort to discussing recent books. Hellie has just finished *Swimming Lessons* by Claire Fuller; she thinks I'd like it. I've been relatively unadventurous and completed *Pride and Prejudice* for the tenth time. The conversation turns to our favourite topic – how women are treated by society and how much has changed since Austen's time. It almost normal till the end, and neither of us can quite say goodbye without our voices breaking. We agree to call again in the morning and then it is time to leave.

Yan is waiting in the car. I feel a rush of warmth towards him. I can open up to him, in a way I couldn't to Hellie.

Perhaps because we are in it together I can confess my terror, and anger about our impossible situation, even if I don't admit the irony of my possible contribution. The journey helps me regain control, to realize that, tonight, these new friendships are all that life has to offer me now. It is time to return to the others. My place, from now on, is at the beach.

James

I have never thought much about death before. I've never really had to. I didn't know Dad's parents and I was quite young when Mum's parents died. They were far away in England, so I don't really remember them. One or two of my friends have lost a parent and one, a cousin. Such events have been so outside my experience, I just haven't known what to say, apart from an inadequate 'sorry', before they, or I, have moved the conversation on. Death has never featured in my life before now. But now it is looming so large, it is all I can think about. Now I know there really is no escape, underneath the casual chatter, every moment is drenched in thoughts of mortality. I stare into the glowing flames of the campfire, joining in the conversation automatically when required, amazed how this strange social situation is following the norms of human behaviour. We've talked comedy programmes, guilty pleasures (I'm rather glad Yan had gone when I admitted to my sneaking admiration for love for *Twilight*), our first kiss, last kiss, pet hates, pet peeves, as if we are just a group of friends hanging out on the beach. On the surface, everything feels peaceful, but underneath, I can sense surges of panic if I allow myself to think about tomorrow.

Before dinner, I stupidly checked my Facebook page, and immediately wished I hadn't. There were over forty comments in response to my post, most of them from people I barely know. 'Friends' with whom I share Trump and Brexit memes, music videos or rant with about how crap the *X Factor* is when I'm drunk. All of them, suddenly, full of concern at my situation, which was touching, but only served to underline the hopelessness of my predicament. The direct messages were the worst. They were from real-life friends, horrified by what was happening. Tony and Jim, from uni, an old flatmate, Sue, Helen, from my days in the City – people I hadn't heard from in years. *Shit – are you OK? Sorry to hear the news. Anything I can do?* Multiple variations on the same theme. All of which spelt out, in black and white, that I am going to die and no one can help, that no one could prevent it from happening and no one could be besides me. And what could I say in reply? *Doing as well as can be expected. Thanks for the thought. Thanks for being there.* Meaningless bullshit to make them feel better, to give me the illusion that I was coping with it. When all the time what I really wanted to do is let out a scream of rage that could be heard from here all the way to Aberdeen. And all the time, the one person I wanted to hear from – Lisa – was the one person not to get in touch.

I'm way too English to do anything so embarrassing as

shout about my feelings, so I put my phone away and took myself down to the seashore, where I pushed my feet through the sand, watching the indentations I made fill with sea water, over and over again. The relentlessness of the incoming tide always infuriated me when I was a kid. I used to stand, Canute-like, yelling, 'Go back, go back', furious that the waves would never obey me. Standing there, I realized it infuriated me still and I found myself kicking sand at the tiny breakers that rushed towards me. All of a sudden I didn't care how stupid I sounded. 'Go back' I yelled. 'Go back.'

A hand touched me on the shoulder. 'Are you OK?' It was Nikki, who had come upon me so quietly, I didn't hear her.

'Facebook messages. They made me want to—'

'Scream?'

I nodded.

'I've had a few of those,' she added. Much to my regret she took her hand away, before asking, 'Have you spoken to your parents yet?'

'Sort of . . . Mum cried, Dad was gruff. We said we'd speak later. Difficult to know what to say in the circumstances. And they're in Lusaka, so the connection wasn't great. You?'

'They're on the plane now. They texted from Lagos airport before they boarded. They said that even though the coast won't be that badly affected, everyone is still leaving the city, including my grandparents. Mum and Dad were happy because they thought I was on my way to safety, God knows what I'm going to say to them when they land. How am I going to tell them I didn't make it?'

We stood in silence for a short while, a happy silence, the kind of silence that in normal circumstances would have made me think anything was possible between us. Then she said, 'I nearly forgot, Poppy asked if I'd sort the campfire out, but I'm a bit rubbish. Could you help?' That had to mean something I thought, as I followed her back to the camp, that she'd sought me out, understood, asked for my help? There was something too sad about it if I thought too hard about it, but as we laid the firewood out together, occasionally bumping arms, or smiling in encouragement at each other, it felt for a little while like we were a team. A thought to keep the dread at bay . . .

Now, though, the conversation has lulled, and there is nothing to stop the panic from swelling inside me. Conscious that I'm about to make a fool of myself – and I really don't want to do that, particularly not in front of Nikki – I do what I always do when I'm feeling tense. I pick up my guitar and begin to sing. I start with an old favourite by Green Day. It is only when I begin 'Tenerife Sun' that I become aware that Nikki is looking at me. I know, then, that I haven't misread the signs: she is reading the meaning in the words that I intend. I throw everything into the music, am glad of her smile of appreciation when I finish. I sing another, and another, before picking up 'Chasing Cars'. By now I am 90 per cent certain she understands; she holds my gaze and I'm sure her smile is just for me. I could keep singing like this for ever, reaching out to her, anticipating her response, when I am conscious of voices on the path. Yan and Margaret are back. I finish the song and put my guitar down, with a final glance at Nikki, as we rise to welcome them back.

'There are four tents, and seven of us,' says Poppy, 'So, me and Nikki, James and Yan, Shelley and Harry, and Margaret on your own?'

That makes sense to all of us, except Harry. He has spent the last hour in intense whispered conversations with Shelley and now he says, 'This is ridiculous. You're just going to go to sleep like normal, wake up and *drown*? What is wrong with you? Why aren't you trying to escape?'

'I tried,' says Margaret. 'It was no good.'

'There was no way out of Penzance,' I say.

'No way by road or rail, maybe. We should be looking for a boat,' says Harry.

'But that didn't work either,' says Shelley.

'We're wasting time here.'

'Help me with the tent,' she says. He looks like he is about to refuse, but thinks better of it.

'We're going to need rocks to pin down the tent pegs,' says Poppy, taking the lead as usual. It's impressive how she's kept us together – it helps to have someone calm and authoritative to follow in these circumstances. Nikki offers to get the stones. I think of joining her, but it feels a bit too obvious, so instead, I start gathering tent poles, trying

109

to pretend this is a normal summer night, camping out on the beach. The others join in and before long we've formed into teams. Me and Yan, Poppy and Margaret, Shelley and Harry.

I'm glad to have the chance to work with Yan. It's not just because he knows what he is doing and I don't. It's the first opportunity I've had to spend time with him since Nikki and I got here. I want to let him now that I'm grateful for telling me about the beach, for making us welcome, for not gloating, but I don't quite know how to. We've never been very good at communicating our feelings to each other. As always, it's easier just to focus on practical matters and assume he'll understand. We're halfway through when Nikki returns with the stones. She hands them over to Poppy before walking down the beach again. I'd like to watch her, but the wind is building up and Yan needs all my help to hold the frame upright as he piles rocks on the guy ropes and places. It is only when we are finished that I can gaze in Nikki's direction. I can tell by the way she is sitting that the conversation is intense. She looks like she might be crying. I want to cry too. This is all so—

'Fucking pointless!' shouts Harry, as the tent he and Shelley are trying to erect falls over for the fifth time.

'Want some help?' Yan asks.

'I'm fine,' says Harry. He looks a long way from fine, but he makes it clear we are not needed, so we return to the fire. Poppy and Margaret are already there, engaged in an intense discussion about the Catholic Church. As I sit down, Nikki approaches us, so I wave at her to join me. She slips beside me, leaning against me as if it is the most natural thing in the world. Her hair smells of wood smoke, her skin of coconut cream. For a second I hesitate to put my arms around her because it feels like I am betraying Lisa. But then I remind myself that Lisa left me and I am a free agent. Whatever this is, I deserve a chance to take it where it leads. I put my arms around her and it feels as if I have held her always.

'Forgive me,' says Poppy, 'I do believe in God, sort of, I think. It's just churches I can't bear. Why should I go and worship with a bunch of people who think loving women is wrong?' Yan cannot hide the startled look on his face. Oh no, poor Yan, did he have hopes in that direction?

'Most church goers don't think that any more,' says Margaret. 'A lot of people in my generation are far more relaxed about sex then you might imagine. And the younger generation are so tolerant, they're teaching us a lot. Plenty of priests disagree with the hierarchy.'

Poppy snorts. 'Paedophiles . . .'

Margaret sighs. 'That's such a bigoted view.'

'What?'

'The assumption that because *some* wicked priests have sinned, all of them have. It does a great disservice to the many good priests who quietly go about their business, preaching, counselling, supporting their parishioners through crises, constantly in demand, with no life outside the parish door, asking no thanks for it. It's terrible when a priest is uncovered as an abuser, and I agree, the Church has covered up too many cases, and is not covering itself in glory even now. But it's not the only institution that's done that. Look at the BBC, public schools, government, the film industry.'

'Fair point; no women, though,' says Poppy.

'Another thing I'd like to change,' says Margaret. 'But churches can do great things too. All those volunteers in food banks, religious leaders challenging the government – and the Pope, for all his faults, talking about poverty and tackling climate change. That's got to count for something, hasn't it?'

Poppy suggests the Church's moral failures mean it has no right to lecture others, besides it isn't the Church's place to get into politics. Margaret disagrees, and then somehow Yan is involved and off he goes on his soapbox. Things are so mucked up in politics these days that social democratic policies are considered hard left, when actually the centrists are soft right, and the right are getting as bad as the National Front. It's not that I disagree with him particularly, it's just his po-faced relentlessness. Every time I say anything to counter his world view, I'm called a Blairite, a neoliberal weasel, or a vassal of the 1 per cent. And the thing that is so infuriating about all of it, is we have more in common then he gives me credit for. He's so tiresome in this mood – I wish he'd stop shouting and actually listen to me, or anyone else, for that matter.

Poppy clearly hasn't seen this side of Yan yet and makes the mistake of challenging him about the economy. When she argues that Labour caused the financial crash, he is red with fury.

'No. They. DID. NOT!'

'I'm sure Poppy's right,' said Shelley, as she joins the circle, 'Isn't that what you always say, Harry?' Harry nods. 'Of course.'

'It was the bankers. The wanking bankers.'

There is a pause and I think that Poppy has got the message, but the woman is made of stern stuff. Off she goes again, this time daring to suggest that, never mind who was to blame, austerity was necessary, at least in the beginning. At this Yan looks even more devastated then when he realized she is gay. I know him well enough to read his mind right now. *A fucking Tory, I fancy a fucking Tory?* Luckily, she turns it round, at least for now, when she adds, 'I do think it might have gone too far, though. My colleague's mum has had a terrible time with Social Services lately, I think the government needs to do something about that.'

Nikki says, 'Perhaps politicians should live with people who are on the receiving end of their policies. It might make them a bit more careful.'

'I'd agree with that,' says Poppy. 'Politicians on *all* sides should know what it's like for ordinary people. It should be a condition of being a politician that you take a day a week shadowing someone in at work your constituency.'

'I'd like them to have to try and apply for benefits,' says Yan. 'And live on them for over a week, without any handouts or help from friends or family.'

'Phew, something we can all agree on,' I say, thinking I will tell Nikki later she's a miracle worker to have stopped that argument in its tracks.

'I wish . . .' says Nikki, 'I wish we had some time. To do something about it . . . It's terrible we don't have any time.

And then she lets out a yell, right from the gut. Poppy joins in, followed by Yan, Shelley, even Margaret. Soon everyone is sobbing.. Only Harry and I remain silent. It's not that I don't want to join them, but I'm all cried out from earlier. I don't know what Harry is thinking, but he doesn't seem too impressed. And, when the noise dies down, and Shelley suggests a hug, he doesn't join, but stands to one side, scrolling through his phone, frowning. I turn away from him, hold on to Nikki on one side and Shelley on the other. Despite everything, we are united by the embrace. The six of us against the terrors of the night.

Nikki

I'm almost enjoying myself tonight. As long as I don't think too much, I can pretend that life is normal. That our diverting chat about films and politics is normal, that tomorrow I will go home as normal and start another day in the crap job, serving horrible people who will be rude or racist or both. I have hated my job all summer, but how I long for tomorrow to be a day where people will be rude to me, my hair will smell of fried fat and my legs and back will ache after a day serving burgers. How I long for people to be rude to me. How I long for that to be possible.

But that will not be the day I will have tomorrow. That will not be the day I will be allowed. Tomorrow everything ends after breakfast. Even though that still feels impossible. Life still seems to be going on as usual, the hours passing in idle chat, making what I know to be objectively true feel emotionally false. How can we be about to die when we're sitting around the fire? How can I have no tomorrows when James sang a love song that I was sure was directed at me and I'm feeling something that could almost count as falling in love? Despite the fact that I've sworn off white men, his music is slaying me. I know the words he is singing right now are for me, alone; that he wants to lie down with me, just the two of us against the world.

I stare across the flames at his face, so new, but already so familiar. His eyes are closed, allowing me to study his white, sculptured cheekbones, elegant nose, strong mouth. He looks like Bowie in his Thin White Duke phase, but without the whiff of racism. He opens his eyes as he repeats the line about lying down together, gazing directly at me. When he looks at me like that I want to shout, 'Yes, yes, yes!' crazy as it is, I want to forget everything but him and lie in his arms even for a short time. Above me, the sky is totally black, pricked with thousands of tiny stars. I can see the familiar constellations: Orion, the Great Bear, the Pole Star, Cassiopeia. And, because a couple of thousand miles away a bunch of rocks is about to fall in the sea, this will be the last night I will see them. And I have to ask myself, is the 'yes' I want to shout because James is gorgeous, or because I'm so damned terrified I'll cling to anyone tonight?

I do not have the opportunity to answer my question as Margaret and Yan reappear with tents, the song ends, and the mood dissipates. Soon everyone is busy, even me. I volunteer to collect rocks because I'm rubbish with tents. It is quite soothing, wondering among the pebbles, choosing stones that are large enough. And it whiles away the time until my family arrive at Gatwick. But once I have gathered enough rocks, I know I can't put it off any more. I find a spot away from the others and stare out across the water. The air is still warm, the moon is rising above the sea, lighting up a silver path across the water. Mum answers after one ring.

'Are you in Manchester?' she asks.

'No Mum. I couldn't get away.'

'Nikki, Nikki, Nikki,' She doesn't ask me how I am, but I know that's what she means.

'I'm OK,' I say trying to be brave, but my bravado disappears quickly. 'I'm sorry, Mum, I tried to leave, but . . .'

'It'll be all right.' Even from a distance, Mum always has the capacity to make me feel better, even though there is nothing all right about this.

'Are Granny and Grandpapa OK?'

'They're fine, they've gone to stay with friends in Ikeja. Where are you?'

'On this beach . . . I've found some people . . . they're nice.'

'I'm glad for that. I'm sorry we're not there.'

'It's not your fault.'

'It doesn't stop me being sorry.'

'I suppose not.' Then, thinking that it will make Mum feel better, thinking that I need to say it aloud to someone, 'The weird thing is, that I think I've met someone.'

'Really?'

'He's called James. He works in an antiques shop.'

'How old is he?'

'Twenty-nine'

'He's a bit old.'

'Mum!'

'Though I suppose it doesn't matter now.'

'I wouldn't put it as top of my important list. Is Dad there?'

'I'll hand you over.'

Dad comes to the phone. 'Hi, Nikki.'

'Hi, Dad.'

'This is all wrong.'

'What do you mean?'

'I expected you to be at my deathbed . . .'

'Oh.' I wanted to be strong, but I am crying before I can stop myself.

'Nikki . . .' His voice cracks too. 'I'm not ready to let you go.'

'Nor me, Dad.' I can't bear hearing the pain in his voice. 'You'd like it here, Dad, you'd like it. Reminds me of Devon. Do you remember?'

'We searched in the rock pools and jumped over the waves.' This is better.

'You held my hand, and I felt safe . . . It's just like that here. I've found some lovely people. And I know it sounds weird, but I'm feeling quite safe and almost happy.'

He clears his throat. 'Then I'm almost happy too.' He hands me to Ifechie, who tells me a stupid joke about Trump before passing me to Ginika. She holds the phone without saying anything I realize she is crying. 'It's all right,' I say, although it isn't. 'I'm all right. I'm having a nice time. I love you.' She whispers, 'I love you too,' and gives the phone back to Mum. 'We have to go through customs now. Call us later?'

'I will. And Mum? I love you.'

'I love you too.'

They are gone. I hold the phone to my ear still, not wanting the connection to be broken, but she has hung up. I can see that the others have nearly finished with the tents. I should be getting back to them, but I find myself wanting to be alone. Now I am away from James, I have to stop and wonder whether he'll be like all the rest of the white boys I've known. However well such romances have started, they've always ended badly. Should I step away before it spirals into disaster? He seems lovely, but so did Patrick, and I vowed I'd never have another Patrick ever again. But when I come back to the fireside and James waves to me to join him, I can't stop myself. I sit beside him, leaning my head against his. It feels the most natural thing in the world.

'Family all right?' he whispers.

'Just about.' He squeezes my hand and I feel as safe as I could be in the circumstances.

Oh great, I've arrived just as Poppy and Yan are having an argument about politics. It starts off reasonably, as most do, but soon descends into anger and fury. I don't think I can bear it. They seemed so close when we arrived, united in a desire to make us all feel better. It really helped, which is why I can't bear seeing them argue now. If they fall apart, I think we all will. Thankfully, Poppy acknowledges that some cuts have gone too far, which gives me a way in to suggest politicians should live by their policies, and the argument comes to an end as we all agree that if they did the world would be a better place. Which is fine, until it dawns on me that it doesn't matter, because after tonight none of us will have a say in politics or changing the world. Suddenly I am assaulted by the feelings I held at bay when talking to my family. My body shakes as I let out a wail of terror and despair. Then it's like everyone has been waiting for this moment, because we are all overcome with emotion, howling like small children. I suppose it is a form of group hysteria, that affects everyone except Harry and James. I'm not sure how long it goes on for, but eventually I find my tears are subsiding. As the sobs subside, Shelley suggests a group hug. I've always thought group hugs a bit lame, but somehow, tonight, it feels right. We may be terrified and lost in the darkness, but at least we have each other. Harry is the only one not to join in. He remains seated, scrolling through his phone. Poor Shelley, I think, as I sit back down with James, who'd want to be stuck with a man like that?

The talk turns to God and whether there is life after death.

'I've always thought heaven was a story to keep kids happy,' says Poppy. Her scathing tone, is a surprise. Even when arguing with Yan she seemed respectful.

120

'I'd like to think it's real,' says Shelley, 'but I'm not sure what it looks like.'

'Believe me,' says Poppy, 'when the dead are dead, they stay dead.'

'I hope . . . think . . . believe there is something beyond this life,' says Margaret, 'That tomorrow, what comes after will reunite me with people I've lost. I could be wrong, of course.'

I remember something I heard in church recently. I raise my head to speak. 'My minister was preaching the other week about this. He has an idea of eternity that I quite like. He says that every moment is eternal. So that each part of us – baby, child, grown-up – exists beyond today and yesterday and in the future. I don't know why, but I find that comforting.'

James looks at me, surprised, and I wonder if my Christianity has put him off. But he simply says, 'I've never really thought much about it, to be honest. Though I did see this article by a scientist who suggested our conscious-ness might live on beyond us. That appealed to me. And it's not too far from your idea, Nikki.' He smiles at me, as if to say that my beliefs are my business. I settle back down on his shoulder, relieved.

Margaret says, 'And the thing is, tomorrow, we'll know one way or another, but we won't be able to share that knowledge.'

Poppy laughs. 'You mean, if heaven exists we won't be able to say "I told you so" ?'

Margaret says, 'I'm not sure it will matter that much.'

There is a lull in the conversation, then someone, I'm not sure who, stupidly mentions Brexit. I groan inwardly. These conversations never end well, and this one is no different. James and I are staunch Remainers, Shelley didn't vote and isn't sure what the fuss is about. Harry, predictably, is a Leaver, but I'm surprised Margaret is. She's sick, she says, of interference from Brussels, though when James challenges her, she admits it's mainly that she doesn't like the Common Agricultural Policy. Poppy and Yan are on opposite sides again, but not in the way I expected.

'The whole thing was a huge mistake,' says Poppy, 'David Cameron pandering to the Ukippers, and now Theresa May desperate to keep her right wing happy. I'm with Ken Clarke on this one.'

'It's the one thing I can agree with David Davies on,' says Yan. 'The EU is unwieldy, undemocratic, full of unelected officials trying to impose TTIP and a gravy train that supported UKIP.'

Oh, how funny. She's a Tory Remainer and he's a Labour Leaver.

'What about the Working Time Directive?' I say.

'And the Human Rights Act?' James adds. I appreciate him working with me on this, it feels like we are together, a team.

'They're good in their way,' says Yan, 'but workers would be better off outside, creating their own institutions. Besides, leaving the EU will bring house prices down, making them more affordable'

I'm about to tell him that's bullshit, when Harry puts his phone away and stands up.

'Well, this has been fun,' he says, 'but I think it's time we went.'

'I thought we were staying,' Shelley says.

'We're wasting time, there's a boat out there, I'm sure of it.'

'But—'

'No buts, we're done.'

I think, for a moment, that she's going to refuse to go with him, but she sighs and says, 'I'm sorry. Thanks everyone. It's been lovely.'

'I wouldn't be too sorry,' he says. 'One of these bastards is responsible for this mess. I'm not staying here a moment longer.'

'What?'

'They're not your friends, Shelley. And they're not going to help you escape. Only I can do that. *Come on*.'

She looks at us, and then at him, whispers, 'Sorry,' again, and follows him up the beach. The rest of us gaze at each other warily.

What on earth did he mean?

Harry

I can't believe I let Shelley persuade me to stay here this long. I only stopped in the first place because we were tired and hungry. It seemed sensible to grab an opportunity to eat while we had the chance. And despite myself, despite the company, I have to admit it was pleasant to sit by the water, enjoying the calm of the evening, pretending for a little while that we didn't have a care in the world. I just shouldn't have allowed myself to get this comfortable I should have insisted we leave after dinner. But I can be a stupid fucking idiot sometimes and tonight has been like the pub on a Friday. There are always annoying people and inane conversations, but once I've had a drink or two, I always find myself staying longer than I intend. I've been convincing myself it was OK, because I'm one of the few people who've got a good signal at this spot. So while we've all been doing our Famous Five bit, I've been able to check message boards and put out requests on Facebook. Even though I've got nowhere, I've been pretending to myself that this is more efficient then driving in the dark.

But I've got nowhere and now I'm beginning to regret not leaving hours ago.

I need to catch Shelley's eye, tell her it's time to go, but I'm beginning to sense she's reluctant to leave, that somehow she's been persuaded by the others there's no point trying to get away.. I don't understand it.

Why they are so passive in the face of the approaching danger? Why aren't they trying to escape? I tried to throw a curve ball in earlier, suggesting we think of our worst moments, just to shake their complacency. It didn't work. Some of them seemed discomforted, and I'm fairly sure Poppy wasn't telling the truth, but they acted as if the question was reasonable and continued to play happy campers. It's not as if they're stupid. Particularly Poppy. In other circumstances I'd quite admire her drive and organisation. She's throwing everything at making this beach party a success, why isn't she using her energy and talent to get away? There she goes again, arguing about Brexit as if any of that matters right now. I zone out, doing one final scroll of social media in the hope of finding a boat. Still nothing, but I do discover an interesting item on a political website.

Downing Street's confirmation that the Natural Disaster Early Warning Unit was cancelled in the 2010 'Bonfire of the Quangos' failed to provide some essential details. Namely, the officials responsible. We think it's in the public interest to know and have tracked them down. The decision was made by a team within the

Department of Science and Technology: Professor David Hollidge, Andrew Gray and Margaret Anderson from the Cabinet Office. David Hollidge and Andrew Gray are still at the Department of Science and Technology and can be contacted on twitter at @ ProfDHollidge and @Andrew_Gray5, if you care to let them know your thoughts. Margaret Anderson isn't on social media and appears to have retired. Some sources suggest she now lives in Cornwall. Now wouldn't that be ironic?

This is perfect. Margaret hasn't mentioned her surname but surely it's her? She's the right age and didn't she say she used to work for the government? She's just the type to do something this crappy, I knew there was a reason she wound me up. It's not just because she speaks in self-important Theresa May tones that demand we listen to her. It's because Shelley has latched on to her big time. She always does this with older women. It's like she's looking for a mother figure or something. I'm sure it's one of the reasons she wants to stay. Well, she'll think differently about Margaret when hears about this, when she sees what a self serving superior cow she is...

This is it. Time to go. As I announce our departure, I decide I'll let them know one of us did this, though I don't say who – they can work out easily enough. Shelley looks like she might argue with me, but when I tell her to come on, she follows me as usual. I didn't expect her not to; she may protest a little, but she always takes my lead in the end. It is only when reach the car park, that things get weird.

'Well, I'm glad that's over,' I say, as I open the car door. 'What a bunch of wankers.'

'I thought they were nice.'

'You think everyone's nice, Shells. Trouble is, they're not.'

'What did you mean back there? Saying it was someone's fault?'

'It was.' I show her the website.

'We don't know that it's her.'

'She's an ex-civil servant, living in Cornwall. Bit of a bleeding coincidence.'

'Cornwall's a big place.'

'And you trust people too much. I bet it's her. Superior cow. Serve her right if she drowns.'

'Stop it!' Shelley rarely raises her voice, so her anger catches me by surprise.

'Don't be so soft, Shells. We're better off without them.'

'Even if we don't find a boat?'

'We'll find a boat.'

'No.' There's a look on her face I've never seen before. 'No. I don't believe we will.'

Normally, she'd cave in by this point but tonight something is wrong. She's arguing with me, she's actually arguing with me. I don't like it. She never argues with me. This new Shells, with dishevelled hair and blazing eyes is unnerving

'We'll discuss it in the car.'

'I'm not coming.'

'Why?'

'I don't believe you'll find a boat.'

'You can bloody well stay here and drown then.' I climb into the driver's seat.

'Come back,' she says.

'Too late. I'm off.'

'No, I mean . . . if you find a boat, or if you don't, come back.'

'Whatever.' I slam the door shut. Even if she's right, there's no way I'm staying now. I'd rather be on my own. I put my foot down and shoot off into the darkness. It is just after ten. That bloody volcano is about to collapse and if I don't get a move on, I'm going to be stuck along with rest of them. I drive up to the main road where I stop, take out my phone work out a route. There are several bays between here and St Ives. I'm sure to find something on the way. I just need to keep steady, focus my mind, stand firm. It's what has got me through life so far. No one else in my family made anything of themselves. No one from my neighbourhood. No one from my school. I'm the only one. I got myself from a market stall to running my own business by the time I was Shelley's age. Now I have a string of companies and hotels to my name, and am pulling in a healthy profit, despite the 2008 crash, austerity, even Brexit. Why? I'm clever. I think, I plan, I foresee obstacles. I know how to survive. It's what sets me apart from everyone else, particularly that pathetic bunch on the beach. It's why I will get through this and they won't. *Rely on yourself and only yourself*. I learnt that early in life and it's always stood me in good stead. There's never been anyone in my corner, except for my sister Val. Even after she married that jerk of a husband, Val has always been there for me. But she can't help me from London and now Shelley is out of the picture, I'm back where I've always been. Having to get through this alone. Well, I've survived worse. I'll survive this, I'm sure. Just got to keep focussed on the task in hand. I put the phone away, take a sweet out of the glove compartment, and set off again.

The hedges are high and the moon is low on the horizon. I turn the car lights up to full brightness so I can see as far ahead as possible. The road is full of sharp bends and sudden turns, so I drive carefully. I've had a couple of glasses more than I intended and the last thing I need is an accident. I reach the next bay twenty minutes later. It is smaller than Dowetha, without a proper car park, but I stop just in case. I climb out of the car, walk over to the cliff edge where I find a tiny path down to the beach. I can see already there is nothing there. Just sand and stones and the sea surging and retreating below. It would be pleasant to stop here for a while. In other circumstances, Shelley and I might have had a bit of fun here, skinny dipping and sex afterwards. I've always liked that she's been up for that sort of thing. Oh Shelley, I think, why couldn't you come too? Why did you let yourself be taken in by that lot? Why choose despair rather than hope? Why stay with a bunch of strangers rather than me? It's not fair.

After all I've done for you. I find that I am shouting my questions in the dark. Stupid idiot! As if that is going to help. Focus Harry, focus.

I glance at my phone, thinking perhaps she might have sent a message, but there's nothing. I wonder if I should phone Val, let her know what's happening. She's probably sitting at home with Ed, right now, watching repeats of *Love Island*. She loves all that reality TV stuff. She'd enjoy hearing about our beach gathering. It might be fun to talk to her about all the personalities. She could help me guessing what clever Poppy might be hiding, mock Yan for his leftie earnestness, place bets on Nikki and James getting it on tonight, be outraged at Margaret's actions. It would be good to get her take on it. Though I have to admit that I wouldn't want to tell her about Shelley, that even if she had decided to come I think she may have broken up with me. I'm not ready for that conversation yet. Besides Val doesn't even know I'm here. Is it fair to freak her out with this, just when the news will be full of the imminent volcano collapse? I think not.

I've stopped too long. It's time to get moving again. I have to face the fact that Shelley is my past now. It's just me, the open road and the boat that will get me away from here. I get back in the car and turn the music on. 'The Wind Between My Wings'. Shit, it's on one of Shelley's slushy compilations. I can't stand that song, but she always insists on playing it – says it reminds her of her dad. Well, I never liked her dad, and her dad never liked me. And

Virginia Moffatt

I'm done with Shelley, so I'm done with her stupid music too. I switch tracks to Steppenwolf: 'Born to Be Wild'. That's much more my style. I put my foot on the accelerator and, throwing caution to the wind, I race off into the night.

Shelley

I thought he said we could stay. Right after we got here. Harry said that maybe I was right for once. Maybe there was no boat to be found. I said we might as well stay here, eat, drink, enjoy just being together, and tomorrow would, well, be tomorrow and he nodded. I thought that meant we were staying. I should have known that he meant just for tea. When has Harry ever properly agreed with me? I should have known that he was always planning to leave. Particularly when he was so sneery after supper, when all they were doing was being friendly and kind. Maybe I just wanted to believe it to quell the doubts that have been growing, not just today, but for the last two months. The fear that I've made a huge mistake being with him all this time. Maybe I wanted to think that I was wrong, that our relationship was worth holding on to. When he helped with the tents, I genuinely believed that he had decided to stay, so it's a shock when he suddenly says it's time to leave. And even more of one when he accuses one of the group of having caused this crisis. Of course, I don't object As always, I trot after him – old habits die hard, and Harry is a very old habit; difficult to shake off. I've been with him so long, I've forgotten I have the ability to choose, that I don't have to follow him all the time.

It is when we reach the car that something snaps. We haven't even left the others five minutes and he is calling them wankers. Next he claims Margaret was the civil servant who cancelled the volcano monitoring unit. He's got no proof, just her name and the fact she lives in Cornwall. He can't be absolutely sure it's her, yet he's happy to claim he knows it's true. And now I come to think of it, he has always judged everyone like that. Has always told me I'm naïve to trust people, that I've led too sheltered a life, that the real world is full of liars and cheats and I should get used to it. Even though I don't believe that really, I've always nodded and gone along with it to avoid a row. Tonight, though, I find that I don't want to.

'Stop it,' I say.

'Don't be so soft, Shells,' he says, 'We're better off without them.'

'Even if we don't find a boat?' I can't quite believe I've aired the treacherous thought.

'We'll find a boat.'

'No,' I find myself saying. 'No. I don't believe we will.'

'We'll discuss it in the car.' That's assuming a lot.

'I'm not coming.'

'Why?'

'I don't believe you'll find a boat.'

'You can bloody well say here and drown then.' He climbs into the car, lowers the window and glowers at me.

'Come back.'

'Too late. I'm off.'

'No, I mean . . . if you find a boat, or if you don't, come back.'

'Whatever.' He slams the door shut, speeding out of the car park. I watch till the red tail lights have disappeared into the night, and the sound of the engine is a faint noise in the distance. He is gone. I cannot believe it. He is really gone, leaving me in a clifftop car park in the darkness. I am sick with the shock of it, I feel like someone has kicked me in the stomach, I stagger to a bench and begin to cry. Below me the waves crash on the beach. Normally I love the sound of the sea at night, now the noise feels menacing, a prelude to the horror that will come in the morning. How has my life come to this? Yesterday I was in a holiday cottage feeling cross that my boyfriend had abandoned me for work, now he has done it for real, leaving me alone to my fate as he chases an illusion. How could he do this to me? I cry and cry until there are no tears left and I am shivering with the cold. That's when it hits me - he isn't coming back.

It's time for me to go back to the others. After all, isn't that why I didn't leave with him? Harry may have gone, but I'm not alone, I have my new friends, I am sure they'll help. And since the bastard has taken all my clothes with him, I'm going to have to borrow a jumper from someone.

I stand up and take a deep breath. I go into the clubhouse toilet and try and sort my face out. My make-up has run and my eyes are a bit blotchy, but once I've got a bit of soap and water on it, I look passable and am able to make my way back to the beach. I want to show them all that I can hold it together, not let this disaster break me. I'm almost feeling cheerful till I I reach the campfire to discover the atmosphere has completely changed. The friendly camaraderie is lost; now it feels as if I have walked into a court. They are all sitting where I left them, focussing their attention on Margaret. Oh shit, it's because of what Harry said. About the woman in Cornwall, Margaret Anderson. They've worked it out. Fuck Harry for being right. Fuck him.

I sit down beside Poppy but she barely acknowledges me. The others don't even notice I'm there.

'You should have told us when we met,' James is saying. I've been thinking he was quite sweet, but now his tone is accusatory.

Margaret flushes. 'I didn't know how to . . . what to . . .'

Nikki reaches over and touches her hand. 'We understand.'

'Do we?' I've been jealous of her closeness to James all night. Now I'm aghast that, they are on opposite sides . Harry's words have poisoned everything. James turns back to Margaret, his voice hard. 'Explain then, why did you cancel the project that would have saved our lives?'

'Yes,' says Yan, equally cold. 'Tell us. I'd love to know.'

Margaret is nearly in tears. 'You have to realize what it was like in that job at that time. Before 2008 I loved working there. I really felt that I contributed to making things better. I helped set up all sorts of research bodies, and independent organisations which really made a difference . . .'

'And?' James doesn't seem much more sympathetic.

'And the financial crash. And the Coalition Government. And austerity. And "The Bonfire of the Quangos".'

'What was that?' I ask, feeling a bit stupid that I'm the only one that doesn't know.

'Quasi-autonomous non-governmental organisations, they needed scaling down,' says Poppy sharply. She seems as angry as the rest of them. I'm none the wiser but too shy to ask another question. 'So many undemocratic bodies, wasting taxpayer resources. Some had to go. You can't really be saying it was George Osborne's fault you made the wrong choice?'

'You weren't there,' says Margaret, furious all of a sudden. 'The job was impossible. We had to retain, merge or abolish bodies that were all doing vital work. We had five months in which to decide what to keep and what to get rid of, with George Osborne breathing down our neck so he could make a splash with his Autumn Statement. Every single decision was difficult. Do we keep Public Health England or the National Housing and Planning Unit? The Health and Safety Executive or the Advisory Council on Libraries?

A volcano monitoring unit was the least of our priorities. How was I to know?'

'Seriously, you're blaming the government?' Poppy shakes her head.

It is Yan's turn to be furious, but this time he turns on Poppy. 'Well she's got a point. That was a typical Tory mess that cost us more than it saved, dressed up as success. And left us with no one to sort out housing and speak up for libraries.' Margaret looks relieved but Poppy is still not convinced.

'That's ridiculous. The government did loads to help first-time buyers. Quangos couldn't stop library closures, those are local decisions. Besides, we were talking about *Margaret*.'

'It's not only *her*,' screams Yan. 'It's the Tories. And you're defending them.'

'After the mess Labour left behind, we had to make tough choices,' says Poppy.

'And look where it got us,' yells Yan. 'Stuck on a beach with no hope of rescue.'

'It's not that simple . . .'

'Poppy's right,' says Margaret, but Yan is having none of it, 'Oh fuck off all of you!' he shouts and strides off down the beach. Shit. This is going from bad to worse. Margaret is properly crying now. Nikki puts her arm round her despite James's angry glance.

'Oh dear, I didn't mean to upset him, should I go after him?' says Poppy.

'I wouldn't bother,' says James. 'He always gets like that after a few drinks. Leave him to cool off for a bit.'

Poppy nods and we settle back down into our places, but something has changed. The air is thick with recrimination. Poppy can hardly look at Margaret and James and Nikki have moved apart. I hadn't expected to return to this. Fuck you Harry, look what you've done. We sit in an uncomfortable silence that is only broken when I ask if I can borrow a jumper. Nikki jumps up and gets me one. While she's gone I consider calling Alison and Dad to update them on my situation, but they don't know I've abandoned Harry, and my one possible chance of getting out of here. I can't even tell them that it's OK that I've found people and we're fine, because looking at everyone, I can see we're not. Still they'll be worried. I send Dad a holding text saying we're doing OK, as I gaze around the group seeing quite clearly that we are not. They're all good people. Kind. Here's Nikki now with a cardigan, and here they are being sympathetic when I say I've left Harry. But they're as scared and angry as I was when we arrived. They helped me then. Perhaps I can help fix this now, give them a distraction. I've been itching to sing all evening. Now Harry isn't here to mock me, there's nothing to stop me.

'James,' I say, 'Can I borrow your guitar?'

He nods. I pick it up, relishing the feel of wood beneath my hands, the touch of the string beneath my fingers. How have I let this go? This is the most natural feeling in the world. It has been so long that I am hesitant at first, but soon I realize the music is ingrained in me, that the tunes I grew up with say more about me than the last four years with Harry. Tentatively, at first, then with more confidence, I begin to play.

Instagram
LisaLuskOfficial
Image: Lisa kissing an unknown man.

                              10 MINUTES AGO.

LisaLuskOfficial *Just discovered the love of my life is stuck in Cornwall. Seriously worried for him.*

Lisasbiggestfan *Hang in there Lisa, I'm sure he'll be OK.*

WonderWoman2018 *Oh Lisa, how awful.*

AllieSimpson4 *You poor thing. Love & prayers.*

JaysonClark *I'm available.*

SteveSmith5 *This is not the time. Lisa we're thinking of you xxx*

JaysonClark *But I can comfort you Lisa!*

StevenSmith5 *@JaysonClark This is not about YOU.*

Jenny5001 *Hang in there Lisa, maybe he'll get away?*

LisaLuskOfficial *Thanks folks. You're the best.*

Virginia Moffatt

Facebook Messenger
Andy Jones to Seren Lovelace
So . . . are you going to contact her?

10.45 p.m.

Seren Lovelace to Andy Jones
Been checking her page and thinking about it for hours. But what's the point? What can she possibly say to me now?

BBC Breaking 11.00 p.m.

First images of Cumbre Vieja collapse . . . News'n Truth names officials who cancelled the early warning unit . . . A30 pile up at Launceston adds to driver woes . . . Evacuation continues across UK, American and African coasts . . .

Facebook
Poppy Armstrong

30 August 11.05 p.m.

It is getting late, and I am tired, but I don't want to go to bed yet. I'm too agitated and there's part of me that feels that I shouldn't waste any time. After all, it's hardly going to matter tomorrow if I'm tired. It's been a strange evening. At times, I feel as if I've known these people all my life, at others like we're blank strangers. It's all a bit intense. Too much. I've come away for a bit. I need some space.

I am sitting on some rocks overlooking the sea. It

142

is calm right now, the moon shining on the water. I still can't get my head around what will happen. And what I'm thinking now is what I could have done differently. The friendships that I let drift, the projects I dropped. Why didn't I ever complete that Masters in Economics? I might have stayed in London if I had, and then – well, then I wouldn't be here, would I? I wish I'd kept up the violin. It just seemed such an effort when I was fourteen and I had better things to do with my time. Recently – before today, I mean – I've been thinking of taking it up again. I wish I'd sorted that out. I thought I had plenty of time. It never crossed my mind that my life would be so short, and be cut off this abruptly.

And then there are the relationships. Well, to be honest, one specific relationship. Someone who thinks I treated her very badly, a long time ago. I thought I'd put it behind me, but tonight I can't stop thinking about her. I wonder if I could get in touch. Or whether I should? Is it fair, after all this time, to contact her, in these circumstances? Is there a right thing to do?

Like Share Comment
20 Likes
6 other comments

Jill Hough Brave of you to even consider it, Poppy. I think you should go for it. Have you looked for her on Facebook?

10 minutes

Alice Evans Having similar thoughts about someone. Thinking let sleeping dogs lie is best?

8 minutes

Beverley Lewis I think you should. Maybe she's on Facebook. Look her up.

6 minutes

Poppy

When Shelley begins to play, the tension eases some-
what. Nikki and James, who were at odds during
the argument about Margaret, move closer to each other.
James nods at her and Nikki offers her a drink, as if to
welcome her back in the fold. I am not ready to be so
forgiving. If it hadn't been for her, none of us would be
here, none of us. It's all very well to blame politicians, but
she made the decision – *she* did, not them. And then there's
Yan. All day he has been an ally, a friend, someone to hold
me through this, and now he's stormed off, angry with me.
That's her fault too. We never would have quarrelled if it
hadn't been for her. Even though the music is beautiful
and appears to soothe the others, it isn't helping me. I'm
still too angry. I can't stay here. I decide to go after Yan.

He is sitting on the top of a slope of sand, close to the
shoreline, watching the tide come in. His back is rigid. He
doesn't even look round at the sound of my footsteps. He
is not inviting anyone to come close. I find a rock a few
feet away, hoping he'll soften soon, while I post random

thoughts to Facebook. I don't describe the arguments – I don't want to encourage negative comments, and I certainly don't want anyone identifying Margaret even if I am mad at her. So I write instead about the things I am beginning to regret, the things I never got round to doing. And Seren. I don't name her, but I write about Seren.

Seren. It's a long time since I've thought about Seren. I haven't let myself. I adored her too much, my lover, my friend. The first person since my parents died to make me feel safe and warm. But ever since Harry's question, all I can see is an image of her face, the day she discovered that email. Had she had her suspicions before then? Gone looking for proof? Had I subconsciously left her a clue by not deleting it? Did I want to be found out? Or was it just bad luck that she happened to be playing around on my laptop and discovered the truth?

I had my story ready. Naturally. But she didn't believe me. And once it was clear that my lies couldn't work any more, there was no point pleading. That was the worst thing, watching the face that I loved harden into the coldness of a stranger. I found a hotel that night, and when it was clear there was no going back to her, I decided I was done. I took the money and ran. I moved down here, because it was the only other place I knew, the only place I could remember being happy. I changed my name, used my savings to set up my craft shop, learnt to surf, built a whole new life. A good life, straightforward, no complications. I've never talked or thought about her since. I haven't allowed myself to. But now, tonight . . . well, maybe it's time. Maybe if I explained, she would see why I did it. That I didn't intend for things to go the way they did. I think for a moment that perhaps I could talk to Yan about it, ask for his advice. Then I see his back, remember his rage at my politics, and I let the thought go. He's a lovely guy, but he will never understand this. I don't think many people could.

What good is this doing me? Obsessing over a past I cannot change. I need something to distract me. The sand in front of me is covered in pebbles. I stand up and begin a search for the flattest stones. They smell of fish and rotting seaweed, but they are perfect for my purposes. I put them in my pocket, alongside the beer, and make my way to the water's edge. The sea is calm, the incoming waves barely make a ripple on the surface. The moon has risen behind me, its white beam lights a silver path across the ocean. It looks temptingly solid, reminding me of a folk story my mother used to tell me. If I close my eyes, I can hear her voice, even now . . .

There once was a man who was so lonely that he was unable to sleep in his large old house. Instead he would walk for miles after dark, with only the owls and bats for company. One night he saw lights falling to earth. Deeply curious, he followed them to a glade, where he discovered a group of star women descending from the sky. They took off their star cloaks and danced in the forest until dawn when they dressed and returned to the heavens above. The man was enchanted by their beauty and returned each week to watch them dance. Till one sunrise, one of the women discovered her cloak had disappeared. She was trapped, unable to return with her sisters. The man took pity on her, taking her into his home. Gradually as they got to know each other, they fell in love . . .

One night in bed with Seren, I told her that story and she told me her name meant star in Welsh. I thought then it was a sign we were meant to stay together, I should have known that was tempting fate. For later on, the man finds his wife's cloak and mends it, but instead of returning it to her, he keeps it locked in a cupboard because he cannot bear to lose her. When she finds out he has betrayed her, she leaves him and returns to her sisters in the sky. For a while it looks bleak but unlike us they find happiness in the end The man is so heart-broken without her he travels across the globe to find a way back to her, finally reaching her by means of a moon-beam across the sea. If only such tales were true . . . If only I could walk across that moonbeam to safety, and find a way back to Seren in the process.

A stupid thought. I shake it off. Instead, I crouch down, position myself carefully, and with a flick of the wrist, throw it across the water, watching as it jumps three, four, five times. I repeat the action until my pocket is empty, and then repeat my search for stones. The monotony of the repeated action is soothing, and I am lost in the moment as I was surfing earlier in the day. After a while I become conscious of little splashes in the water besides me. I glance up to see Yan, standing a few feet away, catapulting stones in the water with strong, jerky movements. It does not seem like a good moment to interrupt him, so I concentrate on skimming my arsenal across the waves, watching with satisfaction as I exceed my target each time. Until my final shot bounces ten times, earning me a grunt of approval from Yan. I take it as an invitation to speak.

'I'm sorry. I didn't mean to upset you.'

'I shouldn't have gone off on one. It's why James hates coming to the pub with me. Once I get stuck on something, I can never let it go.'

'I can see what he means . . .' I grin, but I'm relieved. 'I won't make the mistake of talking politics with you again.' Yan frowns for a moment and then grins back. 'I brought a peace offering.' I pull a can of beer out of my pocket as we walk back to the rock. There is just enough room for both of us to perch, though the surface of the stone is cold and hard. The air is still warm, the water ruffles the beach with gentle splashes on the shoreline.

'It wasn't just the politics,' says Yan. 'I'm just angry. I thought I wasn't but I am.'

'About?'

'This.' He stamps his heel down on the surface of the sand, creating a deep print as he moves his foot away. The impression quickly fades as it fills with water, as if he had never made the mark in the first place. 'We're young. All of us. Even Margaret. We're too young for our lives to be over, like this. As quickly as this. I'm only thirty and I haven't even got started yet. It's such a waste.'

There's nothing to say to that.

'I'm sitting down here,' he says, 'thinking it's so fucking unfair. I'm looking at the moon, the waves splash, you come and throw your stupid stones. It's peaceful, and beautiful and the anger just evaporated . . . I can't quite describe it. Just for now, I don't feel quite so angry. Though I'm none too happy either.'

'That makes sense.'

'How are you doing?'

'Brooding, to be honest.'

'About what?'

'Things I could have done differently.'

'We've all got a few of those. Want to talk?' I am tempted by his interest. Of all the people here, I would probably choose him as a confidante. There is something trustworthy about him despite, or maybe because of, his passionate rants, and dopey love sick eyes. But I can't imagine how I might begin – and if I did, he would probably hate me for it and tell the others. They'd take Seren's side and kick me out. I don't think I could bear that.

'Don't mind me,' I say. 'Just stupid nonsense . . .' I kick a stone at my feet, and add, 'You know what's weird?'

'Other than the situation we're in?'

'We're never going to experience cold again. Real cold, I mean. Winter cold when the outside pipes freeze. November cold, when the wind chills your bones. January cold, when the snowdrifts are so deep snow fills your boots. We'll never know that feeling again, ever.'

'I hate the cold, can't say I'm too sorry about that.'

'I've been trying to imagine it. But I can't. Even though it's getting cooler now, it's not like winter time. I can't remember what it's like to feel really, really cold.'

'Miserable is what it's it like,' says Yan. 'The flat is like an icebox because the central heating is on the blink and the landlord hasn't been round to fix it. You put on every last jumper and your old balaclava, and you are cold still. In the end you get into bed with your laptop and a ton of DVDs and a bottle of whisky and wish the weekend away till you can get back to work where it's nice and warm and your feet aren't turning blue.'

'If you put it like that . . .'

'Believe me, if there are any blessings in this – and I am clutching at very tiny straws here – at least we've had warmth, sunshine and moonlight on the water. Speaking of which . . .' While we have been talking, the tide has been coming closer, the sea is beginning to splash up to the rocks.

'I could do with another beer.' I put the empty can back in my pocket. A pointless gesture – it could be floating anywhere tomorrow – but I still don't want to be responsible for littering the beach.

'Race you,' says Yan, lumbering off before I have a chance to get going. He is back by the tents before I have even made it halfway up the slope. He plonks himself down besides Margaret. I wish he hadn't, I'm not feeling as forgiving as he is, but he hushes me when I try and say that. Shelley is still singing.

A North Country maid up to London had strayed,
Although with her nature it did not agree.
She wept and she sighed and she bitterly cried,
'I wish once again in the North I could be.'

People can be astonishing. Earlier James comforted us with familiar tunes and a reasonably competent voice, but Shelley's singing is of a different order. She could be a professional. I can see the others are as surprised and entranced as I am. I've judged Shelley too quickly. I thought because she was dressed up like a doll, and hanging on to Harry, that there was nothing to her. Clearly I was wrong.

'Oh the oak and the ash, and the bonny ivy tree,
They flourish at home in my own country.'

The song makes me ache with longing for times past. For evenings watching telly with Seren, when we did nothing more dramatic then discuss an episode of *The Wire*. Walking holidays in the Lake District. Dinner in our favourite Italian. If I hadn't been discovered, I might have escaped all this. I might be out in a wine bar, talking in hushed voices with friends of the horror that is about to come in the place where I used to holiday. If I hadn't been discovered, I might have been able to, extricate myself, and carry on with our lives. But instead, I am here, among people I hardly know, and there is nothing I can do to change it. A film of water forms over my eyes. I blink it away, wishing I was home, in my own country, with Seren to hold and protect me. But I don't have one. I lost it, a long time ago.

Yan

I don't know what was worse. Discovering Margaret had a hand in the closure of the volcano unit, the humiliation in realising I never had a chance with Poppy, or the fact that Poppy's politics are so despicable. The two people I've had most affinity with today, the two people I've been relying on to get me through this, have let me down. I can sort of forgive Margaret for her part – she must have been in a horrible situation – but I can't understand why she didn't tell me about it when we were alone. I'd have understood it more if she'd explained. As for Poppy, I was stupid to get my hopes up – I never have success with women – but that's not what's killing me now. How can I be friends with someone whose views are the polar opposite of mine?

The anger holds me tight as I sit gazing at the water. The sea is fast approaching, wave upon wave is invading the shore, rapidly overcoming the sand. I know this beach; once the tide reaches the top of the little slope on which I'm sitting, it will be rushing round these rocks in no time.

I'll have to shift soon, but for now I am unable to move from this spot.

I've been here a while when I sense some motion behind me. Perhaps one of the others has come in search of me. I am not in the mood to be talked round. Mum always said I could sulk for England – well, if tonight isn't the best time for having the biggest sulk ever, I don't know when would be. The person doesn't acknowledge me but walks to my right, head down peering at the ground, picking things up. It is only when she pulls herself upright, I see it is Poppy. The last person I want to speak to. I ignore her, focus instead on the black water in front of me, its forward movement as inescapable as the hours ahead. A single moonbeam lights a path across the waves. Above me the moon has dwindled from the enormous globe of earlier to a silver, round ball, no less beautiful. In front of me the waves crash and break on the shore. Out of the corner of my eye I can see that Poppy has crouched by edge of the sea and is flicking stones in the water. I turn my head away, but I can still hear the pebbles landing with tiny splashes to the side of me. Ahead I hear a louder splash. To my delight, I see a seal in the water. It must have been lying so still on the rocks I thought it was a stone. It is bobbing in the waves in front of me. I slip off the rock and walk towards it, paddling into the sea until the waves splash over my knees. I barely notice the chill of the water, drawn as I am to the brown eyes of the animal in front of me. It doesn't seem to be afraid, just sizing me up. Is it under a death sentence too? Will the wave dash it against the rocks or the cliffs? Or do animals have a sixth sense about these things? The seal looks away and then dives for fish; perhaps it will dive at the right time tomorrow and so save itself.

A wave splashes over my crotch. The tide is coming even faster than I expected, washing away the sand and, with it, my anger. It occurs to me that I might, perhaps, have over-reacted. People are more than their politics aren't they? Poppy is still skimming stones. I decide to join her, collecting pebbles, crouching, throwing, watching them bounce off the waves, in silent communion as we did when we surfed earlier today. Only this time I do it knowing there is no hope of romance, no chance that she will ease my pain that way. I'm surprised to discover that I no longer feel disappointed by this. My crush was just that, a stupid crush.

I grunt in appreciation at Poppy's successful ten-bounce skim, which she takes as an invitation to talk.

'I'm sorry. I didn't mean to upset you.' She seems sincere; she *is* sincere. It's not her fault I got her so wrong. And really, why the fuck should politics matter now? It's not like any of us are going to be able to change anything ever again.

'I shouldn't have gone off on one. It's why James hates coming to the pub with me. Once I get stuck on something, I can never let it go.' I have never admitted this to anyone before. Not even to myself. Perhaps that's been part of my problem: I've always put winning an argument above friendship.

She has brought beer and, presently, we are sitting companionably on the rock, sharing our anxieties until it runs out. We race each other back to the campfire. Things have moved on since I left. James is holding Nikki in his arms. Margaret is sitting nearby in a chair, seemingly forgiven. Shelley has the guitar and is singing:

'*Oh the oak and the ash, and the bonny ivy tree,*
They flourish at home in my own country.'

The song reminds me of the Polish folk tunes Mum used to sing – mournful, but somehow comfortingly familiar. I slip next to Margaret, not wanting to break the atmosphere. Poppy slides beside me and we listen in appreciation till Shelley finishes. Everyone claps.

'That was gorgeous,' says Margaret.

'Where did you learn to sing like that?' I ask.

'My dad used to be in a folk band. When I was little he used to let me sing along with him . . .' Shelley says, 'But then we moved to London. And I stopped.'

'Why?'

'I dunno. I was mad with him for making us move. And everything was so different in London. My sister and I, we weren't cool. Our clothes, our accents, our attitudes were all out of place. Folk singing was *definitely* not cool. It was all right for Alison. She's brainy. She never cares what people think of her. But I'm not clever and had nothing to recommend me except a voice that sounded wrong and a poor grasp of fashion. So I dropped the singing, learned to speak south London, and developed clothes sense.'

'Didn't you miss it?' Poppy asks.

'Not really. There was too much going on. Dad was on my case for a while till I started dating boys, and then that was all he'd talk about. After that, I met Harry and . . . well, he wasn't exactly the folk singing type. He was pretty rude about Dad, actually.' Shelley sighs, 'I should have realized then, when he was so disrespectful. I should have known that I was wasting my time with him. But I always felt Dad and Alison were ganging up on me. I know they didn't mean it, but after Mum died, I also felt they looked down on me. Harry told me I was beautiful and made me feel special. So I took his side . . . Now I feel my whole life's been a waste.'

'I don't know,' I say. 'That voice isn't a waste. Not right now, not tonight. Sing us another.'

The others nod in agreement. Shelley picks up the guitar again and tunes the strings. Margaret turns to me.

'I'm sorry.'

'What for?'

'For not telling you earlier. About my job. I was too afraid . . .'

An hour earlier I would have been too angry to listen, but now I just nod, and when I tell her it's OK, I realize it actually is. The talk with Poppy, Shelley's singing have reminded me why I came here in the first place. Life's too short for arguments isn't it? That sentiment has never felt truer than tonight.

Shelley begins to sing again

> *The water is wide, I cannot get o'er*
> *Neither have I wings to fly.*
> *Give me a boat that can carry two,*
> *And both shall cross, my love and I.*

I lie down. James whispers to Nikki and she grins and stands up with him. They walk off towards the cliffs. Earlier I would have resented them, envied James for always falling on his feet, but now I watch them go without bitterness.

> *I put my hand in some soft bush*
> *Thinking the sweetest flower to find*
> *I prick'd my finger to the bone*
> *And left the sweetest flower behind.*

All at once an image of Karo comes to mind. Aged nine, playing in the back garden on a summer's day. Why am I thinking of her? Oh yes. The rose. The day she tried to pick a rose, but pricked her thumb instead. The blood swelled in a large, red globule and she screamed at the sight of it. Screamed and screamed, despite my warning that Mum would not want to be disturbed from the nap she had taken to having ever since Dad left. I was right. Mum came out, red-faced, shouting it was just a little prick, what was all the fuss about? How was it that her Karolina, such a big girl, could be such a baby? She would have to deal with far worse things than a cut thumb. And Karo had cried and cried as the blood trickled down her thumb and Mum had dragged her indoors, cleaning the wound and scolding, scolding all the time. Was it then that Karo's problems had begun? She was always more sensitive than me, feeling every slight, every harsh word, ever tease. As we grew older and Mum's problems became apparent to us both, we worked out different coping strategies. Where I developed a defence mechanism of belligerence mixed with indifference, Karo retreated into frenzied study, her eyes on Oxbridge to the exclusion of all else. My clever, wounded sister, making her escape to the golden city where there were no mothers in darkened bedrooms smelling of alcohol and unwashed sheets and all she had to do was learn. If only, the reality had matched the dream . . .

> *I lean'd my back against an oak*
> *Thinking it was a mighty tree*
> *But first it bent and then it broke*
> *So did my love prove false to me.*

Karo . . . My eyes prick with tears. Ten years haven't dulled the sense of loss, of a life incomplete without the sister I should have saved. Why hadn't I seen it coming? Her emails and texts were cheerful enough, but when I visited, hadn't I had a sense that all was not well? The bags under her eyes, the nervous energy, the clumsiness. I'd put it down to lack of sleep, too many parties, and she hadn't suggested anything otherwise. I should have seen it for what it was, the stress of living up to the perfection she always demanded of herself. On that last night, when she needed me, I missed her calls. She'd tried to lean on me, but I wasn't there, and she broke.

My betrayal was nothing on Mum's. Not content with ruining our teenage years, she'd given Karo nothing but grief whilst she was away. Ringing her constantly, *Karo, Karo when are you coming home?* And when she did, expecting to be waited on hand and foot. Something she never asked of me. Worst of all, when Karo died, she turned back to the God she'd ignored for years, declaring suicide was a mortal sin. She refused to have anything to do with Karo's body, leaving it to me to sort out the funeral. I had to take out a loan to pay for it, deal with distraught friends and family, tried and failed to trace Dad, all while Mum's door was shut in my face. At one time I didn't think I would ever forgive her for it, but when she moved back to Poland we settled into an uneasy tempo of occasional visits and phone calls. It's why it has been so hard to call her tonight. Our relationship is so damaged, it is difficult knowing what to say.

The song finishes.

'Thank you,' says Margaret, 'Your dad would be proud.' Shelley shrugs but looks pleased. I glance at my phone – nearly midnight. Suddenly, I have had enough of company and morbid thoughts. I feel like losing myself in a book, and *The Humans* is waiting for me in my tent. I have a hundred pages to go and I am keen to finish it. I stand up. 'Night all.'

'Bed? So soon?' Poppy says. 'The night is still young.'

'I'm bushed.' I give her a hug, careful to ensure it is within the bounds of friendship, offering no more. 'Thanks for today. It's been . . .'

'Yes.' She gives me a peck on the cheek. I nod goodnight to the others, enter the tent, and jump into my sleeping bag fully clothed. I'll feel grimy in the morning, but who cares? I pick up my torch and take up the book. Soon I am absorbed in the life of an alien trying to be human. Outside I am vaguely aware of the voices of the women murmuring in the night, the ruffle of breeze on my tent, but soon the story takes over. As always, when I have a book in my hand, the anxieties of the world recede.

Margaret

Icould murder Harry, I really could. Throwing that comment into the group as he left, getting everyone riled up. Then, before I had a chance to work out what to say, Yan had found the website, worked out it was me and everything fell apart.

'*You* were responsible for this?' he said.

'What?' said Poppy.

'I'm sorry,' I said. 'If I'd known . . .'

'But you must have,' said James. 'Before cancelling it you must have had all the information.'

'It wasn't that simple,' I said. They were having none of it. Poppy, James and Yan all vied with each other to shout at me the loudest. Only Nikki didn't join in; she moved away from James and touched my arm, saying she understood. Bless her for being on my side.

When I finally got a moment to speak, I thought it might make things better, but it seemed to only set them off more. Then somehow the argument shifted and before any of us could stop it, Yan and Poppy were yelling at each other, till he stormed off down the beach. The rest of us were left feeling awkward and uncomfortable, reminding me of family Christmases when I was a child. So many days that started off so pleasantly then descended into anger, shouting and blame. Grandma always tried to make light of it, and she often managed to calm everyone down, but it was always too late for me by then. Christmas, with all its excitement and eager anticipation was always over the minute the first angry word was spoken. I hope this argument won't follow the same pattern. This beach has been such a haven today. It would be a shame if the last few hours are to be spoiled.

Since I am the cause of the conflict, it is impossible for me to try and make it right, so I'm grateful to Shelley for providing a distraction. When she picks up James's guitar everyone begins to relax. James and Nikki who have been sitting apart, come closer again while Poppy jumps up, saying she's going to try and put it right with Yan. She doesn't look at me when she leaves, but at least she is trying to sort things out with him.

The music helps me too, particularly when Shelley begins to sing. She has a lovely voice. I sit back in my chair, staring up at the stars. She starts with "Scarborough Fair". Grandma used to love this song – she'd sing it in the kitchen, the place where she was most at home. . . .

. . . I am five years old, watching her with her sleeves rolled up, pinny on, hands plunged into a basin, mixing the pastry for mince pies. The air is infused with the smell of Christmas: cinnamon, ginger, cloves and brandy for the cake and pudding she will serve till Easter. Her kitchen was old-fashioned even when I was small. She had no time for mod cons, cooking on the black range that had been there since the house was built at the turn of the century. She had no fridge until the late Fifties when Uncle Eric insisted on buying one for her for Christmas. Until then, she used a cool box in the pantry and bought ice from the ice man until he stopped visiting the street. It didn't matter to me. In winter the range kept us warm. In summer, the back door was wide open, the range only used for the evening meal. The summer scents were fresher, lighter – mint, cucumber, strawberries – but the aroma I most associated with her was of bread rising or bread baking, for 'without bread,' she always used to say, 'a house is not a home.' She always let us help. As the eldest, I always had first stir, followed by my cousin Kath and my little brother Andrew, until, the cake or pie or pudding was ready for the oven and we were dispatched to play in the garden.

When I was little, I never noticed the tension between my father and uncle. It was only as I grew older that I began to observe the strain in Dad's voice when his brother's name was mentioned, the slightly false smile from my uncle when our families met. I noticed Dad didn't seem to enjoy Uncle Eric's tales of selling cars to the rich and famous as much as the rest of the family. I picked up on the sneer in Uncle Eric's voice whenever Dad referred to his job in the tax office. At unwrapping time, I began to understand the true meaning behind the polite *thank yous*: our family's gifts were too mean, Uncle Eric's too ostentatious. Once I became aware of such things I saw that the annual argument was inevitable, So I learnt to take Andrew and Kath away to the conservatory where we could play with our toys in peace away from all the shouting. It was usually over by tea time because Grandma was so good at making them stop. Until the year of the fridge.

Grandma had always had said she never wanted a fridge, she was happy with her ice box. But one Christmas, Uncle Eric ignored her wishes, wheeling in the most expensive model on the market, making my parents gift of plants for the garden look even less impressive than usual. I think that's what set Dad off. He accused Uncle Eric of buying their mother's affection, while Uncle Eric just said he was jealous. This time, no-one was able to stop them from trading insults and harsh words, not even Grandma.

The day ended with Dad dragging us out of the house, yelling he never wanted to see Uncle Eric again. We never went for Christmas after that and things were never the same . . .

. . . The song has ended. Shelley starts another, and then another. Her singing is sad and melancholy, but suits my mood. For years Kath and I had despaired of our father's pig-headedness, but when it came to it, we were just as bad. I thought we'd find a way back to each other, but we never did, and now it is too late. I brush away a tear. How stupid of me, to have left it too late. How bloody stupid of me.

Shelley has just begun 'A North Country Maid' when the breeze blows an echo of a laugh up the beach. To my relief I can see Poppy and Yan running towards us, their quarrel seemingly forgotten. That's one thing less to worry about. And Yan seems to have forgiven me too, he sits down besides me as if our earlier argument had not happened. I wish I could say the same for Poppy, but she doesn't even acknowledge my nod. There's nothing I can do about it, but as I watch her staring at the flames, I wish things could be different. I'd hate for this row to sour the rest of the evening.

Shelley finishes her song to enthusiastic applause, which she acknowledges with endearing modesty.. . I take advantage of the break to apologize to Yan and, to my relief, he really is over it. If only it was as easy with Kath and Poppy.

The air is getting cooler; I pull my sweater on and, as I do so, Nikki and James stand up and wander towards the cliffs, hand in hand. I am not sure if they are lucky or not to have found each other at this moment, but the sight of them fills me with warmth. Richard and I fell in love on a night like this, thrown together by our mutual dislike of our fellow students on a geography field trip. We sneaked away from the campfire, found a spot on the cliffs, and talked till sunrise. I'd known then I wanted to marry him, and although the marriage was cut short so early, I never regretted it. I hope Nikki and James can snatch that kind of happiness tonight. I really do.

When Shelley finishes "The Water is Wide", she puts down the guitar, and though we ask for another, she has had enough. Yan stretches, stands, and announcing he is tired, disappears into his tent. Poppy is silent. Her body bristles with disapproval and I wish I could find a way to get through to her. I try and soothe myself listening to the rush of waves crashing and retreating from the shore.

'I love that sound,' I say

'Who doesn't?' says Shelley. 'It's the best part of being on a beach.' This is the last thing I'd have expected her to say. I am beginning to realize that she is more than she seems. Kath always said I was too quick to judge; maybe she was right. And then Shelley surprises me again, 'I always have to make a sandcastle when I come to the beach, just by the shoreline.' The brittle young woman of earlier has disappeared, replaced by this eager, enthusiastic girl.

'We should make one now,' I say, fired up by the thought of doing something active.

'In the dark?'

'Why not? The moon is bright enough to see. I've always loved making sandcastles too.' I don't add that I don't think there'll be time in the morning, or that doing this is another convenient way of delaying being alone with my thoughts at bedtime. 'Coming, Poppy?' I say, hoping that because she is smiling at Shelley's enthusiasm, she might be willing to forgive me. She declines, claiming exhaustion, though I think it's probably to avoid being with me. I watch her grab her wash things from the tent and climb up to the car park, wishing I could put it right, but I can't think how.

'Come on, then,' says Shelley, 'If we're going to be daft, it might as well be now, as my dad always says.'

I hurry down the beach with her to the firm sand by the high tide mark. With no buckets or spades, we are reduced to scooping it with our hands and placing it on a mound which gradually takes shape. I concentrate on building the base, making the foundations firm. I am not particularly artistic, and my sandcastles are never usually up to much, but it is always the simple pleasure of building something from nothing that I enjoy. Shelley, on the other hand, is an expert. She pats sand, crafts corners and crenellations, forms little windows, creates a moat and a drawbridge across it. It's a work of art. It is close to completion when we hear voices. I glance up to see Nikki and James clambering on the rocks by the headland. They must have got caught by the tide. Nikki reaches the end of the stones and jumps down onto the sand. Behind her James slips and topples head first into the water with a curse. Nikki laughs at him, a warm laugh, signifying intimacy. I am glad to see something good coming out of this wretched situation.

The couple come towards us. I'm a little nervous of speaking to James again, but he smiles at me and is genuinely apologetic, and Nikki is delightfully enthusiastic about our sandcastle. She's so excited by it that though James returns to the camp to get out of his wet clothes, she stays to help. With her assistance we add further turrets and crenallations, decorating the final effort with seaweed and pebbles. When we are done, we are all ridiculously pleased with our creation. It's only a stupid sandcastle, but somehow it feels significant. Shelley takes a few pictures. They're a bit dark, but the castle is clearly distinguishable, so I take one too. I'll send it to Hellie before bed time, to show her . . . what exactly? That life goes on? That imminent death isn't necessarily as bad as all that? That I'm a silly old fool? Maybe all three.

We wash our hands in a sea so icy that it hurts my fingers. As I shake them dry my skin tingles with the cold. How can my life be about to end when I can feel the sensation so deeply? I rub them together to warm them up, remembering another night, another beach, when the children were small. Kath and I had snuck out from the holiday cottage, leaving the Dads in charge. We'd swum in a sea, feeling every part of our body tingle with the cold before sitting by a campfire and drinking red wine. A happy evening, liberated from the burdens of childcare, one of so many Kath and I shared. How had we let an argument ruin all of that? Why had I never tried to put it right?

'Shall we go back?' says Shelley. 'I think I'm ready for bed. And I want to talk to my dad.' Nikki nods

'You go on,' I say. 'I just want to sit here for a bit.'

I sit down on the damp sand, take out my phone, hoping Kath still has the same email address, and begin to type.

James

Shelley has been singing for some time now. Her voice is astonishing, it gives me hope, fills me with life, makes me feel anything is possible. The moon is bright, the air is cool, the flames of the campfire are glowing and all at once I am ready to take the kind of risk I've avoided since Lisa left.

'Fancy going for a walk?' I whisper in Nikki's ear. She nods, takes my hand and we stroll down the beach.

'You were a bit unfair, back there.'

'What do you mean?'

'To Margaret. I mean, how was she to know? She had an impossible decision. Would you have done anything differently?'

I think about this for a minute. 'Probably not,' and then, sensing this is not enough, 'I'll apologize to her when we get back.'

She squeezes my hand and leans into me. We are both barefoot and the sand beneath our feet is damp, but we feel comfortable, at our ease, as if we've done this a thousand

173

times before. The waves crash on the shoreline ahead of us, the white light of the moon sparkles and splits among the rising and falling crests. The tide is coming in, but it has yet to reach the cliffs. We probably have an hour or so before we are cut off. Enough time to show her my favourite cave. I lead her across the damp sands, passing the rocks around the headland. The cliffs tower above me, making me stop for a moment; how could a wave be so high that we won't even be safe up there? Nikki squeezes my hand as if she has the same thought. As we turn the corner, out of sight from the others, I stop and pull her closer. She holds me more tightly, raising her face so that our mouths meet and we kiss, and kiss and kiss, till my phone vibrates in my pocket breaking the spell.

'Come on,' I say taking her hand again, peering at the cliffs, looking for the crevice. 'It's round here somewhere . . .' I find the opening between the rocks. 'The first section's a bit dark, I'm afraid.' She follows me up the sandy shingle. 'Careful. The pebbles are a bit slippy here.' The stones are slimy underfoot, the mouth of the cave reveals an inky blackness ahead. Nikki switches her phone torch on, its narrow light exposing the rock pool ahead, the walls of the cave marked in green seaweed. I do the same. The buzz was Lisa. Of all the times to text me. I try to ignore it but as I say 'Stay by the side, it's deep in the middle,' I am acutely aware that I have done this before, with Lisa. Early in our relationship, when she still laughed at my jokes, told me I had a great singing voice, that she loved playing music with me. Back when I was stupid enough to believe her. That night we'd made our way to the centre of the cave and, though it was a cloudy night, it didn't matter. We'd made love here and she said she loved me. And I believed that too. Fuck you, Lisa, what are you doing texting me now? After all these months. I don't need you now, not when Nikki is with me, when I'm thinking about those kisses, how much I enjoyed them, how much I want to kiss her again. I force Lisa from my mind, concentrating on what I am doing, holding the side of the cave wall as I find may way through the pool. The water is cold, but not icy, and after a while it feels quite pleasant. In the darkness I am aware of Nikki breathing behind me, the splash of her feet through the water. Ahead, I can make out a bright light, which grows stronger until we reach the centre of the cave, where we clamber out of the water onto soft sand that sinks under our feet, leaving deep impressions. Shafts of moonlight illuminate the walls and light up the water. Ahead of us we can see the full, round moon shining through the hole in the ceiling like the iris of a dark-blue eye.

'Wow, it's beautiful,' she says.

'We'll have about twenty minutes before it moves away.'

My phone vibrates again, reminding me of Lisa's text. Weird that I can get reception here. I glance at it. *Dearest James. I'm beside myself with worry. Call me xxx.* I put the phone away, tell Nikki it was nothing. Forget Lisa; I only want to think of the gorgeous woman in front of me. She moves towards me.

'Thank you for bringing me here.' She takes my head in her hands and kisses me on the mouth. I put my arms round her and kiss her back. Gradually we sink to the ground, not caring it's damp, that sand that is getting in our clothes. We kiss and kiss as our hands begin to explore each other's bodies, removing clothes quickly until we are semi-naked in the darkness. I want to lose myself in this moment, forget the wave, forget the past, forget everything. But somehow I can't get a picture of Lisa out of my head. My kisses lose focus, my body tenses, not sure if this is what it wants. In response she falters, and then all of a sudden she sits up.

'Stop.' She is half crying.

'What's the matter?'

'It's just that . . . I don't know you . . . I don't know what I'm doing. I don't normally do this.' She pulls her skirt down, her knickers up, finds her bra and laces it up. Part of me wants to tear it back off, feel those smooth breasts in my hands and mouth again, but as she puts her top on I can feel desire fading too. It's not that I don't want her, it's just that . . . 'Time,' she is saying. 'We need more time . . . I think that you could be somebody. We could be some-thing. But we don't have time.' She starts to cry properly now and I put my arm round her, because she is right. There is not enough time to understand the way I am feeling about her and simultaneously wonder how I feel about Lisa getting in touch. And the sense that I am too old for one-night stands, and if the wave were not coming tomorrow, if it all proves to be a horrible mistake, I'd hate to have slept with her too soon. 'I know,' I say, 'I know.' And now I am sobbing too, for the waste of it all, for the possibilities we are losing, for the knowledge that when this night ends there is nothing left for either of us. And that knowledge isn't romantic and bittersweet like in the movies. It is just so fucking unfair. To be dying before my time, dying before I am ready, dying before I have the chance to get to know this woman who might just be the one for me. And there is nothing I can do but sit with her, sobbing on the floor of a damp, cold cave.

At last, our crying comes to an end.

'I'm sorry,' she says.

'It's OK.' I kiss her on top of her head. 'It's just . . .'

'Too soon.'

'Yes,' and then because I feel I owe it to her to be totally honest, 'And my ex just texted. Bad timing . . .'

'Oh.' Nikki is about to say more when she jumps up as water splashes up from the pool. Shit. The tide is coming in. I should have been more alert.

'We've got to move.' I follow her back through the pool. Already the water is deeper, up to our knees, swirling about us as the waves enter and leave. We need both our hands to cling to the rocks in order to stay upright. When we reach the edge of the cave, the sand has vanished, the sea is at shin deep and has cut off our escape. We will have to make our way back along the rocks at the cliff edge until we round the corner to the safety of the beach. Nikki nods as I explain and she immediately applies herself to the task of plotting out the easiest route, avoiding stones covered in seaweed, carefully navigating the smallest boulders, keeping as far away from the sea as possible. Watching her progress I am grateful that it is Nikki rather than Lisa who is accompanying me. Lisa had her strengths but she'd have baulked at this. She would have made so much fuss that the journey would have taken twice as long. Nikki reaches the end of the rocks and jumps onto the sand. I have just reached the shallows and am thinking that, if Lisa were here, she would be bound to fall in the sea, when I miss my footing and find myself slipping backwards. Before I know it I am sitting in the water as the waves break over my midriff. Nikki turns round and starts laughing.

'You look a bit wet,' she says, running up to me as I emerge from the water.

'I think I'd better get changed.'

'Yup.' She is still laughing and I'm about to get mad, but then I realize that I like the fact she is still laughing. It makes me feel like we're a couple, even if, after the disaster in the cave, we probably aren't. Then she reaches for my hand, smiling, and dispels doubts. Whatever happened there, whatever happens now, we're in it together.

As we turn back to the camp, we come across Shelley and Margaret who are making a sandcastle.

'That was spectacular,' Margaret says

'One way of putting it,' I say and laugh ruefully. She is

OK, really, and Nikki is right, what would I have done in her shoes? 'Look, I'm sorry about earlier.'

'Don't mention it,' she says, and I can see she means it.

The sandcastle is nearly complete, an elaborate construction with towers, windows and crenellations.

'That's fabulous,' says Nikki. 'Need any help?'

'Feel free,' says Shelley.

'I think I'd better get changed . . .' I say again. My clothes are damp and beginning to chafe. There is a cool breeze now and I have no desire to stay here getting colder. I'm a little disappointed that Nikki wants to stay here rather than be with me, but then she flashes that warm smile, gives me a peck on the cheek and says, 'You do look cold. I won't be long. Meet you up there in a bit?'

Whatever has gone on between us, it isn't over. I'm so relieved I race up the beach, diving into the tent, where Yan is reading.

'What happened to you?'

'I fell in the sea.'

'Oh dear.' He turns back to his book as I strip off, find a towel and dry myself as best I can. I am shivering, my skin covered in goose pimples. I grab clean clothes and put them on as quickly as possible. I am about to go out again and make myself a cup of tea, when Yan puts the book down and says, 'Sorry about earlier.'

'That's OK.'

'No it's not. I was an arsehole.' I'm tempted to remark that this is nothing new, when Yan he says, 'But I hate it

when I'm an arsehole to you. You're one of my best mates.'
I am so surprised I sit down, pulling my sleeping bag
round my shoulders for warmth.

'Really?'

'Really. I only ever bother arguing with people I like.'

'Oh.'

'Mind you, you don't half come out with some crap.'

'Only when you're being a self-righteous prick.'

'Am I?' Yan looks so horrified, I laugh.

'Sometimes. We agree more than you might think. I just
hate an opinion shoved down my throat.'

Yan is quiet for a moment. Then he says, 'I'd like to
think I could be mature enough to take that criticism.
Given time . . . That was the trouble tonight. The situation
as much as the issues made me mad.'

'I can understand that.'

'How are you doing?'

'Terrified.'

'Me too. Trying to keep it at bay . . .' Yan holds up his
book. 'You seem to have your own solution.'

'Huh?'

'You and Nikki.'

'I suppose. She's lovely . . .'

'But?'

'Lisa.'

'Please don't tell me you're letting her stop you? That
woman left you in a mess. If you don't mind me saying.'

'I like her a lot. Just difficult in the circumstances.'

'You know what? If I were you, I wouldn't be in my head so much. Seize the day. Or the night. There's not much time left. Make the most of it.'

'Perhaps you're right.'

'You know I am.'

Outside the tent we can hear the sound of voices – Shelley and Nikki, coming back up the beach. Yan puts on a fake American accent, 'Go get her, tiger,' as if we're in some cheesy romcom. Before adding, 'Now let me get on with my book. I want to finish it before tomorrow.'

I unzip the tent, step out still wrapped in my sleeping bag

'Cup of tea?' I say to the women, hoping that only Nikki will accept. Margaret, picks up on my not-so-hidden agenda and suggests to Shelley that the two of them go and wash. They carry on up the beach, leaving us alone. I reach for Nikki's hand.

'Stay with me.' She nods, leaning in to kiss me.

The wind ruffles the tents. The gulls call above us, and as I kiss her back, it feels like coming home.

Nikki

When James takes my hand and suggests a walk, I am only too happy to agree. I have been hoping he would ask me for the last hour; I'm thrilled that he wants to be alone with me as much as I want to with him, and though Shelley's music has helped calm everyone down, the row has left a nasty taste in my mouth. Even so, I'm a little anxious. James was so quick to join the others in condemning Margaret. Have I misjudged him? I was sure of him before the argument, but now I'm worried I might be making a mistake. So I'm pleased that when I challenge him he recognises he was wrong, and is quick to see my point of view. He promises to apologise and I feel I can relax. He really is as lovely as he seems.

We meander down the beach in the darkness and I am taken back to nights like this in the Scouts, in the time when friendships weren't complicated by race or gender and we would run around the woods playing wide games after dark. Evenings filled with laughter and excitement when anything could happen and often did. I have the same sensation now. So I am not surprised when, the moment we are round the corner, he takes me in his arms and kisses me. We kiss and kiss and kiss until his phone vibrates and he breaks away to check it. He doesn't say who it was, just takes me by the hand and leads me to the entrance of a cave.

It is dark, so I use the flashlight on my phone to illuminate the way. There is a pool ahead of us. We leave our shoes on top of a rock, as I follow him into the blackness. The water is cold and the stones slippy, but I am caught by a sense of adventure and I trust him to be leading me somewhere special. And he is. As we move forward, I can see a glow of silver light ahead reflected on the water. We reach the centre of the cave. 'Wow, this is beautiful,' I cry. The moon is shining through the hole in the roof of the cave. Light ricochets off the pool and onto the walls, which sparkle like diamonds. 'Thank you,' I say, taking his face in my hands, kissing him slowly, appreciatively. He kisses back, and soon we are sinking to the ground, our hands roaming over each other's bodies. I unbutton his shirt, he undoes my bra, caressing my breasts, sucking my nipples. It is only as I feel him harden on top of me that doubt creeps in. Who is this man? Why I am I kissing a stranger like this? What am I doing here? I sense a similar uncertainty from him; my kisses falter.

'Stop.' I sit up, pulling my clothes on as quickly as I can. The moon has passed out of sight leaving the cave in darkness, taking with it delight, wonder, excitement. All I am left with is embarrassment, followed by deep sorrow and soon I am crying, huge sobs from the bottom of my gut. My whole body is shaking as it all spills out. The waste of it. The loss of what we might have had. The fact that I almost trust him. I want to trust him, but it's not quite enough. I tell him that time, or lack of it, is to blame, but it is not just that. It is knowing what I know, what I have always known since we met, what he can't possibly know, that to be with him raises too many questions. Too many difficulties.

My whole dating life has been like this. I was popular with the white boys at my posh boarding school, something that pleased me for a while, though I knew it wouldn't please my parents. They sent me there to ensure I got the best education and to prove to themselves they'd made it. But I knew I was supposed to marry a nice Nigerian boy eventually. It was confusing for a long time. As was the difference between the glossy brochures boasting of diversity and racial harmony and the promise that every child mattered, and the actual reality. Kids like me were allowed to win prizes from time to time, but we were never allowed to forget that, however hard we tried, we were never quite up to muster. I never told my parents this, it was too hard. Instead, I kept my head down, worked hard and made my way to Cambridge – accompanied, on the way, by charming white boys, who morphed into the charming white men at Trinity. Until one day I woke up to the fact that I was being used. The ones who boasted they never saw colour yet told me I was exaggerating when I talked about the dangers of racial profiling, or stop and search. Or the other, worse type, who pretended to care about racism, when all the while they were bragging to their friends how they'd bagged another hot black woman. Patrick was the last one of those. I really thought he was different. When he turned up at our Black Lives Matter group, he impressed me by hanging back, acting respectfully, not trying to invade the space. He waited till asked before expressing his opinion, and made it clear he understood what his white privilege meant. He was sweet and funny and so of course I fell for him, before long we were inseparable. We lasted for the best part of a year, till the day his favourite lecturer was caught on camera making racist comments. Despite the evidence he couldn't stop defending him, and making excuses for his behaviour, so we unravelled as quickly as we'd come together and I swore off white boys for good. After that Mum said what I really needed was a nice Nigerian boy. During the summer holidays she set me up with Abeo who I'd known forever, and I have to admit it was nice for a while. He was kind and looked after me and after all the racial tension, it was restful to be in a relationship where none of that mattered. But it fell apart under the weight of too much expectation and I decided I was better off single. I haven't dated in over two years, and haven't missed it till now.

Now here's James with his warm smile and big blue eyes, willing me to trust him. And I want to, I really do, but can I trust he won't be like all the rest? I can't say this to him. I don't know how. So I sob instead, and soon he has his arms round me and is sobbing too. Life isn't meant to end like this. We shouldn't be spending our last night in a damp cave that smells of rotting fish. Life was supposed to be about so much more. A wave splashes us and our sobs abate as we realize the sea is rushing in and we have to leave before we're cut off. The pool is now thigh deep, dampening the edges of my skirt, and when we emerge from the cave, the sea is right up to the rocks. Part of me thinks that we might as well not wait for morning, that we might as well give up now, but in spite of this, I find my earlier spirit of adventure is returning. It is fun to find my way through the rocks till I reach the safety of the beach.

I am just turning to see where James is when he slips and topples in the water. I burst out laughing. He is mock outraged till I run over to give him a kiss and he laughs with me. Despite what happened in the cave, we are still connected; there is something going on here and it feels good.

Walking back to the camp we come across Margaret and Shelley, making sandcastles. It seems both the most ridiculous thing in the world and the most sensible. After the last intense hour, I suddenly feel the need to do something silly. I sit down beside them and join in. James hovers besides me, teeth chattering, unsure what to do. I don't want to send him away, but part of me feels we need a break, so I suggest he'd better get out of his wet clothes. We agree to meet again in a short while and I remain behind to assist the others with their creation. I plunge my hands into the sand as I add to the wall, forming a long ridge of crenallations on the top. The sand is moist and cold, but easy to shape.

'Oh you're good,' I say to Shelley, as she finishes the top of a tall, thin turret.

'You too.'

'I loved doing this as a kid. I'd spend hours on the beach creating what Dad would call, my "works of art" and then insist that he and Mum come and applaud and tell me I was a creative genius.'

'In my case, I was trying to outdo my big sister. She was always so much better than me at everything.'

Margaret laughs. 'I was always rubbish. I just wanted to make the basic shape and then watch the sea come and get it.'

'That part made me cry,' said Shelley. 'Alison always said I was a baby, but I wanted the castle to last. It was devastating when the water began to flow up through the channels and my beautifully decorated towers collapsed to mush.'

'I always cried too,' I say. I don't add that tonight's efforts seem even more pointless than usual in that regard. I've wasted enough emotion on worrying about the future tonight.

'You two seem to be getting on well,' says Shelley.

'He's nice.'

'He seems it. Makes me wish . . .' Shelley pauses. 'I don't think I've been that wise about men.'

'Don't be too hard on yourself,' says Margaret. 'You're very young still, you've got plenty—'

'Of time? I *did*.'

'Sorry, wasn't thinking.'

'It's easy to forget,' says Shelley. 'At the very least, I'm pleased to be rid of him. He hasn't even answered my texts to see how he is. We've been together since I was fifteen, what does that say about us? About him?'

'I've had my fair share of idiots believe me,' I say. 'And it's not as if . . .' I don't complete the sentence, but they seem to understand my meaning. We finish the castle, decorating it with seaweed and stones. When we are done, we stand back with sandy hands, and damp knees, proud of our efforts

'Well, I call that a fine piece of work,' says Margaret. We nod and all take photos. *Look what I made*, I text my parents, hoping it will make them remember, make them laugh. Then, though he probably won't get a signal in the tent, I send one to James, *Miss you!* I say, and I mean it. I am glad Shelley suggests going back, the half an hour's absence confirms for me that we need to be together again. We leave Margaret by the water's edge and walk back up to the tents. Poppy and Yan have gone to bed, and for a moment I think James has, but he emerges from the tent, wrapped in a sleeping bag, and offering tea. Shelley says she is going to bed and heads up to the clubhouse to wash. We kiss each other, and I know that I don't want to be separated from him again. I grab my sleeping bag and sit by the fireside next to him, watching the glowing embers like an old married couple. When the fire finally dies, and Shelley and Margaret have returned and entered their tents, we decide we are not ready for bed yet. We take a bottle of wine and move to a spot by the cliffs, above the tide line. We talk in quiet voices, telling each other the story of our lives. Our beginning is our ending, and yet it feels like it must have always been this way.

Harry

It's been two hours since I left the beach and still no sign of a boat. I have given up on the coast and have come inland, searching through the villages for a garage or garden where one might be found. I've had no luck so far. I can't believe it is taking me this long.

And now the engine light is flashing. Sod it. Not now. The bloody thing has really chosen its moment. I'll have to stop before it cuts out. Sometimes it does this after a lot of driving, particularly up and down hill. I've been meaning to replace it but I am exceptionally fond of this old Maserati. I picked it up an auction for an exorbitant price because it was the same model as the first car I ever bought. Shelley couldn't understand why I spent so much money on it, she can never know what it was like to finally have a set of wheels, the sense of power and control it gave me. I love this old car and have put up with its foibles because it reminds me of a time when I was young, without a care in the world. It's just a bloody nuisance that it has failed me tonight. But there's nothing I can do. I switch off the engine and push my seat back. I might as well take a rest while I can. Knowing the way this car works I have half an hour or so. I check my phone. Shelley has sent me a couple of texts. I wonder whether to call her, but what is the point? I asked her to come, but she decided to stay. She decided she doesn't need me any more. What's the point of ringing her to hear her say it again?

It's making me mad though. The knowledge that she is sitting on a beach with that bunch of sneering bastards. They all looked down on me the minute we got there, yet she's thrown her lot in with them. Worse still she doesn't seem bothered that it's thanks to Margaret that we're in this awful situation. I can't believe she chose them above me. I can't. It'sdoing my head in.

I need a distraction so I check the BBC website. It's still reporting on the evacuations, and the situation in Cornwall looks pretty grim, but there's no mention of Margaret. And although people are sharing links to the Dowetha Facebook page, no one seems to have spotted the connection with the News n' Truth story. I look at the timeline. There we all are, sitting around the campfire and there she is, Margaret, with a glass of lemonade in her hand. All the fury I felt when I left comes back to me. On an impulse, I download the picture and send it to the website telling them who she is. That feels better. Satisfying. Let them deal with that.

It makes me feel better for a minute or so, but not for long. I'm back thinking about Shelley, how we were in the beginning. We used to have such a good time together. I've noticed lately, even before we came down here, she seems less content than before. Before we moved in together, she didn't seem too bothered that my work entailed lots of nights out entertaining. But once she was in the flat, she started complaining that I was always out, and when I went abroad she was forever angling to come with me. She's been begging me for a holiday for so long that in the end I gave in and said she could accompany me on this trip. There seemed no harm in staying an extra day but now I'm kicking myself. If I hadn't given in to her I'd have been home from that meeting last night. We could be in the jacuzzi right now, not even giving the poor sods down in Cornwall a thought. I wouldn't be here sitting on my own, desperate to get out.

An owl hoots and I shiver. I am not really one for being alone in the dark and this road is surrounded by trees on all sides, making the night even blacker. When I was young, the lights were always on at home and there was always someone around. It may have been too crowded sometimes, there may have been too much noise and too many siblings. But there was always someone about. Night was scary in a different way, back then. Night was a fight breaking out between Mum and Dad, Dad drunk, coming upstairs belt in hand, Mum running out of the house screaming that this time Dad was going to kill us all. Night was Val holding on to me, promising me that Dad would never do it and Mum would come back and everything would be all right in the morning. And she was right. It always was. But now I am on my own. The hedges of the road on either side make the night seem blacker, the only light is the moon whose rays illuminate the road behind me. Ahead, I can barely make out the shapes of the trees. I try not to think about what tomorrow might bring. I try not to think that I won't achieve my mission, find a boat, get out of here. I'm only forty-two, for Christ's sake, no age at all. Too fucking young to die.

It is twelve thirty. Give it another fifteen minutes and the car will be as right as rain. I try to think of something positive. The boat, discovering the boat. The wind in my hair as I push down the jetty and speed away to safety, laughing at the idiots I have left behind. I will do it, I *will* get away: I will survive. I always survive. Didn't I escape the family home, make something of myself? Unlike my loser family: Ann, Karen, even Val repeating Mum's mistakes with men, Evan on drugs, Paulie and Stevie inside. I haven't seen them in years. Only Val. I still have a soft spot for Val. It was Val who helped me get away from the house, bearing the brunt of Dad's rage after I'd gone. I keep up with her because of that. Even if her Ed is a prick as big as my dad, and she's as stupid as my mum about sticking with him. She's my big sister and she's always been there for me. Thinking of Val renews my hope. I may have lost Shelley, but I'll never lose Val. Things are going to work out for me. They always do. I check my watch again. Time to get moving. I rev the engine. It starts first time and I am off.

The Wave

I am driving so fast I almost miss it. A single bungalow, appearing out of nowhere. There is a trailer in the driveway and on it . . . Oh. My. God. It's a boat – a beautiful, beautiful boat. Tempted as I am to just to run in and take it, I check first to make sure the owner is gone. The lights are out but I knock several times until I am satisfied that there is no one around. The boat is all mine.

In triumph, I send Shelley a text, *Found a boat!* Let her stew on that. She should have more faith. She replies straight away, *Are you coming back?* I will have to think about that. The road ahead leads to St Ives one way and the A30 the other. If I go back to Dowetha, we'll have to find another launch spot and we'll have further to travel till safety but if I go to St Ives, it will probably take longer to go round the coast to get her. *If I can,* I text, and then, to soften the blow, *I love you.* She doesn't respond, presumably because she is put out. Well, fuck her. She should have come with me when she had the chance. In the meantime, I have work to do . . .

It looks simple, but it isn't. The first complication is figuring out how to lift the blocks so I can attach the trailer to the car. Still, it is only one o'clock. I still have six hours.

But it takes longer than I thought I need screwdrivers, a jack and wrenches, and I have to break into the garage to get them. After an hour of sweat and hard work, I am finally done. Triumphant, I drive out of the lane, glad to be finally on my way. I have gone two miles when the car falters and shudders to a halt. I try the ignition. Nothing. I try it again. Still nothing. Has it finally given up the ghost? I glance down at the dashboard and see that I'm an idiot. A total fucking idiot. I have been so intent on my search for a boat, I haven't checked the petrol gauge. Now I've run out. I hit the dashboard in frustration. How could I have been so stupid? I try my phone to see if here is a garage nearby but I've got no signal. There is no way out of this mess. All night I've not let myself feel fear, but now I'm alone in the dark it breaks over me, I curl up on the seat, shaking and sobbing . . . I'm back home in the cupboard under the stairs, hiding from Dad, while Val holds me . . . except this time there is no one to comfort me.

I don't know how long I am like this. I haven't cried since I was a child. I'm simultaneously embarrassed and relieved to let the emotion out. But at last I calm down and start thinking again. My phone was working fine when I texted Shelley, I must have just got into a bad spot. I climb out of the car, walk a little way up the lane and bingo, Google returns. I search for petrol stations and find there is one on the A30 about a mile and a half away. That's not too bad, and I should be able to get some food too, I am starving hungry.

I take the petrol can and stride off into the dark night. The moon is high in the sky, but the trees cut out most of its light. Soon I have the feeling I am in a long, dark tunnel going nowhere. Around me there are rustles as the wind whispers through the hedges and small creatures scuttle in the darkness. I have forgotten how much I hate the countryside in the dark. Ever since I was a little kid and we were once taken on a Special Holiday for Poor Children from Estates. All the leaders thought it was exciting to take us out into the forest, an experience that we'd not get back home. My brothers and sisters loved it, but I hated every second. I spent my time longing to be back in the smelly high rises, with the noise of traffic and police sirens to send me too sleep. There were terrors there for sure, but they were known and manageable. The forest was full of fear and I longed to go home, the whole time. Night walks were terrifying. All I could think of were Evan's horror stories of men with axes that linger on country roads to surprise their unsuspecting victims. Of vampires and ghouls that live in the forest ready to suck your soul dry. Stupid stories to frighten kids. They were awful then and, even now, I feel uneasy walking alone in the dark. I keep my eyes on the road ahead where the moonlight occasionally flashes on the path focussing on that, trying to ignore the rustles and night noises. I am relieved when I reach the end of the woods. The moon is half obscured by cloud, but there's enough light to see me to the footpath across the fields to the A30.

It takes about ten minutes to reach the main road, and there, thank fuck, is the garage, the pumps left unattended, the shop door left open. The staff must have just decided to leave everything and go. The road is deserted, according to the news the tail end of the jam has reached Truro, so there is nothing to stop me running across the road to the shop. I grab a plastic bag and fill it with food, stuffing down a pork pie and swigging a drink of coke. That's better. Much better. I turn the pumps on at the till, and take the can outside to fill it up. The petrol pours in so fast it is quickly sloshing over my fingers, leaving a metallic tang. I am tempted to stop and rest a bit, but time is pressing, I cannot afford any more delays. When the can is full, I twist the lid tight, grab the bag of snacks and drinks and march back into the dark night.

Shelley

I can't quite believe that I have been singing in public again. After all these years, I'm surprised how easy it was. I wasn't embarrassed, it didn't feel lame. People appreciated it, they applauded, reminding me how good I am, how much I used to enjoy this. I feel so pleased with myself that I text Harry to see how he is doing. He doesn't reply. I try not to read anything in to that, perhaps he is still driving.

Nikki and James have drifted away, Yan has gone to his tent to read. But I am wide awake and so is Margaret. We are restless feeling the need to do something physical and before I know it we have decided to go down to the shore and make a sandcastle. Everyone I know would think me silly for suggesting it, but she doesn't and pretty soon we are kneeling in the damp sand, scooping out a large trench. We don't have a spade, and my hands are quickly cold, but I don't mind, not even when a nail breaks. Tara and Liv would laugh if they could see me now, but I'm having the most fun I've had in ages. I'd forgotten how much I love to make these towers and shape turrets, and windows. How when I was little I'd make up stories of princes and princesses, dragons and fairies determined to impress my parents and outshine Alison in her creativity. That all stopped when we moved to London. After Mum died, we didn't have enough money for holidays. And by the time we did, I was fifteen, beaches were boring, sandcastles childish and my mind was full of Harry. I always thought that being a grown up meant giving up silly things like this, but, looking at the enthusiasm with which Margaret is attacking the castle, I wonder if I've been entirely right about that.

A splash and a shout from the sea cause me to raise my head. James has fallen in the water and Nikki is on the sidelines, laughing at him. They look happy, in love. I'm pleased for them, but I feel a bit sick too. I've been with Harry four, no five years, and we've never laughed like that. It's been fun being with Harry, I've been to great parties, met some interesting people, but it's never been anywhere near that joyful. It has taken till tonight for me to understand that. It occurs to me that if I hadn't gone back with Harry that first time, we probably wouldn't have got together and my life would have been very different. I wouldn't even be here on the beach. One stupid decision five years ago, has led me here to this beach, my final destination.

I am pondering on the unfairness of all of this when Nikki and James reach us. Thankfully her enthusiasm drives away my self pity, and I'm glad she joins us while he goes back to the tent to change. I've been slightly in awe of her all evening. She's like Alison's friends, clever, thoughtful, seems in total control. I thought she, would be like them and not have time for me. But she's just as keen as we are to make this work and she's great at sculpting sand, so I quickly lose my nervousness. When we've finished – well, it's only a stupid sandcastle but I feel really proud of it and the three of us for building it. I glance at my watch, it is nearly half past twelve. I have been putting off the inevitable but it's time to ring Dad. He keeps late hours and it's Alison's night to be with him, so I should be able to catch both of them. My phone needs charging, so I leave Margaret by the water's edge, Nikki with James at the camp, and I climb up to the clubhouse. I plug the charger in and ring home.

'Shelley, where are you? We've been so worried. I'll put Alison on speakerphone.'

'It's been a bit . . .' I hesitate.

'What do you mean? Weren't you getting a boat?' Why does Alison always sound like she is scolding?

'We couldn't find one; we searched for hours, but we couldn't find one.' I try not to cry as I explain. Dad is sympathetic though Alison, typically, doesn't hold back. 'Why didn't you wait till you were safe to leave him? Honestly, Shells—'

'Because I don't believe he'll find a damned boat!' I yell. 'And I was fed up trailing round after him. It's not that I don't want to escape. I just don't believe I can. And these people are nice. If I can't leave, I might as well stay here.'

201

'Your sister didn't mean it,' Dad says quickly, trying to put things right. He's been trying to do that ever since Mum died, but he's never had her knack for it till tonight. Tonight, for once it works. 'Sorry, Shelley, just worried that's all.' There is nothing to say to that. We chat for a bit longer, all making an effort to be kind, but we are exhausted, and soon the conversation peters out and all we can say is goodnight and lots of love. I get ready for bed and return to the camp, glad that Margaret offered me a space in her tent to save me being alone in mine.

As I reach the entrance I can hear her saying her prayers. I don't want to disturb, so I hover by the entrance. She is reciting a Psalm I vaguely remember from primary school.

The Lord is my shepherd; I shall not want.
  He makes me lie down in green pastures.
He leads me beside still waters.
  He restores my soul.
He leads me in paths of righteousness
  for his name's sake.

Even though I walk through the valley of the shadow of death,
  I will fear no evil,
for you are with me;
  your rod and your staff,
  they comfort me.

The Wave

You prepare a table before me
*   in the presence of my enemies;*
you anoint my head with oil;
*   my cup overflows.*
Surely goodness and mercy shall follow me
*   all the days of my life;*
and I shall dwell in the house of the Lord forever.

I unzip the tent. Margaret is sitting up on her Lilo, her prayer book in her hand, a lantern beside her. I sit down on mine and begin to undress. Nikki has lent me a pair of pyjamas which are slightly too big. I pull the trousers on and climb into my sleeping bag. 'Does it do any good, praying?'

'Well, it's not like magic . . . It won't change anything, but it helps me. I feel like I'm speaking to God, putting all my hopes and fears, my regrets in front of him.'

Margaret seems so assured, so calm, I cannot imagine her having regrets. 'Cancelling that unit?'

'Obviously. Though, to be honest, I don't think I could have done anything different.

There was overwhelming evidence that the chances of something like this happening were incredibly rare. Faced with the choice I had at the time, there's nothing else I could have done. No, I'm worrying about something else.'

I lie back, glad we are camping on soft sand, not hard earth. I'd never thought of real grown-ups like Margaret having things they wished they'd done differently. I always imagined that once you got past thirty life was pretty much sorted.

'It's my cousin, Kath' she says. 'We haven't spoken in years.'

'What happened?'

'Family stuff. So stupid, really. We were close when we were children. But our fathers fell out one Christmas so we lost touch. It was only when I started working in the civil service and moved near Grandma, that we met again. Kath was living with her parents in nearby Chingford so I began to spend time in their house, much to my father's annoyance. He told me Uncle Eric was untrustworthy, but I just thought he was jealous. Uncle Eric was younger then him, rich and handsome. Aunty Sue was glamorous, they had a huge house, a swimming pool, and three cars in the driveway. They were dazzling, and I was dazzled.

'Even so, after a while, I couldn't help noticing they weren't visiting Grandma that much and when I asked why she never came to lunch at theirs, Uncle Eric shrugged and said she was more comfortable in her own home. Still when she was diagnosed with lung cancer he was quick to act, taking care of everything, so I thought he was all right. I even thought her illness might bring him and Dad back together again, but the enmity ran too deep . . .'

'That's sad.'

'Yes,' Margaret sighs, 'Grandma had been in hospital for a few weeks when she asked me to cook her some bread, on her range, using her favourite recipe. She said it was the only way to guarantee it tasted good.

I hadn't been to the house for ages, and I was shocked to arrive and find two men throwing wood into a large skip at the front. It turned out Uncle Eric had given them permission, and there was nothing I could do about it because he had the power of attorney. When I entered the house it was to find the kitchen was gutted, the range gone, and the recipe book thrown on a pile of rubbish. I took it home, baked the bread there, pretending to Grandma I'd cooked it on her range. By then the drugs had taken hold, so I don't think she noticed, but I was none too keen on Uncle Eric after that.'

'I'm not surprised.'

'She died soon after. Uncle Eric and Dad just about managed to keep the peace till the funeral, when Dad found Uncle Eric had inherited the house and was giving it to Kath as an engagement present. He accused Uncle Eric of all sorts, and they never spoke again. I was tempted to do the same, but Kath made a point of going out of her way to make sure we stayed friends. So we did. For years. Right through marriages, babies, Richard's death, family holidays.'

'What happened?'

'She didn't show up to Dad's funeral, even though I went to Uncle Eric's. It turned out she'd promised her Dad that she wouldn't mark his death in anyway. I pushed her and she said it was because my Dad was always looking down on hers, on them, and to be honest, she'd always felt the same. I suppose I was a bit irrational with grief because I accused Uncle Eric of being irresponsible, and exploiting

Grandma, and she said a load of stuff about Dad I'm sure she didn't mean. It ended up with her chucking me out of the house and we haven't spoken since.'

'I'm sorry.'

'It's stupid. I should have tried to sort it out. But we're both as stubborn as our parents so here we are. I've emailed her tonight. I don't hold out much hope of a reply.'

'I'm sure she will.'

'How about you? What do you regret?'

I tell her everything. How life took a wrong turn after Mum's death and no matter how hard I tried I lost my way with Alison and Dad. How Harry had seemed like the answer to a prayer but now is beginning to feel like a waste of time. And how much I regret having given up my music, not made more of myself. She reaches out and holds my hand as I talk, is sympathetic to my tears, and I feel a sense of comfort that I've missed since childhood.

'It's not your fault, you know,' she says. 'You're just young, you haven't had the time I have.'

That's true. I haven't. And it's not like life has been terrible in my family. Alison and I may have argued all the way through our teens but she's still my sister. When I look back on it, we were constant companions in Yorkshire and always did everything together. We were wild and reckless back then, challenging each other to be the best at everything. Who could swing higher, who could climb higher, who could run faster. And even years later, when she was getting all those A stars while I was bottom of the class, she did what she could to help. All these years I've resented her bossiness, and yet, when I think about it, isn't that what big sisters do? Particularly a big sister who felt she had to replace her mother. Maybe I've been looking at her through Harry's eyes for too long. And forgotten that, deep down, we love each other very much. Maybe we're just like Margaret's Dad and Uncle, Alison being the responsible big sister, me the resentful younger one. It's just my bad luck to have only worked it out now.

'Thank you,' I say, but Margaret is already asleep.

I let her go of her hand and am about to turn off the lantern when my phone flashes with a text from Harry *Found a boat*. I reply immediately *Are you coming back? If I can*, he replies. A few seconds later, he adds *I love you*. An afterthought, as usual, but it reminds me that he can be kind. Maybe Alison was right, maybe I should have gone with him. But at least he hasn't forgotten me. Perhaps this will be the time he surprises me, perhaps he will come back for me, perhaps he will be my knight in shining armour after all.

Instagram
LisaLuskOfficial
Image: Unnamed man

THREE HOURS AGO

LisaLuskOfficial *Am out of my mind worrying about him. A friend says he texted he was leaving but that was hours ago.*
Lisasbiggestfan *Praying for you.*
AllieSimpson4 *Hopefully he's nearly at Plymouth? Perhaps his phone needed charging.*
LisaLuskOfficial *You're probably right. I can't stop thinking that if we were still together, I'd be down there too.*
AllieSimpson4 *Well, that's something to be thankful for.*
WonderWoman2018 *Can I ask, is Never Leave Me about him?*
LisaLuskOfficial *Yes. I never normally talk about him,*

but he was the Love of my Life. I've never got over our break up.
StevenSmith5 *Hope he's on his way home and back to you.*
Jenny5001 *We're all rooting for that to happen.*
LisaLuskOfficial *Never Leave Me, Never Leave Me/ Believe me when I say to you/ James, my darling James/ I'll never ever be leaving you. xxxx*

Facebook Messenger
Seren Lovelace to Andy Jones.

2.00 a.m.

Are you still up? Am freaking out. She's just messaged me.
Andy Jones to Seren Lovelace

2.02 a.m.

I'll call you.

2.05 a.m.

News n' Truth
The website that never lies

Image: A smiling woman sits on a beach drinking. An eagle-eyed citizen has spotted this rather surprising image on Facebook. Margaret Anderson, the woman who created the tsunami crisis, at Dowetha Cove earlier this evening. It is indeed ironic that she will be a victim of her own misguided actions, but here she seems to be celebrating the fact. Do the brave souls on that beach know they are there because of her? Perhaps someone should tell them?

Facebook
Dowetha Beach Live

30 August

Image: A smiling woman sits on a beach drinking.
Ten other comments
Tommy Fairbanks: Do you know who this is? Margaret Anderson, the woman who caused the tsunami. You should make her pay.
Jay Palmer: Drown the bitch.
Hannah Samuels: How dare she sit there like that? All that suffering. You ought to kick her out. Let her die alone.

Facebook
Poppy Armstrong

30 August 2.15 a.m.

I can't sleep. I tried earlier, while others went for late night walks, I suddenly found myself overwhelmed with exhaustion. But the minute I lay down, I found myself wide awake. All day long I have acted as if tomorrow is something that I have accepted, come to terms with. I have been the cheerleader for our little group, trying to create a party atmosphere, bring people together, have stimulating conversations, swim, eat, surf. I have comforted and encouraged, and behaved as if the world isn't just about to end for all of us. I've always been a good hostess, and I think tonight I have played my part well.

But now, as everyone has drifted off to bed, or for late night walks, perhaps even for romance, I cannot hide how alone I feel. I tried to sleep, but I can't. I am scared, really scared. I have only a few hours left until the wave comes. Even as I write it, I can't think that it is really true. It still feels as if this is some horrible hoax conceived by some stupid joker who will reveal all tomorrow. I still find it hard to believe I am going to die. And yet, if I chose I could spend the rest of the night looking at the images which are hard to avoid. I am trying not to click on them, but they keep popping up on my timeline. The long line of cars fleeing coastlines everywhere, the moment the volcano erupts spewing burning orange lava from its summit. And the worse moment, when the mountain collapses in on itself, splitting in two, sending tonnes and tonnes of stone into the water, creating the wave that is right now crossing the Atlantic towards us. There is no way out. I cannot escape it. That moment has long passed, if it ever existed in the first place.

In other news, I've contacted my ex. Let's hope she responds.

10 Likes

3 more comments

The Wave

Beverley Lewis Hope so. x

8 minutes

Andy Carroll Very brave of you, even if she doesn't it's the right call.

5minutes

LAUDS

Poppy

The wind has built up and even with a jumper on, I am shivering. I really should be getting back to bed, but ever since I sent my faltering message to Seren, I've been unable to move. I have to see if she replies. Any response, will do, even a negative one. I sit on the bench, willing the message to appear, aware that is getting colder. It is not the ice cold of the winter days that I will never have again, but cold enough to be uncomfortable. I wish I'd brought a jacket, but I'd was hot in my sleeping bag, and when I couldn't sleep I stupidly wandered up here without it. I could go back to the tent, of course, but my network only seems to get a strong signal up here. Instead I stand up, stamping some life into my feet, and wander over to the wall of the car park, staring down at the beach as I had earlier in the day. All is quiet now, just the ebb and flow of the waves, the tide turning back once again. The moon has risen high in the sky, half muffled by cloud. Earlier, the sky was full of stars, but now only a handful are visible. Down on the beach I can make out the shapes of the tents, huddled against the rising wind. The campfire has gone out and the site looks alone and defenceless; it would probably be kinder if none of my friends woke up tomorrow, probably be better for them to be swept away, oblivious. What have I been thinking of, encouraging people to come here? Harry had the right idea: we should have tried to escape when we had the chance.

I check my phone. It's 2.30 a.m. It's stupid to think that Seren is awake right now, and if she is that she has nothing better to do than check Facebook. Stupid to imagine that Seren might be thinking of me, might remember me telling her how much I love it here. She has no idea where I am, how could she? Even so, the thought that she might, perhaps, still be up; might, perhaps, at least remember how much I love this part of the world and wonder if I might be down here, is incentive to stay up another half an hour just in case.

I check my Facebook page. Nothing. I check the Dowetha Live page. To my dismay there are loads of messages from trolls. They've found out about Margaret and all the bile of the internet has been unleashed. I block every nasty comment. I'm still mad at her for what she did, but no one should be subject to this kind of crap. She doesn't do Facebook, but all the same, I don't want these things being said about her.

It is getting colder. The car has a heater and maybe some toffees in the glove compartment; I decide to sit there for a bit, listen to the radio. It's a good move; soon I'm feeling warmer, and I find a station streaming undemanding pop songs of the Seventies – my parents' era. And I was right, there are toffees in the glove compartment. I take one out of its wrapper sitting back to listen to Karen Carpenter sing of birds and stars and being close to the man she loves. I can still picture Mum and Dad dancing in the living room on a Saturday night after a couple of glasses of wine, all giggly and flushed. We were happy then, even if I hadn't yet plucked up the courage to come out to them. How would it have been, if they had lived? I was their only daughter, I know they loved me, I hope they'd have accepted me, but it was the Nineties when that was still a big ask. So, I kept my teenage romances far away, hoping that one day I could explain. I never expected sudden death would take them from me before I got the chance. It wasn't fair. My whole life has been so unfair.

I was in my first year at Bristol, in a world that was feeling scary as shit after 9/11. I was a long way from home, veering between loving my independence and missing my parents daily when the police came round. I don't remember much of what followed. I somehow made it back to Barnsley where Aunty Barbara and Uncle Tim were busily arranging the funeral. The house was in negative equity and I couldn't afford to keep it. They said I could stay with them for as long as I wanted, but there were six of them in a small terrace, and, besides, we'd never been that close. I went back to feeling depressed and in debt, and spent the next year, eking out a miserable existence on my grant and crappy bar job. When Alisdair, one of my lecturers offered me 'research' work, I jumped at the chance. At first, it was just that. Researching student attitudes to the war on terror, Islam, security. But soon they asked for a bit more. Could I keep an eye on this student, or tell me where this one went at night? Was that person a fan of Bin Laden, did the other one mention attending a particular mosque? It was easy money, taking the pressure off so I could concentrate on my studies. They told me I was helping keep the country safe. And I believed them. The job lasted as long as my course. And when I graduated with my 2:1, I went to London to find my fortune. I thought no more about it until a couple of years after Seren and I got together, when Alisdair came looking for me again . . .

If only my parents hadn't died, none of it would have happened. None of it. Seren and I would still be together, or at least not have broken up so catastrophically, and I wouldn't be here. My life has just been one set of disasters. Before I know it my face is wet with tears and I cannot stop.

'Are you all right?' Margaret is tapping on the window. I am about to tell her to leave me alone, when it occurs to me that company might do me some good.

'Get in.' She climbs in beside me. Karen Carpenter has been replaced by Neil Diamond – 'Sweet Caroline' – Mum's song, I can still hear Dad serenading her at the breakfast table. I cry harder. Sobs that come from deep inside my body and I cannot stop them; I sob and sob so hard that my whole body shakes. Gradually, I am aware that Margaret is reaching towards me. I find myself leaning on her shoulder, her arm is round me and I sense a comfort I haven't known in years. At last, after what seems like hours, but is only really a few minutes, the sobs subside, and I sit up and find some tissues in the side pocket.

'Better?'

'A bit. Sorry. I hate crying like that.'

'It's been one of those evenings.'

She's kind. She really is. And I realize that's why I've been so angry with her. That the person I felt I could lean on has let me down so badly.

'I know you blame me,' she says, as if reading my thoughts.

'If you'd not got rid of that unit . . .'

'Even if we'd kept it, monitoring volcanos might not have been the priority. It would probably have been focussed on climate change. And there's no guarantee that the technology would have caught it anyway.'

'Really?'

'Really.' Margaret looks at me. 'What's bothering you? I know we're all overwrought tonight, but I was watching you earlier. You seem to have something on your mind.'

'It's about someone in my past. I've tried to get hold of her but . . .'

'Now it's probably too late?' Margaret's smile is sad. 'I've got someone like that.'

'Have you got in touch?'

'Yes, and she's replied. Not the answer I wanted, I'm afraid.'

'Oh.' That's not very comforting. Margaret leans over and puts her hand on my knee. 'I'm still glad I did it though. I'm leaving this world having tried to make amends. Better than doing nothing. This woman . . .'

'Seren.'

'She may or may not respond. Her answer may or may not be what you want to hear, but at least you will know you tried.'

'Maybe.' I want to tell her more, but I am afraid that she will judge me, as I judged her earlier. I say nothing as I check my phone. There have been a few more encouraging messages on my page, but nothing from Seren. I let out a big yawn. I can barely keep my eyes open, and my body is aching from the earlier exercise. I need to sleep, even if only for a couple of hours.

'Time for bed.'

'Yes.' We get out of the car. Yan meets us at the top of the slope, like us, he's been struggling to sleep

'Have you seen the Facebook page?'

I frown at him, I hadn't wanted to mention it for fear of upsetting Margaret

'Yes.'

'What's the matter?' says Margaret.

'A few trolls,' I say. 'I'm sorry. I deleted some nasty comments already but looks we've had a few more.'

'How did they find out?'

The Wave

'There's a picture of you from earlier today. It was shared on a website . . .'

'It can't have been one of us?'

I think about it, Nikki and James are too interested in each other, Shelley wouldn't have, and it's none of us. 'I wouldn't put it past Harry,' I say. They nod. Margaret sighs, 'At least my daughter doesn't share the same name. The last thing she needs is to be harassed online.'

'It's just a few idiots,' I say. 'I'll put them right in the morning.' We say good night to Yan for the second time and I follow her back to the tents. It is 3.00 a.m. If I'm lucky, I'll catch three hours or so. 'Thank you,' I whisper, giving Margaret a hug before unzipping my tent and diving in. I pull myself into my sleeping bag and lie back, closing my eyes. Pictures form: my parents singing to each other, the day I received the phone call about the accident, Seren's face when I first saw her at the concert in Hyde Park – and the last time, full of rage. No, this is no good. I can't sleep with that image in my mind. I think of my mum telling me stories at bedtime, remember the moon on the water earlier, the silver path streaking to the horizon. I think of the star woman and the husband who pursued her to the ends of the earth. I imagine following a silver path across the water, and reaching the heavens to find Seren there, willing to receive my apology and forgive me. The image soothes me as waves of sleep come, sending me into a blessed oblivion.

Yan

It is a hot and sunny day; the sky is blue and cloudless. Karo and I are covered in suntan lotion and wearing hats for protection, but we are not really aware of the weather. We are too busy building a huge sandcastle at the bottom of a red and white striped cliff. We have been doing so all week and today's effort is the best yet. There are turrets, tunnels, shell escarpments, seaweed flags, a large moat, which we are filling with water, and a drawbridge. When the tide comes in, we will take great pleasure in trying to defeat its passage. We will fight till the very end to block its path up the channel and round the moat, until the inevitable happens – the final wave will overwhelm it and we will watch as it crumbles into the sea, fading away as if it never existed. But this is some time away. For the moment, we are enjoying the sheer joy of working together to complete our masterpiece. The water in the moat has drained away again, leaving a pile of gooey sludge. It is my turn to fetch some more. I pick up the bucket, and wander past my parents, who are half lying, half sitting, watching us play. This is a good day. The best day. The wind is rising as I walk down the beach, but I don't notice. I am more interested in the tiny spiralled fossils I can see on the ground. I pick up a few and put them in the bottom of the bucket for decoration as I make my way to the water's edge. I am just intending to fill my bucket, but the wind has whipped up the sea into a white foam, and though Mum always says to wait for her and Dad, I cannot resist, I jump in the water, enjoy the exhilaration of the waves crashing about me. I am drawn deeper in. There is a strong undercurrent and, before I know it, I am up to my waist. It is then that I hear a warning shout from Mum and spot a huge wave coming towards me. Panicked, I try to turn, but the undercurrent is strong and I slip. Suddenly I am under the water which is trying to force its way through my nose and mouth. I push myself up, sink, push up, gasping, and sink again. And suddenly Mum is there, grabbing me with her strong arms, pulling me out, just before the wave would have come crashing down on my head . . .

I wake with a start. That was weird. Though Karo and my dad regularly feature in my dreams, Mum never does. And while I struggle to recall those Karo and Dad dreams, waking only with a deep sense of loss, I can remember every detail of this one as if it had just happened. The beach felt familiar too. Was it a real place? Did we actually go there? I try and think back to family holidays. We couldn't always afford them, but before Dad left we had two that were particularly memorable – one in Rye, the other in Hunstanton. There was something about one of those places that was a bit unusual . . . it's at the back of my memory, something to do with the cliffs . . . That's it! The cliffs at Hunstanton were striated, red and white, a mixture of sandstone and clay. Just like the cliffs in my dream. There were fossils there too. Now I think of it, we used to love collecting the ammonites. If the beach was real, was the incident? Did Mum really rescue me from the sea? So much of family life before Dad left is a blur I really can't remember. Is it possible that I have I forgotten this story? Did it actually happen? Or is it a fantasy I've come up with to convince myself she has always loved me?

Oh, this is pointless. I'll never know the answer because, when I do call her in the morning, I can't ask her about it. I'll have to spend most of the call preparing her for the news that I am going to die and the rest of it dealing with the fallout. I doubt there'll be an opportunity to discuss whether she actually saved my life when I was a child or whether it is wishful thinking on my part. To be honest, I don't dare put the question to her; I'm not sure I want to discover it's all in my imagination. I'd rather leave this world with the comforting belief that there was one day in my childhood, one day when it *really* mattered, my mother was there for me.

I turn over to see if James is awake, but his sleeping bag is gone. He must be with Nikki somewhere. Lucky sod. Still, my earlier resentment has gone. Something good needs to come out of this. Somebody deserves something good to happen. I'm glad it is him. I'm glad it is them. I wish I had someone with me now, to talk to, to take the edge off the fear that's building again. But it's nearly three and I am alone. Everyone else must be asleep. I am alone in the night with the flap of the tent in the wind, the menacing roar of the ocean. I'm not sure why all those meditation tapes use the sound of the sea to relax – tonight the noise of crashing waves feels like a threat. I am exhausted but I cannot sleep now. I am too anxious. I switch on the lamp. My copy of *The Humans* is beside me. I finished it just before dropping off. A satisfying end to a great book that will stay with me for a long time. Well, would have stayed with me if I had a chance of living beyond tomorrow. The book falls open and I pick up my torch and read, 'If there is a sunset, stop and look at it. Knowledge is finite. Wonder is infinite.' Perhaps it's a sign that I should go out and look at the stars. Fuck it, it's better than staying in this tent, tossing and turning.

I grab a jumper and jacket and step out onto the beach. To my disappointment, the night is cloudy, the moon only partially visible. As for stars, I can see a few dotted about, but most are obscured. So much for seeing the wonders of the cosmos one last time. I stand, uncertain what to do for a moment. I don't want to go back to bed; perhaps a walk would help. I grab a beer and a bar of chocolate for sustenance, aware of voices speaking quietly. Heading up the beach I notice James and Nikki have found themselves a spot under the cliff. Not for the first time, I wish I had someone to be that intimate with, to help me keep the fear away. Before I wallow in my own misery, my phone begins to buzz with Facebook notifications. Lots of them. Oh fuck. The trolls have found Margaret. The Dowetha page is full of horrible comments. It doesn't matter that I'd thought the same as some of them earlier. I, at least, had a justification. I'm stuck here with no way out. I had every right to be angry with Margaret. But these sick bastards are sitting at home in safety. They don't know her, have no understanding of what she had to do and aren't going to be harmed by that decision anyway. Instead of being sympathetic to her for the awful situation she is in, they pile insults and death threats on her. Why do they have to be so vile?

I'm wondering what to do about them when I see Margaret and Poppy coming towards me. I don't intend to mention the posts, but somehow, when they reach me, I can't stop myself, I blurt it out. Poppy frowns at me, but it is too late, Margaret has heard and I am forced to explain. It dawns on me as I speak that only one of us could have made the connection between that photo and the stories in the media. I can't think which one. Even though we were all angry with her, I don't think any of us would be that vindictive, The only person I can think of is . . .

'I wouldn't put it past Harry,' says Poppy. Me neither. I knew he was an arsehole. This proves it. I wish I had his number so I could tell the bastard what I think of him, but then I think what good would that do?'

I'm tempted to ask the women to walk with me, enjoy the night for a while, but I can see they are exhausted. It would be selfish to ask them to come with me. I say good-night again and continue up to the car park. I could walk along the cliffs, but the pounding waves are too much of a reminder of tomorrow. I decide to walk along the road that Margaret and I drove along earlier this evening, or technically last night, because we are already in the tomorrow that ends today. I walk purposefully, as if I have somewhere to go because that is easier than acknowledging that nothing I do really matters now, that there's very little I can achieve in the hours that remain.

The hedges seem higher on foot. The moon has disappeared behind black clouds, I take out my phone and put on the flashlight to guide my way. The night is full of rustlings: the wind in the grass, small creatures in the bushes, sheep walking through the fields. I walk and walk, until at after about a mile I reach a footpath. I am sick of the road, so I climb over onto a path that leads to a small mound. The wind catches my breath as I make my way to the summit just as the moon reappears, lighting the ground around me. At the top, I sit, take the beer and chocolate out of my pocket and gaze out across the fields. I can just make out the sea beyond, a black strip beneath the horizon. The clouds are breaking up, revealing the stars behind them. I lie back on the damp ground, gazing upwards as more and more stars appear. I'd swear I can see millions, though I recently read somewhere that it's only about 4,000.

The Wave

It doesn't really matter how many there are though, because they are magnificent, and the sight of the sky is glorious and fills me a hope that I don't have any right to and the same joy I experienced in my dream. The familiar constellations dance across the sky, reminding me there is time to wonder, even now.

I am still here. I am still alive. Tomorrow is a long time away.

Margaret

The wind wakes me and for a moment, I think I am on a camping trip with Hellie. Then Shelley rolls over and I see the long blonde hair tumbling out and remember. Dear God, in a few hours' time I will be dead. We will all be dead. Even so, I'm tired and I want to go back to sleep, but the flapping of the tents is irritating and I'd like to know if Kath has replied. Bugger, there's no signal. I should try and get back to sleep, but the thought that she might have responded is more pressing. It is enough to have me scramble out of my warm sleeping bag, throw some clothes on and step out into the night air.

The signal kicks in halfway up the beach. There's a message from Kath. My mouth is dry. I sit on the sand to steady myself. It is damp and cold, but I barely notice, I am too intent on scrolling through the words slowly, reading them and re-reading them in the vain hope they will say something different.

Dear Margaret,

You certainly have some nerve. Last time we spoke, you told me I was selfish, like my dad. That I'd always been selfish. That you didn't want to be part of our family any more. You walked away. YOU WALKED AWAY. Not a bloody word for years and now this devastating news. I didn't even know you were in Cornwall. You left without a trace. And here you are offering your patronising forgiveness in the hope I'll care for your family after you've gone. Your apology, such as it, doesn't even stop to reflect on the hurt you caused me. And now you want me to be there for Hellie and the kids? How dare you?

But that's always been your trouble, hasn't it, St Margaret? You always did love the moral high ground, didn't you? You and your dad, judging me and mine always . . .

You said we abandoned Grandma, but we didn't. I know you saw a lot of her when you moved but you hadn't lived with her over the previous years as we did. Maybe it was old age or the beginnings of a tumour, but she was so cantankerous. We stopped having her over for lunch because she was always so rude to Mum . . .

Grandma . . . Rude? That can't be right.

We tried to keep going round, but I can't tell you the amount of times she told us to go away, and all she ever talked about was you.

The Wave

I am about to protest at this, but I have a sudden flash-back of Grandma telling me that I was the only one who really cared about her, that the others never came. I took her at her word, never thought to question it. Had I been wrong all this time?

As for the house, she gave it to me. She told me loads of times that she wanted me to have it. She always said you were the kind of person to make your own way in the world, that you didn't need possessions or houses to make you feel happy. But she knew I was different, I needed security. And I loved the place. You may not have liked the way we redecorated, but it doesn't mean I did it out of disrespect. You think we were pulling the wool over Grandma's eyes – we weren't. We knew she couldn't come home, we were trying to protect her, pretending nothing had changed so she didn't have to worry.

Oh Lord, am I wrong about this too?

Don't believe me? Well I'm still here, living out her legacy, loving her house whilst you pretend you had the better relationship because of some damned cookery book.
Damn you, damn you, damn you.
The answer is no.
Kath.

I put my phone down as I stare out into the darkness, listening to the rush of the waves, back and forth, back and forth. I can still feel the impact of Kath's fury. All these years, I've been so convinced I was right about what happened, that mine was the story that was true, the one that mattered. I had never stopped to consider it from her perspective. And while, I think her version is coloured by how much she adored Uncle Eric, I have to admit, she has a point. I didn't see how things were with Grandma. I was young, I didn't understand then, as I do now, how ill health and old age can change the way people behave. Oh Kath, I'm so sorry. I got this so wrong. I have to let her know, I understand. She may reject me again, but I can't leave things like this, and Hellie will need her. I type out a reply immediately.

Dearest Kath,

You are right. I have gone about this all the wrong way. Forgive me for not being in touch for so long – for waiting for you to make the first move. For leaving it till this crisis forced my hand. For making the mistake of thinking there was plenty of time to put things right between us.

You are right. I have misjudged you. I had no idea that Grandma had behaved like that to you. Otherwise I'd have never said what I did. Forgive me. I walked away because I was angry and hurt. I didn't look back because I thought you'd chase after me. I was so sure

I was right. I thought I could live without you. I was wrong. I need you. But more importantly Hellie, who doesn't deserve to be caught up in our fight, needs you.

You may think these are the meaningless words of a dying woman, who is offering too little too late. Perhaps they are. But please don't punish Hellie for my mistakes. You love her. I know you do. Do it for her. Please.

I hope, one day, you'll look back and remember me with love and affection. Please believe me, when I say that is how I remember you.

Margaret.

I press send. It probably won't make any difference and it is unlikely Kath will see it till the morning now, but it's better than doing nothing. I look out across to the black sea. Tomorrow the spot I am standing on will lie under hundreds feet of water. Afterwards – though how long afterwards no one has said – when the ocean finally retreats, the beach below will be the sole witness to the destruction. Huts, cars, boats strewn across the shoreline in its wake. It is still hard to imagine that I won't walk away from this, that my body will lie somewhere among the debris, waiting to be identified. What a terrible legacy to leave Hellie . . . My phone buzzes. There's only one person who would call me at this time, only one person I'd want to speak to.

'Mum . . . I was hoping you'd be awake.'

'I can't sleep.'

'Me neither.' I try to find . . . not the right words, for there are none, but the best words I can. Hellie is quiet for a moment, and then her wail floods the phone, 'Oh Mum!' Last time I heard her express such pain, was the day she had appendicitis. Five-year-old Hellie, screaming at the top of her voice, as I drove as fast as I could, steeling myself not to feel the cries as I made pointless soothing noises that were the only way I could let her know I was trying my best. Tonight, the torrent of sobs fills me with the same sense of helplessness, the knowledge that there are limits to the protection a parent can offer her child. All I can do is offer the same meaningless noises until the tears subside and Hellie is able to speak again.

'Sorry, Mum . . . Last thing you needed.'

I can hear music above me; someone must be in the car park. Poppy, maybe? I look at my watch, half past two. 'It's wonderful to be so loved.'

'You'll start me off again.' Hellie's voice wobbles.

'Try and get some sleep. We'll talk in the morning. Everything is always better in the morning.' Hellie's laugh is weak; I always say that, and I'm usually right, though how it can possibly be true in these circumstances is anyone's guess. We say good night for the second, the last time, and then it is my turn to scream silently to the skies. To God. The Universe. Life. For ripping me away before I am ready. Without being able to hold my daughter ever again. It's not fair, I think, as the emotion drains away, leaving me with my other parental truism – *Life never is.*

And, on the whole, I've had a good life, even the bad bits can't outweigh that fact. I must remember to tell Hellie this in the morning.

I should go back to bed, but Hellie's phone call has unsettled me. I cannot face going back to my tent. Above me I can hear the Carpenters on the radio. I might as well investigate, and if it is Poppy up there, maybe I'll have the chance to clear the air with her. I arrive at the car, to find it is her, she is crumpled over the wheel sobbing. I knock on the window. For a minute, I think she's going to tell me to go away, but she lets me in as 'Sweet Caroline' comes on the radio.

'My mother's favourite song,' she says through her tears.

'Ah . . . What's the matter?'

She cries even harder, the sobs causing her body to shake. It is natural for me to reach out to her, let her rest her head on her shoulder, as the tears tumble. For a moment, I can pretend my daughter is with me after all. I hold her tightly, drawing comfort from her warmth and her need. It is better than being alone with my own fears.

I close my eyes. The words of a prayer come to me, 'O, God come to our aid'. I used to find it reassuring on the long nights after Richard died, when I'd say the office to myself to get me through till morning. I repeat the words over and over again, though tonight I have no confidence the prayer will be answered. Still, it has a soothing effect on me, and somehow I transmit this to Poppy. Eventually she stops crying and breaks away. She seems embarrassed by her show of emotion, and I can see the distrust of me returning in her eyes. I am sick of explaining it, but I try again. I cannot bear that she, who has done so much to make the best of this situation, still thinks badly of me. She listens and though I'm not sure she believes me, at least she has stopped being hostile. And when I ask what's bothering her, she tells me – well, some of it, anyway. She talks about her former girlfriend and how they are estranged but she seems reluctant to say why. I don't like to push it, so I don't ask, simply grateful that she is letting me in.

Poppy yawns, I follow suit, time to go back and catch what sleep we can. I'm feeling almost content until we run into Yan who blurts out that people have been leaving nasty comments about me on Facebook. I feel sick. Why would they do that? Who gets so angry that they post vile statements about a stranger on social media?

'It's just a few idiots,' says Poppy, 'I'll put them right in the morning.' I am touched by the fierceness in her voice, her willingness to defend me. It is all the proof I need that I am forgiven. And as I climb back into my sleeping bag, it crosses my mind that perhaps my prayer was answered after all.

James

The wine is half drunk. After the sadness and terror of earlier, the world is as peaceful as I can hope for now. With my arm round Nikki, her head leaning on me, sheltered from the wind by the rocks, I can almost believe in our future. A while ago we saw Poppy leaving her tent and, soon after, Margaret. They both headed to the car park. The wind has grown in strength, it whips the waves so they crash into a mass of white foam on the shore. The tide is going out and the path round to the cave is beginning to emerge again. The night has clouded over, and the sky is darker, but I am not afraid. I feel warm and safe. We have not spoken for a while, but now, as Nikki passes her mug for a top up, she says, 'Tell me about your ex, then.' I pour us both a drink, staring into the dark liquid in my cup. 'That's if . . . if you want to,' she adds. I take a gulp of wine. 'Difficult to know where to start.' I take my arm away and lean forward, looking ahead at the dark waters; somehow it feels easier not to look at her.

'Have you ever had the experience of wanting something,

someone, so badly that everything else fades in comparison?'

'Can't say I have, no.'

'If I say she is the artist known as Lisa Lusk, you might have a clue.'

'Her?' Nikki splutters.

'You see the attraction?'

'If you like super-skinny, over made-up white girls,' Nikki snorts, and adds, 'Well, I suppose there's something behind the foundation.'

'There is, there was. I met her on the pub circuit, before she went all indie techno on me, in the days where her image was more flowing skirts and bright colours than elaborate make-up and fantastic costumes. We were both in groups which were going nowhere, and one day, after a gig, we got talking, and decided to join forces.'

I continue to stare out to sea, turning my cup round in my hands, remembering that night back by the fireside in the King's Arms. I can almost hear the crackle of the flames, smell the smoke, see Lisa leaning towards me. For a moment I hesitate, and then it all pours out. How she talked about her dreams for the future, her eyes shining as she touched my arm to emphasize her points. How she invited me to form a duo and I returned home, unable to believe my luck. How, in the next blissful months, I raced through the days, living for the evenings in the shed in her back garden where we rehearsed, the nights in pubs where we sang to tiny audiences until, one Saturday I walked her home in the pouring rain. And how, outside the tiny Victorian cottage she shared she drew me towards her and invited me inside because her friend Daisy was away. How we got as far as the staircase before tearing our clothes off, making love in a messy, frenzied tumble, ignoring the friction burns from the carpet, the discomfort of the stairs, caught in the moment. And how, from that day onwards, every waking moment was spent thinking about her.

I pause as, below us a tent unzips. It is Yan. Only Shelley is left sleeping. Yan lumbers off up to the top of the cliff. I take a deep breath, it is hard to talk about the point at which it all went so badly wrong. I refused to admit to myself the signs that were there right from the start. Lisa always asked me to leave before dawn and, even when we were seeing each other regularly, we never went out with her friends. She began to critique my performance making it clear she was the one with talent and I was lucky to be in her presence. She started to experiment with music I hated, and began to cut me out of rehearsals. But I was besotted with her, so I put up with all of that just to spend an hour or two in her company. Then one day, she announced she was leaving for London, just like that, no discussion, no suggestion I might come too, and though she never exactly said this was it, it soon became clear that it was over when she stopped texting. Soon after that she burst onto the pop scene with a look and sound so far removed from the woman I had been with that I realized I had never known her at all. The knowledge had crushed me, leaving me in such a state of such despair that for a while I abandoned everything I loved – music, going to the pub, seeing friends – because, after all, what was the point? And even though it's been eighteen months, she still has the capacity to stop me in my tracks, as she did with that text. I begin to cry, not the hard, painful sobs I cried in the cave, but sad, slow tears, at my own stupidity, the time I wasted on her, the fact I let her still affect me . . .

Nikki touches my arm. 'I'm sorry. If it's any consolation, I always hated her music.'

That makes me laugh. I think Nikki could be good for me. I sit up straight, wipe my eyes and say in a more normal voice, 'Me neither. What I can't forgive myself for is that I let myself be her doormat for so long, let her departure wreck me for weeks, and even when I started putting my life back together it was always at the back of my mind that she might come back. So tonight, when I received her text, just as I was getting her out of my head, there she was, right back at the forefront. But you know what?' I feel in my pocket for my phone, 'That's it. It ends here.' I pull up Lisa's message and send a text, *Thanks, I'm fine. I've met someone. I'm doing OK. No need to text again. Appreciate your thoughts.* I press send. 'There. That's over with, I'm all yours if you'll have me.'

Nikki smiles. 'That's an offer worth considering.' To my disappointment, she says nothing more. I'm not quite sure what I expected from my revelations – a declaration of love, perhaps – but it wasn't this quiet withdrawal. I take comfort from the fact that though she is silent, she snuggles back against me; perhaps she needs some time think. The waves crash and recede below us, and soon I am mesmerized by the ebb and flow, the patterns they create in the water, the foam-flecked shore they leave behind as they recede. Margaret and Poppy return to their tents. It is very late. Perhaps we should call it a night too. I am about to suggest it when Nikki sighs.

'What's the matter?'

'Just thinking about my family. That I won't see them ever again. Or Lagos. I'd have liked to go back to Lagos.'

'Tell me about it.'

'It's a beautiful country. Mind you, I didn't think that the first time I went. I was a total brat. My parents were always telling me how wonderful England was, how glad they'd escaped Nigeria during the war. All I knew of Nigeria was that it was violent, full of poverty and very different from my world. So when they said we had to visit Grandma who was sick, I refused to go. Of course, there was nothing I could do about it, but I was furious we were leaving before the end of term. I was going to be the first black Mary in the nativity play. I was furious that I was going to miss it

'I was grumpy and bad-tempered as only an eight-year-old can be, and when we arrived and we drove to my grandparents' house and they didn't have a telly and their house was so small, I was rude and obnoxious and told everyone the place was horrible. Ifechi was three, and cute, so everyone fussed over him, while they expected me to be grown up. I hated it. Nothing smelt right, and it was hot all the time. I just wanted to go home . . .'

I love this: the sound of her voice, her head resting on my chest, listening to her story as I stroke her hair. 'Go on,' I say.

'So we'd been there a few days during which time we were either visiting grandma or I was being sent to my room constantly for my bad behaviour. My parents told me afterwards that they were totally mortified by me and at their wits' end at how to proceed. Then, one day my grandfather took me aside, and said, "I hear that you do not like our country, little Nkiruka."

' "My name is Nikki," I said and scowled at him.

' "I am so sad, that you feel like that, Nikki, Nkiruka is such a beautiful name. You know what it means, don't you?"

' "No." Despite myself, I was interested. No one had ever talked to me about my name before.

' "It means 'The best is yet to come'. You see, my little Nikki, you were born after our family had many struggles and much heartache. Your grandmother and I, we had to leave Lagos, our home city, and fly to England, where you now live. I remember feeling like you do now. It was cold in London, the streets were crowded, and the people unfriendly. It didn't smell right. It wasn't my home."

' "Lagos isn't my home."

' "But it could be . . . and you see, my darling girl, you

are lucky. Because although at first London made me very unhappy, and I worried for my mother, who we had had to leave behind (her name was Nkiruka too), and I worried for your grandmother because it was hard for me to find work, and though I had money in this country the government froze my assets and I couldn't get at it. So I was forced to take what jobs I could, portering and cleaning, doing anything to keep a roof over our heads, put food on the table, help your grandma, and your mother and her sisters. But I found, after a while, these English, these people I thought as cold as the weather, were kind when you got to know them. We made friends at our church who helped look after our children so Grandma could get some work. And when someone found out that I had once been a lecturer, they told me a job was going at the university. And so, after a while, this place that had once been cold and grey became something of warmth and light and colour. I missed my homeland, I missed the rainy season, and the sun and the beach, but I learnt to love my new city and have my heart in two places too. So when the war was ended, and it was safe to go home it was a wrench for me, a heartbreaking wrench. Your mother and her sisters were fully grown by then, confident young women making their way. But Grandma and I wanted to come back here to the life we left behind, and we needed to take care of my mother who was near the end of her life. We returned to our city by the ocean, to the sunsets and rainy seasons. But we never forgot the place that had adopted us. We loved to visit your mother and father once they were first married, and it has only been Gran's health that has stopped us returning, to meet our little Nkiruka and Ifechi. So let me show you some places in my second home because you are old enough and he is not. Then you can tell me if you like them and, if you do, why then you will have two cities, two homes, just like us."

'So he took me through his city, showing me its secret places, telling me of the war and it's after-effects, of the impact of colonialism, of the story of his childhood; and I realized then that he was right. I did have two cities and Lagos was mine. Ever since then, I've been conscious of my dual nature, dual nationality. As my parents embraced England and left their past behind, I have taken the reverse journey. I have been to Nigeria as often as I could, because in some ways I have never entirely fitted in either country, but I know that I am deeply connected to both. And now I can never go back.' She begins to cry, soft tears, that run down her cheek, and onto my shirt.

'Sorry,' she says, wiping her tears away with her arm.

'Don't be.'

'It's just . . .'

'Shhh.' I kiss the top of her head. 'You know, it's funny, but I think I get a little bit of what you mean. I don't mean the racism. I'll never know what that is like. It's just that growing up in Zambia, going to school in England, neither place was ever quite home, but both absolutely are.'

'I never thought I'd hear a white boy say that.' Nikki is recovering herself.

'I'm not your average white boy.' I kiss her. 'The best is yet to come. I like that.'

'If only it were true.'

There are only a few hours left, but somehow, in this moment, I feel, perhaps, it is.

Nikki

I'm not sure how long we have been sitting here, watching the white foam as the waves crash on the shore. The wind has picked up, ruffling the surface of the water so it constantly moves and changes. The tents are still flapping in the wind. I hope now Poppy and Margaret are back, they will be able to sleep. I am getting tired myself yet I cannot bring myself to go to bed. I need to ask James something and I am screwing up the courage. If this is to work, even for a few hours, I need to know that he is as he says, not the usual kind of white boy.

'Tell me about Zambia,' I say; I need to work up to this conversation.

'My parents met in a village outside Luangwa whilst working for a charity. He was a conservationist, she was a teacher. They were supposed to be there for a couple of years, but when they came back to the UK, they found they couldn't settle. So the minute they had me, they returned. They've made their home in Luangwa. She still teaches and he works for the safari park. So that's where I

grew up, went to the local school, where Mum taught, the
only white boy in the class. Not something I noticed till I
came over here for school. My parents thought it best, but
like you, I wasn't so convinced. The racism horrified me,
still does.'

'Glad to hear that.' I swig the last of the wine for Dutch
courage. 'We need to talk about this.'

'What?'

'Race.'

'We do?'

'We do.'

'I was kind of hoping it wouldn't be an issue. Given the
situation . . .'

'It's always an issue.' Now I feel anger rising. Does he
not get it?

'I just meant: here we are. The end of the world. Two
people falling in love. Can't we ignore it?' I stop myself
from thrilling at the suggestion he might be falling in love.
I cannot allow myself to admit this, until I am sure of him.

'We can never ignore it. I need to know . . .'

'What?'

'That I can trust you to understand that, even if we're
here isolated from the world, we can't ignore it. That if we
posted on Facebook, someone somewhere would comment.
That we'd have to respond. I need to know that you get
that.'

James turns towards me, 'I get that. But . . .'

'What.'

'Who cares about comments? I'd block anyone who was shitty.'

'It's easy for you to say that. Easy to block out what you've never had to deal with.'

James bristles at this. 'I hope you're not saying what I think you are saying.'

'No, of course not. But, if we're going to be together, for however short a time, I need you to understand this.' He thinks about it for a moment.

'All right. Let's do it.'

'What?'

'Post our pictures on Facebook. See what happens.'

'Even if it means unfriending someone you really like?'

'Especially if.'

We pose for selfies, James with his arm round me, me kissing him, him kissing me, both of us pulling faces. As if this is an ordinary night, as if we haven't a care in the world. James posts it on Facebook with the message. *Strange old night. Best thing to happen today. Best thing to happen for ages is meeting Nikki Anekwe. Wish it was in better circumstances but wish us luck.*

He sits back. I look at him, as if seeing him for the first time. I want to think he'll go through with it, be as true as he says he will be. Before I go to sleep with this man, this stranger, this white, beautiful man. I need to know that I can trust him.

'Thank you.'

'Of course, there might not be many people up at this

time,' he says, and then his phone pings, and pings again. 'Two likes already. There, you see?'

'Wait.'

'I don't want to sit around here, waiting for my phone to prove you right. Let's go for a walk,' he says.

'OK.' We rise, climb up the beach, past the car park, and take the cliff path. The moon is high above us. It lights up the grass, the shrubs, and shimmers in the dark black sea below. Despite the wind, the night is peaceful, tranquil. His hand feels comfortable in mine. I can almost believe in happy ever after up here. No former girlfriends, no race issues, no wave to come between us. We walk on in companionable silence; I have never felt this easy with anyone before, black or white. I want to believe it can last. We find a bench and sit down.

His phone pings, again and again. 'Better switch that off,' he says, sitting down on the bench. 'Ten likes, five shares and . . .' He scrolls down. 'Eight comments. Who'd have thought so many people were still up?'

'Let me see.'

Alex Harvey Look at my man! Picked himself up a honey.
Sue Edwards Gorgeous. Happy for you.
Robert Smith Wow. Exotic babe.
Andrew Stanton Lovely. Good luck to you.
Sandra Smith Didn't know you were into ethnics.
Paul Earley You like it hot, hot, hot

Lisa Lusk: Wow. Didn't expect that. Good Luck.
Tony Edwards A dusky beauty indeed. How lucky are you?

I give it back to him, 'Unfriend, keep, unfriend, keep, unfriend, unfriend, unfriend, unfriend.' He views the comments, clicking on each one. 'Yep, yep, yep, yep, yep, yep.' And pauses. 'You want me to unfriend Lisa?'

'You said she was in the past.'

'She is, honestly, we haven't spoken on Facebook in months. But this is nice, don't you think?' I'm not so sure. I saw how distracted Lisa's text made him earlier. I want him to focus on me alone tonight. He frowns as he looks at the last name. 'I can't unfriend Tony.'

'You said . . .' First his ex, now this; suddenly I am furious with him. 'You're just like all the rest.'

'Hold on a minute,' he protests, 'I meant I'd unfriend Facebook friends – I can't unfriend Tony. We've been mates for years. We used to house-share at Uni. I'm not unfriending him on the last night of my life.'

'That's even worse. Tolerating the racists in your actual real life.'

'I'm not! I'm just saying I can't unfriend him just like that.'

'Fuck you.' I push him away, and march off shaking with rage, disappointment, heartache.

'Nikki!' He starts to follow me.

'Leave me alone, I mean it,' I am shouting now, 'Leave

me alone.' He takes me at my word, sits back down on the bench allowing me to walk along the cliff till I reach a path down to a little cove. All that hope I had wrapped up in him, all a delusion, a fake happy ending. I will die tomorrow, alone as I have always been. The shingly path descends steeply. My pastor has always said that life is full of ups and downs, stiff climbs, painful descents into the abyss, but that God is always with us. I've believed him up till now but standing here alone on this rocky seashore I'm filled with fury. *Fuck you, God, fuck you! You take away my life before I've even begun to live it. You give me false hope in the form of a man who is just like the rest. You abandon me to my fate. Call yourself a loving God? Why the fuck have I wasted my life following you?* I scream at the sky until my throat is sore and my anger is spent. I find a damp rock, shivering as the water moves backwards and forwards up the beach, coming closer with each wave. *What's the point of staying alive now? For a few hours more? I might as well just enter the sea now. Lose myself beneath the waves. Let myself go. It's going to happen anyway. Why wait any longer?* Without stopping to think, I stand up and move along the beach, placing pebbles in my pocket. I reach the water's edge. I am about to step into the sea when I think of my parents. How will they feel in the morning if I don't ring them? How will Ginika and Ifechi feel? It's bad enough me dying, but leaving them without a word. That's too cruel of me. And then James's face comes to me. Not just now when he disappointed me, but yesterday when we met, and earlier this evening when he was playing to me, and in the cave when we kissed. It occurs to me that I'm expecting a lot from him. And, of course I should, but I ought to give him another chance. I am emptying my pockets of the stones when I hear him on the cliff path.

'What the fuck?'

'I was going to walk in the sea.'

'Why?'

'Because I was upset, because I didn't see the point . . .'

'I'm sorry, I messed it up, but I couldn't bear it if you did that.'

'You're part of the reason I didn't. You and my family. It would have been too cruel.'

''Thank God. Listen, about Tony. You're right. What he said was racist, and I won't defend it. But before ending a decade long friendship, I've got to give him the chance to put it right. He shows me his phone. He has sent Tony a message:

Dear Tony, thanks for your congratulations, but what you said was racist and upsetting to me and to Nikki. Please delete the comment and think before you write next time. James.

Tony has replied. *Dear James, God. I'm sorry. I didn't even think how that would come across. I feel so mortified. She's gorgeous and I'm very happy for you. I've taken it down, please apologise to her for me. Tony..'*

Tony has taken the comment down, and he has been forced to think. That might be enough for now. I lean up and kiss him.

257

'Am I forgiven?'

'You are. Come on. Time for bed.' I collect my head scarf and oils from Poppy's tent, quietly so as not to disturb her. Though she is fast asleep, she is still holding onto her phone. I follow James to a corner of the cliff, where the rocks have formed an almost complete circle, providing a private space just for us. I massage my hair with oil as he sorts out the sleeping bags.

'Seems like an effort.'

'With this salt air, sleeping on sand? It'll be so dry in the morning.' I don't add that the ritual itself is comforting. A pretence at normality to end the day. I wrap the scarf round my head and lie down beside him. It is when he kisses me good night, I realize something has changed. I have never shared my hair routine with anyone.

'I love you,' I say. And I mean it.

'I love you too.' He gives me a final kiss.

This is what commitment feels like. Drifting off to sleep, safe, warm, ready to face tomorrow, no matter what it brings. Thinking, maybe, God has been gracious after all.

Harry

On the bad nights, Val was always responsible for us little ones. The minute things kicked off downstairs, she would gather us up to the girls' bedroom, pile furniture in front of the door to keep Dad out, and sit us on the lower bunk. While the storm raged beneath us, we would cuddle under a duvet as she told fairy tales to distract us. To keep our interest she'd do different voices and inject humour into the darkest of stories. Hansel and Gretel was my favourite, perhaps because the children were so resilient in the face of their parents' abandonment of them. I loved Hansel's cleverness with the pebbles, how Gretel was able to trick the witch into the oven, and how they made it home to find the wicked stepmother dead. And Val was so strong on those evenings. No matter how much shouting went on, she'd keep reading, distracting us from our parents' rage, and if Dad came upstairs looking for a fight, she'd keep us quiet until he gave up trying the door and went downstairs. Val was my hero, she gave me the courage to survive. I wish she was with me tonight. I need her comforting voice to keep me going, particularly since I've lost my way and haven't got a trail of stones to guide me back.

I'm kicking myself for not paying proper attention earlier. I was so focussed on getting to the garage that I didn't memorize the route. I took the right fork instead of the left. The woods looked familiar, so I didn't realize my mistake till now when, faced with a large field of cows to my right, I have had to admit I didn't pass this way before. Fuck. It will take me twenty minutes to walk back to the junction and it's another twenty from there. It's another delay I could do without.

The cows are still awake, huddled bodies in the field, lowing mournfully. Even though there's a fence between us they make me nervous. Ever since Shelley and I got stuck in a field with some heifers on a rare country walk I've always given cattle a wide berth. I suppose it was quite funny in retrospect, the way we had to cling to the fence because we were intimidated by their rolling eyes and stomping feet. Shelley was actually a lot braver than me on that occasion, but then, growing up walking on the Yorkshire moors, she had more experience than me. It's strange that Shelley is so much on my mind tonight, I don't usually think of her this often when we're apart. But since she decided to stay behind, she's been constantly in my thoughts. If she were here, she'd probably be giving me a hard time about our predicament, but even so I wish she was with me now. I'd rather be walking with her by my side, prattling on about the Kardashians, than this lonely journey in the darkness, spooked by every sinister rustle. I need her with me to tell me it's ridiculous to be afraid of walking at night. That I shouldn't let the stories Evan told me when I was eight still fill me with dread. But she is not here, so all I can do is tell myself to toughen up and keep moving, it's not far. There's nothing to worry about, nothing to worry about at all.

I am halfway back to the crossroads when a buzz from my phone tells me my signal has returned. I stop to check and see if it is Shelley but it is just an automated message from a supplier. I have a quick look at social media to see if she has posted anything but her twitter feed hasn't been updated since midnight. For some weird reason she shared a picture of a sandcastle she'd made. She's grinning wildly as if she hasn't a care in the world. What the fuck has got into her?

Shelley might not have posted, but the rest of the world has; my timeline is full of videos of the eruption of the volcano followed by it crumbling into the sea. Someone must have got a drone up there, because the footage captures the exact moment it begins to break apart. A path of red lava is flowing from the summit, illuminating the cliff face allowing us to see the first small rocks chip off, followed by large chunks falling into the sea, exploding in a cloud of grey and white dust. More and more pieces break away until, eventually, the mountain itself splits in two, boulders and stones tumbling in the water, leaving a huge trail of smoke and generating the start of the wave that is coming for us. If that's not an incentive to keep going, I don't know what is. I put the phone away and march forward with more purpose. I've got to get back to the Maserati, get the boat to a harbour and get moving as soon as I can.

Thank fuck, there's the turning. My mood improves. At least I'm in the right place now. Spurred on by images of the turbulent sea, I up the pace, eager to get back to the car as soon as I can. But I'm not as fit as I'd like to be, so I am out of breath quickly and I keep stumbling. Everything aches and I have to put the can down every few minutes. And still the rustling trees, movement of wildlife, hooting of owls fills me with a fear I cannot shake off. I am so tired of this walk; why is it taking me so long to get back? I have almost given up hope of ever arriving when I finally see the outline of buildings, the shape of the Maserati on the road. I am almost sobbing in relief as I run up to it, opening the hub cap to pour the petrol in. The liquid rushes through the pipe like rain after a very dry season — the sound of my salvation. I climb back into the driver's seat. Now I am back in the Maserati I feel safer, but I will have to decide soon which road to take. Do I go right and collect Shelley, risking not getting far enough around the coast, or left to St Ives and the certainty of reaching safety? I can't work out what to do. Despite my uncertainty and the fact I have to drive more slowly with the trailer attached, my earlier confidence returns. My eyes feel heavy but, I almost feel happy and I am no longer panicking. Even with the boat bouncing behind me, I love driving this car. I remember the first time we took it out for a spin. We pulled the top down and shot down the A23. The sun shone all the way and we picnicked on the beach on French bread, cheese, tomatoes, washed down with champagne. Shelley isn't much of a swimmer, so she spent the afternoon sunbathing, but I've always loved the water and was in and out constantly, making her laugh with my Craig Daniel impressions. And then, later, we booked into a hotel where we had steak and chips and sat out on the beach watching the moon rise and send a silver path across the sea, just as it has tonight, before returning to our room where we had the best sex we ever had. That was a day that was; we were so close, then. What happened to us?

Oh Shells, I think, failing to suppress a yawn, why did you have to stay behind? Why did you choose to leave me for a bunch of strangers to make sandcastles at midnight? Why didn't you trust me to get us both out of this alive? You should be with me now, joining me in my triumphant escape instead of waiting for death in the darkness. I wish you'd come with me, I really do.

God, I'm knackered; my eyes are struggling to focus on the road ahead. I glance down at the clock, the blurry numbers say half past three. I am not far from the turn when I make my decision. I'm going back for her. We can drive up to St Michael's Mount and go from there. We probably have room for one more too. I think it has to be Poppy. Behind that jolly bossiness and organisational skills,

I detect a ruthlessness that I admire, a kindred spirit, a fellow survivor, who, in other circumstances might have been a friend. Yeah, Poppy can come if she wants, though Shelley is all I care about. It's taken tonight and this absence to make me understand that. She maybe a bit dippy at times, but she's kind and caring and I'm too old to be on my own. Fuck it. Maybe I should be thinking of settling down, giving her kids. All these years I've avoided the family life – at first, because my own was so crap. Later, because watching my sisters settle for a life of nappies and demanding children, my brothers and mates restricted by domestic duties, I was sure it wasn't for me. But tonight it occurs to me that maybe it's time. Living through this has shown me I don't have long left on this planet and I have to leave more of me behind then a string of hotels and big fat bank balance, don't I? Yeah. I'm definitely going back for Shelley.

The road bends sharply to the left and I think I've slowed down in time, but I've misjudged the distance, and I have to pull hard to get round the corner. Something jumps out in front of me. Jeez, where did that come from? I slam on the brakes to see a deer running off into the night. I should get going again, but now I've stopped, I can barely focus. I just have to lay my head on the wheel for a minute. There'll be no harm in that; I'll just close my eyes for a bit . I am so tired . . . I won't be a minute. I just need to rest my head. I lean forward, clasp the wheel with both hands, my head resting on top. Just for a minute, just for a minute, and then I'll be on my way.

Shelley

I have slept in fits and starts all night, drifting in and out of consciousness as the minutes pass. At some point I wake to discover Margaret has gone and I turn over and doze off again, coming to at the sound of voices approaching. I hear Margaret whispering 'good night' to someone, Poppy I think, before entering the tent. I don't say anything; I'm talked out and I suspect so is she. I close my eyes and force myself asleep. Sometime later I can hear voices murmuring by the cliff, it sounds like Nikki and James. I sleep, I wake, I sleep, I wake, I sleep awake . . . Normally, I would feel frustrated by now, but every time I look at my phone I am aware I am still here, I am still alive. I am so grateful to be still alive. Let the night last fore ever. Let me stay alive – please God, if you exist, if you have any thought for me, please let me live.

Eventually I reach a point where no matter how much I close my eyes and breathe deeply, I cannot sleep. It is dark, but I sense morning is not far away. I check my phone; five fifteen. Margaret is snoring beside me. I had hoped that perhaps Harry might be back for me by now, but looking at his texts again I don't think they're very encouraging. Though he's on his way, he doesn't seem eager to come and get me; maybe it's not even possible. He might be much further up the coast, not able to make it back round to Dowetha. Besides, I'm not even sure he knows how to steer. Even if he did want to get back to me, he might not be capable of managing the journey.

Shit. Alison was right. I should have gone with him. After all this time with Harry, why did I choose tonight of all nights to leave him? I should have stuck it out, trusted he wouldn't let me down, seized my only opportunity for escape. I shouldn't have let my frustration and tiredness and the lure of good company keep me here. I know I was right to leave him, but why didn't I wait till we'd reached safety? I should have known that he would find a way to get out. Now I am left with the grim reality that, in a few hours, my life will be over, because I lost faith in him at the crucial moment. But haven't I always got it wrong at every turn? I've been a constant disappointment to Dad ever since we came down south. Unlike Alison the Perfect, who has never made a misstep ever. Alison, with her endlessly good grades, her university degree and promising career in marketing. Her words from last night ring in my ears, *Why didn't you wait till you were safe before you left him?* Only this time, she's not exasperated, she's sneering; my older sister, superior as ever, shaking her head at my foolishness.

The Wave

Suddenly, I am filled with anger. At Alison. At Harry. At my own stupidity. I want to scream at the top of my voice, but I can't do that. Nor can I go back to sleep. I think of waking Margaret, but she is sleeping so peacefully it doesn't seem fair. Instead, I unzip my sleeping bag, quietly slip out of the tent and make my way down to the sea. The waves rise, fall, crash on the shoreline with a soothing rhythm *rise, fall, crash, rise, fall, crash*. The sky ahead is still a deep dark blue but, behind me, the clifftops glow with a golden light, sunrise is coming. The air is cool, but not unpleasant, the wind has died down, the waves lap at the shore gently. The sound is soothing, and as I let the noise wash over me I can feel my anger evaporate. I rarely think of Mum but all of a sudden her voice comes back to me loud and clear, don't be too hard on your sister, she loves you very much. When I think about it, I was a gobby little sister at times. That must have been so annoying. If I'm honest with myself, I often got away with murder, playing on being the youngest, pretending to be more innocent than I was. It wasn't her fault she's cleverer than me, or mine that I struggled to study. It's just how it was. And I know she doesn't mean to criticize me really; it's just a force of habit. I check my phone, five thirty. Harry hasn't sent me any more messages, so it doesn't look like he's coming back for me. Bastard. He really is a bastard.

'Morning.' I jump. I hadn't heard Yan approaching. All of a sudden the sick feeling in my stomach returns. 'Can't sleep?' he asks.

'No.'

'Me neither. I've been stargazing.'

Now he is here, I cannot avoid the truth. I can hardly look at him because he is living confirmation there has been no mistake. We have less than three hours left. I don't think I can bear it.

'Have you looked at the Facebook page?' he says, hesitantly.

'No.'

'It's just that someone has told a website about Margaret and there are loads of nasty comments.'

Someone . . . 'Harry.'

'We thought so.'

'It's just like him. I could bloody kill him. First he gets everyone angry with her, and then he does this.' I pick up my phone and without stopping to edit, I send a message *How dare you tell people about Margaret? What a foul thing to do. Unforgivable. Fuck you.* That feels better. Though he'll definitely not for me now.

'That's probably another stupid decision I've made,' I say, 'to add to being with him in the first place and not leaving when I had the chance.'

'Seems to me like you've made the right ones,' says Yan. 'Besides, if he's not on the water by now, I can't see how he can get out of the danger zone at all.'

I shiver. The danger zone. That's where we are right now, and unless Harry gets a move on, that's where we're going to stay.

'It'll be here soon,' says Yan. I nod miserably
'I can't believe it's happening.'

He reaches over to me and we hug in silence, tears falling. We have so little time left. And there is absolutely nothing we can do about it. At last we break away. I stare up at the cliffs. A red-gold light is shining just above the horizon, the night is nearly gone.

'It is so beautiful here,' I say, looking back at the sea, which glows orange and red in the reflected light.

'Yes.'

'This won't look beautiful though . . . afterwards. The beach, the land. I've seen pictures after tsunamis. It will be a hell of an operation to clear up . . .' And then the idea comes to me. 'We could do something, we could help. *I* could help.'

'How?'

'I could sing. You could video it, and we could ask my dad and sister to use it for fundraising.'

'That's a brilliant idea.' He isn't laughing at me. He genuinely thinks this is worth doing. 'Come on.'

We run back to the campsite. I, for one, am pleased to have something to focus on, to have the energy to do something, no matter how small. We grab Yan's iPad and James's guitar and then I go and spruce myself up in the bathroom. I don't have any make-up – I left that in the cases – so I wash my face and sweep my hair to one side. I'll look a bit pale on the video but it will have to do. When I emerge, the sky ahead takes my breath away – red, gold, orange, blue, over the vivid green fields. It doesn't seem possible this will all be gone soon, taking me and everyone on the beach with it. I push that thought out of my mind and walk with Yan to the clifftop.

I strum the guitar as Yan sets up. It takes a while to get started. At first I cannot get through 'The Water is Wide' without crying, and then, at the fourth attempt, I have an inexplicable giggling fit. We get it right for the seventh version when my singing and playing are in perfect harmony and I hit the right emotional beats. Better still, Yan captures the moment that the sun rises, a fiery red ball, lighting up the sky behind me. I'm stunned at how good it is, that we have done this together. I have never done anything like this in my life. Yan gives me the iPad so I can send the video and heads back to the beach to start on breakfast.

As I email Dad, I check the time: six thirty. The sun is warming me already. Below me the sea sparkles invitingly. It is going to be a gorgeous day. Despite my lack of sleep I feel alive, and though it seems strange to say it, in this moment, I feel happy. I will follow Yan in a minute, but right now I want to appreciate this feeling of the peace while it lasts. I am still sitting there, enjoying the sound of birdsong, the splash of the waves, the slight breeze on my face, when Dad rings.

"What are you doing up this early?' I ask.

'Couldn't sleep.'

'Me neither.'

'We can see. Shelley, love, that's such a beautiful video, such a beautiful thought.'

'We're proud of you,' Alison chips in on the speaker-phone.

'Really?'

'Honestly, it's a wonderful thing to do.' It's been such a long time since Alison has been this nice to me, I don't know what to say. 'And . . . sorry about last night. I was a bit of a cow. I've just never liked Harry and couldn't believe your bad luck.'

'I've not been much better. Fancy that, eh? Takes the end of the world for me to see what an idiot I've been.'

'You're not an idiot,' says Dad. 'You're my girl and I'm so proud. We'll make this video go viral, you'll see.'

I don't quite have the heart to say I won't see, but when they hang up, after I promise to call later, I am almost skipping back down the path.

I stand on the slipway looking down at the campsite below. Only yesterday morning I had no idea who these people were, but if it wasn't for them I wouldn't have thought of singing, wouldn't have made that video. I may have made the wrong choice staying here, but at least something good has come from that choice. At least I can say my life hasn't been totally wasted. Though I am terrified, I know I am with friends, people who care about me, who appreciate me. It shouldn't make that much of a difference, but as I walk down to breakfast, I know that it does.

Instagram

LisaLuskOfficial *I'm heartbroken. He's on that beach, and there's nothing I can do. Thanks for being with me on the longest night of my life. Can't bear to wait for the next part. Going to bed.*

Image of couple by rocks.

StevenSmith5 *Found this on Facebook. That's him, isn't it?*

AllieSimpson4 *OMG he's been cheating on you tonight?*

StevenSmith5 *It's not right.*

Jenny5001 *Let him know what you think folks. He can't treat Lisa like this.*

5.45 a.m.

News 'n Truth
The website that never lies

Image: Couple cuddling on a beach.

Seems like Margaret Anderson is not the only one at Dowetha Beach who's got some explaining to do. As pop star Lisa Lusk has kept an Instagram vigil for her boyfriend James, he has been consoling himself with a new friend. We'll say this for you James, you've certainly got a way with women....

Facebook Messenger
Seren Lovelace to Andy Jones

5.45 a.m.

Thanks for the chat last night. I did what you said and wrote it all down. I thought about making it public, letting the world know who she is, what she did. But then I saw footage of the volcano and thought . . . Poor Penny. Whatever she's done, she doesn't deserve this.

Andy Jones to Seren Lovelace

5.51 a.m.

You're a better person than I am! Still, I know what you mean. Those poor people. So many of them still stuck on the roads. How awful for them. And their families.

Facebook
Dowetha Live

30 August 6.00 a.m.

Due to unpleasant comments about two members of our group, we have disabled comments on this page.

The Wave

Facebook
Poppy Armstrong

30 August 6.05 a.m.

After my last post I did manage to grab some sleep. I didn't think I would, and my dreams were troubled, but at least I'm a bit more rested. Hangover, sort of, rested but better than a few hours ago. I'm studiously avoiding pictures of the eruption and collapsing volcano, but I can't miss the news which is as bad as I feared it would be. The earliest escapees are reaching safety, giving breathless interviews about the panic and chaos they have left behind. In their wake they have left gridlock. Many have abandoned their cars, in the vain hope that their feet can transport them where their vehicles could not. Those at the head of the traffic, who are within a few miles probably have a chance, but the majority are too far away. And yet they are marching like so many tiny ants, their eyes fixed on their destination, still hoping to outrun their fate. My friends are not with them. Alice texted half an hour ago, to say they have left the road and found a pretty spot where they will sit it out like we are doing. I was doubting a few hours ago whether I had made the right choice, but it seems as if I have. Or at least, made the best out of bad choices.

And, I have had a response from my ex. She's asked me lots of questions, and I am going to attempt

275

to answer them. I'll send and then wait, hoping she
will get back in touch soon.

In two hours, there will be no waiting ever again.

Like Share Comment

PRIME

Poppy

I wake sometime before six. I still feel tired, but sleep is impossible. I emerge from the tent to see Yan walking down the beach to Shelley who is sitting by the water's edge. Above me the sky is getting lighter, the air is warm, and the wind has died down. It is going to be a glorious day. I walk up to the car and check the news websites. I avoid looking at pictures of the volcano, but the pictures of the evacuation are everywhere. Thousands of cars are fleeing coastlines from Morocco to the Congo Republic, Mexico to Brazil, the Eastern Seaboard in the US, and in the UK all the way from here to the top of Kent and Wales. There are stories of problems of evacuating vulnerable people everywhere, but the worst traffic is in Cornwall. Cars are still crammed on the roads from Exeter down to Truro. No one south of Dartmoor has a chance, and even those who reach the moors will be at risk of flash floods from over-full rivers. All night I have been questioning whether I did the right thing coming here, but seeing these pictures, I'm thankful we stayed. There's no way we could have escaped, and at least the last few hours have meant something, as I hoped they would.

I open Facebook to see I have a message from Seren; I can't quite face reading it yet. Instead, I check the Dowetha page. More vile people. What is wrong with them? Now they are after James and Nikki too; the racism and misogyny is depressing. I suspend comments, delete the worst remarks and steel myself to read Seren's letter.

Dear Penny,

It is odd to be called Penny again. After so many years being Poppy, I'd almost convinced myself Penny no longer existed.

Thank you for your message. I was not sure last night when I received it, whether I should reply. For so many years, I have wondered what I would say to you if you ever got in touch. I have thought often about writing to ask for an explanation of why you did what you did. Several times I started a letter, or an email, but I never finished it. Because, in the end, what was the point? What could you say that could make it possible for me to understand? Possible for me to forgive? You abused my trust, and that of all our friends. The fact that you never reported on me was beside the point. All those times people came to the house, all the times we were at parties, the pub, or just hanging out, you were watching, listening, and noting any tiny thing that could be of use against us. All the while saying you loved me and wanted to build a future with me. How could any of that possibly be true?

I put the phone down, blasted by her fury. I can't disagree with this, yet I want to make excuses. I had good reason, I didn't mean it, I wish I could have done it differently . . . But I didn't, which means I have to face this now.

And now, you are about to die. Suddenly the conscience that has lain dormant all these years has been stirred. When you wrote to me last night, my first instinct was bully for you. Too little, and way too late. You are in a shitty situation and I'm very sorry about that, but you can't possibly expect my sympathy now.

My eyes prick with tears, but seriously what did I expect?

Last night, I was so angry I had no intention of giving you the satisfaction of a peaceful death. To get in touch after all that time and lay that guilt on me? Made me think you're still the same selfish cow who betrayed me. However, this morning I changed my mind. I slept badly. I don't suppose you got much sleep either. I kept checking my phone and seeing pictures of people fleeing the disaster zones, the images of the volcano falling and the wave that is coming for you. Yesterday, like everyone else, I watched the panic, the fear, feeling that detached horror you get from seeing disasters you can do nothing about. I cared, of course I did. But to be honest, I was relieved I wasn't anywhere near. Realising you were there changed all that. And your message connects me, even if I don't want it to. I cannot ignore that.

So I went to your Facebook page. I have to admit, it's a good thing you are doing. I admire your courage in the face of what is coming. I admire the fact you have brought people together. From your posts, it seems you are worrying about what you did. Maybe it's for effect, to make us sympathize – you of all people know how to lie more than most – but maybe, just maybe it's genuine. It occurred to me I have the power to refuse to respond to you, or to communicate. I could have chosen cruelty. I could have left you lingering in your last hours, but I have opted not to. I just have one question left, really: Why did you do it Penny? What was in it for you? Tell me that and we're done. Seren.

Seren is more generous than I deserve, but then she always was. That was part of the attraction. Part of what I miss about her. I owe her the truth before it is too late. I begin with the devastation of my parents' death, how my money troubles led me to work for Alisdair. When I moved to London, I thought that was behind me, particularly when I met Seren. It was when I started a Masters in

Economics at King's that he found me again. He offered me the same deal as before – keep an eye on that student, report what that lecturer said. I knew Seren wouldn't approve, but I didn't have her income, and London was expensive. It was easy money, and it was just work. Besides, unlike Seren, I thought the war on terror was a good thing, and wasn't doing this helping keep us all safe?

I pause, gazing across sea. There is a blush of pink on the water, reflected from the sky above me. It is quite beautiful. I wish . . . I wish . . . I wish . . .

I wish that what happened next never happened and that when it did, I had said no. But when Alisdair wanted information on Seren's friends, Amy and Jake, I was tempted. It wasn't only that rent and tuition fees were due and he promised he'd pay double. It was also the fact I always felt they looked down on me, thinking I wasn't good enough for Seren. I'm not proud of the fact that part of the reason I accepted was because I wanted to pay them back for sneering at me. And so, when Alisdair said they were violent animal rights activists, I was happy to believe that was true, justifying my behaviour because I never reported on Seren, and because I'd stop people being hurt. Justifications which fell apart the day she found out.

I end by saying I don't expect her to understand, but I want her to know I'm sorry. I think of leaving a kiss but I know it's too much. I send it before I can admit the worst thing. The thing I don't ever want her to know. The thing I can barely admit to myself. I don't want to even think about that now. I put my phone away to see Shelley disappearing into the clubhouse, as Yan walks towards the cliff path; he is on the phone so I don't disturb him. Now I've heard from Seren, I have nothing left to worry about. The sky is burning red and gold, anticipating the sun that cannot be far away, and I realise if I hurry I can squeeze in one more swim. I run back to my tent. To my delight, when I emerge I find Margaret has the same idea. We rush down to the water together and dive between the waves. The sea is bracingly cold, but once I get used to it, refreshing. We swim up and down, splashing each other as the sun rises above the cliffs, until the cold drives us back to the tents to change. Yan is cooking breakfast. Just like yesterday he is very good at taking care of us. I smile at him before going to find a quiet spot to see if Seren has replied. She has, though as I read, I wish she hadn't.

Dear Penny,

I refuse to call you by any other name. Thank you for your message. Congratulations on your shiny new life. Glad to hear you have made peace with your past. Bully for you. You may have moved on from this, but I haven't. You lied to me, you spied on my friends, and then walked away from the wreckage. And now you come with this pathetic bullshit. Poor little Penny, the orphan with no money whose rich girlfriend's friends were mean to her. Loads of people get into debt at uni, loads of people struggle with the rent, loads of people hate their lover's friends. They don't fucking spy on them.

You say you are sorry, but this is the sinner repenting on their death bed. What is such repentance worth?

I pause, tears streaming down my cheeks. What else could I have expected? What else did I deserve? A gull swoops over my head, diving down towards the sea. The sun is high in the sky now, a reminder of how quickly time is passing. I force myself to continue reading.

What is that repentance worth? A couple of years ago, I would have said nothing. But, today, I find myself unable to be quite so harsh. Today, I find that despite the fury and bitterness I still feel towards you, there are some remnants of affection left. Not enough for mercy, not yet anyway, but enough to say this.

Penny. You still don't seem to understand the harm you did. Your betrayal will haunt me for the rest of my life, making it hard for me to trust people, particularly lovers. When you left, I lost friends who couldn't believe I wasn't helping you. I lost the flat because I couldn't afford the rent alone. I became depressed and took months to recover. You have no right to my forgiveness, or even to ask for it. I am not done with being angry with you, even if my anger looks like it will be reserved for a ghost.

Even though I can't forgive you, I can at least wish

your last few hours are peaceful. I find myself thinking it is unbearable that you are going to die like this, and no matter how angry I have been, no matter how angry I still am, I wouldn't wish this on you, none of it.

No mercy, then. But, from the bottom of my heart, I am sorry for what you are going through. I salute your courage, and I am glad you have people with you to comfort you. Maybe one day forgiveness might be possible, but in the meantime, I will be thinking of you. I hope the end comes quick and that you feel loved, not by me, but by others. I want you to know that the love we once had was a splendid thing. One day, I hope, that is what I will remember when I think of you, Seren

Another seagull sweeps overhead, or perhaps it is the same one returning from the beach. It was clearly too much to ask her for forgiveness, and most of me can't blame her. I just wish it didn't leave me feeling this desolate. I reply that I am sorry, because I truly am and then I have to acknowledge that that's it, there is nothing more we can say to each other. Time for me to move on.

An inviting smell of bacon welcomes me back to the campfire. I take some food, and my place at the fireside, joining in the conversation. I have experienced so much loss in my life, some of it self induced, but here, at the end, as I look around my new friends, I can see that in the last twenty-four hours, I have gained something too. It's a small comfort, but right now I'm glad to cling to it.

Yan

I fully intended to go back to bed, but once I lay looking at the stars I was too entranced to move. I stared for hours at the little beams of light travelling across the galaxy from tiny suns that died centuries ago. Which, when I think about it, put my situation into perspective. My lifespan is miniscule compared to the length of time the light of a star lasts. What does it matter if I die today or in forty years?

It is only as the sky is beginning to lighten, and the stars to fade, that I sit up. I am stiff and cold; it is time to go back to the beach. The march back warms me up and when I reach the beach, despite my lack of sleep, I am filled with energy. I walk down to the shore where I find Shelley at the water's edge. She, too, has been struggling to sleep, wrestling with her decisions, wondering if she should have gone with Harry. Although I don't tell her that I think he's an arsehole, I do let her know that he's exposed Margaret, and am secretly pleased by her reaction. The Shelley of last night has completely disappeared. I much prefer this newer version. And then I am overwhelmed by the realisation that this could have been a brilliant friendship, but it is over before we start. We hug, and weep until, at last, she breaks away.

The sun will soon be here; the cliffs are glowing gold and red in anticipation. It is so beautiful here, though as Shelley says, it won't be later. It is typical of the new, improved Shelley, that she comes up with the idea of recording a song to help fund the clean-up efforts. I don't need persuading to help her. She grabs James's guitar from the tent, and I take my iPad as we make our way up to the cliffs. It is nearly six. Mum will be up by now. I can't put off this call any longer, so while Shelley is getting herself spruced up, I ring her.

'Yan,' she says. 'What are you doing up so early? When are you coming to see me?'

'Mum . . . have you heard the news?'

'The news is I'm old, and my son never comes to visit.'

'About the volcano.'

'Volcano? Why are you talking about a volcano?'

'It erupted Mum and now it has collapsed in the sea, and . . .' I take a deep breath, 'It's created a wave that is coming towards Cornwall.'

'So what?'

'The thing is . . . I can't get away.'

'Father Piotr is coming to see me later. For coffee.'

'Mum, did you understand what I said?'

'He is having such trouble with his housekeeper. I said to him, "Father Piotr, loyalty is important, of course it is.

We all know the Lord rewards good, loyal servants. But when you cannot get a decent meal cooked on time, and your toilet is not clean, the Lord will forgive you taking the necessary action." '

'Mum.' This is no good, she has always had this tendency to run on and on with her latest obsession and not listen to a word I say.

'Poor man. He isn't getting any younger, and every night his supper is cold and he sits in his study coughing the dust. It isn't right.' She could go on like his for ever. Shelley has come out of the clubhouse and is waiting for me to finish. I lose the thread of Mum's words, a tsunami of ill will and harsh judgement. I was wrong to call her; she will never change, not even when I am dying. Above me the sky is lighter now and a sliver of red is apparent above the horizon.

Mum is still talking, 'No wonder her daughter left her!' She takes a breath and I seize the opportunity. 'Did you hear what I said about the volcano?'

'So what? Rocks fall into the sea all the time.'

'It's the wave, Mum, I can't get away from the wave. I'm going to die.'

This time, I get through to her. 'Have you said your prayers?' Her voice is shaking.

'I don't pray any more, Mum, you know that.'

'I will say them for you.' She seems to gain some strength from this thought. 'I will go to church now. Father Piotr and I will light candles. I will pray for you.'

There is clearly nothing else to be said. 'Goodbye, Mum.'
'I will pray for you.'

I hang up as Shelley arrives. She smiles at me. And we begin to film. It takes a few attempts, but the final version is just brilliant, particularly as it captures the rising sun in the background. It is quite a sight. A slender red arc, that becomes a semi-circle, and finally a whole fiery globe. I'm glad I caught it on film, that Shelley's voice will be a legacy of our time here. I hand her the iPad so she can send it to her family and return to the camp to make breakfast.

Soon the bacon is sizzling on the pan. I turn it slowly. If I close my eyes it as if the last few hours have not happened, it is the beginning of yesterday evening and we are about to have a barbecue. Why can't I fix time, so we return to that moment again and again like Bill Murray in *Groundhog Day*? Me enjoying the cooking, with the possibility of something happening with Poppy stuck in a constant time loop so the wave never comes for us at all? I open my eyes again, staring at the blue sea ahead. Poppy and Margaret are in the sea, their heads bobbing in the water. I had thought of joining them but I couldn't quite summon up the energy. Now the moment has passed. And I am left with the thought that the cruellest thing is I am about to be killed by the thing I love the most. And then, even that thought fades, leaving me by a campfire, cooking for my companions, breathing in the fresh sea air, feeling the warmth of the sun on my back. . . .

The Wave

My life is receding before me, Karo, Mum, seem as far away as the swimmers in the sea. The politics I argued so passionately about last night are remote and unimportant. Even the film I just made for Shelley feels a long time ago. The bacon spits fat, the smell wafting up my nostrils taking me to a happier place – the campsite in Devon overlooking the sea, Dad cooking, Mum reading in the deckchair, whilst Karo and I run around the tent laughing.

The sound of Margaret and Poppy giggling brings me back to the present as they run up the beach and dive into their tents. Nikki and James have emerged from their hideaway and Shelley has returned from the clifftop. It is time to eat.

'Mmm, bacon,' says Shelley, as she grabs a plate. 'Thanks.'

'Sent your video?'

'Yup.' She is beaming. 'Dad said he was proud of me.'

'So he should be.'

Poppy and Margaret both reappear, with damp hair and glowing faces. Poppy disappears up the cliff for one last call, but Margaret takes her breakfast and sits down by the new fire. It is barely needed, the sun is warm and the food hot. Still there is always something encouraging in seeing orange flames flicker from last night's ash.

'Nice swim?' I ask.

'Wonderful,' says Margaret. 'You should have joined us.'

'Somebody had to do breakfast.'

'Happy to.'

Poppy returns, I give her breakfast and sit down with mine. I find myself telling them about previous camping trips in woods, on beaches, by the base of the mountains. Poppy describes a journey she once took through the Rockies, Margaret remembers a holiday in Portugal, Shelley recalls the misery of being under canvas in a gale. The fireside mood is good-humoured and I realize that, if it is possible to miss life when you're dead, I will miss this when I am gone. Mum would say that I am going to a better place, but I've never really believed that, and even it were true, in Mum's heaven there's no room for suicides. Why would I want to go anywhere that Karo isn't? If I'm going to choose one version of the afterlife, I prefer James's – my consciousness released on the universe, so I can rest here, in the warmth of the sun, feel the spray over and over again. That's certainly an eternity that appeals. No pain, no suffering, no . . .

'Trolling,' says Poppy. 'Margaret's had it, now Nikki and James. You'll probably get some too with your song, Shelley. It's bloody horrible. I know we don't have much time, but I think we should do something about it.'

'What do you suggest?' says James.

'A statement and a joke.'

'How about we do a video of "Shake it Off"?' says Nikki.

' "Shake it Off"?' Margaret asks.

'Taylor Swift,' says Shelley, showing Margaret on her phone.

'That's a great idea,' I say. Someone plays the music and we pass the iPad round, videoing each other in stupid poses as we scream 'Shake it Off' to the sound of Taylor's sick beat. Even Margaret joins in, gamely trying to model some of the more ridiculous moves. The song finishes and we all fall on the ground, laughing hysterically.

'That was so much fun,' says Shelley presently.

'It will give Hellie a laugh,' says Margaret.

There is a lull in the conversation. James and Nikki grin at each other and then they say, ' We've decided to get married.'

For a moment, no one says anything. It's seven o'clock – there is just over an hour to go. I bite back a comment that they're cutting it a bit fine, as the campfire erupts with question and congratulations.

'On the clifftop,' says Nikki in answer to a query. 'We'd like to film it to our parents. Can you do that, Poppy?'

'Of course,' says Poppy.

'We should find you some flowers,' says Margaret. 'There are some bushes by the car park.'

'I could do your hair,' says Shelley.

'We were wondering if you'd be our best man?' James says to me. *Only because I'm the only man left,* I think sourly, before remembering our night-time conversation, and that we do have this connection, no matter how fractious.

'Honoured,' I say.

'You need a ring,' says Margaret. 'Here, have mine.'

Nikki smiles as she takes it. 'You're all so wonderful. Thank you.'

'Sorry I don't have two.'

'It doesn't matter,' says Nikki as she hands the ring to me. 'Can you take care of this?' I nod and put it in my pocket. 'We need to get moving,' says Nikki, She grabs her bag from Poppy's tent and, gathering the women with her, says, 'I'm going to get ready. See you at the top at 7.20?' She kisses James and the women run laughing up the beach.

We sit in silence. I find myself playing with Margaret's ring. That was generous of her, to immediately give up the ring she'd carried for years, the mark of her love for her husband. James needs one too. I should offer Karo's ring, but I find myself strangely reluctant. It's my last link with my sister and I'm not sure I'm ready to let go.

'You know, I might have asked you even if these weren't the circumstances,' says James.

'Really?'

'Yeah. Like I said last night, you're beyond annoying sometimes Yan, but you're honest, you care – and I trust you. What more do you want from a best man?'

I don't know what to say. I look at the ring on my finger, think of the awful, awful day when I picked it up with the rest of Karo's stuff. Sometimes, you just have to let go of things. You just do. I take it off my finger and give it to him.

'Wow, thanks,' he says. 'Can you keep it with Nikki's?'

'Of course.' I check my phone. 'Come on, it's time we got ready.'

'Get me to the church on time,' James says and grins.

'It will be my pleasure.' I say, as we make our way up to the cliffs for the very last time.

Margaret

I wake for the second time to an empty tent. It is quarter to six. The sun is already strong and the tent warm. I could stay snuggled in my sleeping bag or get up to face the day. I cannot face the day. Facing the day means facing my death. I am not ready for that. I am just not ready. I dive down in my sleeping bag, like a child avoiding school. And then, just like a child avoiding school, I hear a voice in my head telling me it is time to get up. I try to ignore it, but it is loud and incessant. When I emerge from my sleeping bag I bang into my prayer book at the head of my Lilo. I pick it up. It is old and battered, my Father bought it for my Mother when they first got married. It seems a sign that I should pray, though I am far from in the mood. Out of force of habit, I open it up. This morning's prayer of thanksgiving sticks in my throat,

Let us give thanks to the beneficent and merciful God, the Father of our Lord, God and Saviour, Jesus Christ, for He has covered us, helped us, guarded

us, accepted us unto Him, spared us, supported us, and brought us to this hour. Let us also ask Him, the Lord our God, the Almighty, to guard us in all peace this holy day and all the days of our life.

Really God? You expect me to think that today? I plough on though, because even as I argue with the prayer, I find the practice of it soothes. Even as I pray for a good start to the day, and for the Lord to deliver us and know it is impossible, the familiar ritual is comforting. And though I've been saying to everyone all night, that prayer isn't a wish or magic, that it doesn't always provide what we want, it doesn't stop me praying for a miracle. I wish the Lord could deliver us with a boat, or a helicopter or something. Deep down I know that there'll be no such rescue, or deliverance, I know we are on our own but I can't stop praying for escape, even though Psalm 13 reminds me.

How long, O Lord? Will you forget me forever? How long will you hide your face from me?

Yes, God, have you forgotten me? Maybe I have made mistakes with Kath, but do I deserve this? Do any of us? The final prayer does for me:

As the daylight shines upon us, O Christ Our God, the true Light, let the luminous senses and the bright thoughts shine within us, and do not let the

darkness of passions hover over us, that mindfully we may praise You with David, saying, 'My eyes have awakened before the morning watch, that I might meditate on Your sayings.' Hear our voices according to your great mercy, and deliver us, O Lord our God, through Your compassion.

Sod you God. That doesn't help in the slightest. Despite the approaching dawn, I am deep in darkness, I have no confidence in your luminosity and no desire to praise you. I throw the prayer book across the tent in frustration and climb out of bed.

I consider ringing Hellie, but if she is up she will be attending Toby's needs; it is not worth calling her for another hour when he'll have had breakfast and be settled watching CBeebies. I need something else to get me out of this black mood and decide a swim will do it. I put on yesterday's shorts and T-shirt and grab a towel. As I unzip the tent, I meet Poppy who has the same idea.

'Great minds think alike,' I say. She laughs and we run down the beach. Though the tent was warm, there is still a chill in the air, and the water is so cold my skin tingles. The tide is coming in again and the strong undercurrent means every stroke is an effort, but I'm glad of it. It helps take my mind off what's about to happen, helps to focus on what I have right now, rather than what I am about to lose. I don't go out far. I swim a circuit in parallel to the beach, *stroke, breathe, push, stroke, breathe, push,* back and forth from one side of the cove to the other. The sun rises above the cliffs, lighting up the water. It helps soothe my restless mind. Stretching my limbs also relieves muscles aching after a night under canvas and helps me keep in the discipline of the here and now. I am so focussed on my path that I don't see Poppy until I'm nearly upon her. We collide and both go under, come to the surface spluttering, and laugh at our idiocy. For a while we splash about in the water, until cold and hunger drive us back to the campsite, where Yan is frying bacon.

I change quickly, folding damp clothes neatly through force of habit and emerge to be handed a plateful of food by Yan and a cup of tea by a smiling Shelley.

'You look pleased with yourself.'

'I recorded a video.'

'It's terrific.' Yan says. 'And a great idea. To fundraise for the clear-up operation.'

'The best thing is, Dad says he's proud.' Shelley is beaming. 'It doesn't change anything, but it sort of does . . .' I smile back. She is a different girl from the one who arrived yesterday, even from the one who made sandcastles in the middle of the night. My own mood lifts. The sun is shining, the food is good, this could be the start of a perfect day. Energized by the swim, I can even let myself think perhaps it won't be so bad. Maybe the waves won't be as high as they say. Even if they are, maybe it will be possible to survive the onslaught of water. Miracles happen sometimes.

But I know in my heart of hearts that this is a false hope and I let it die, trying to make enjoy the conversation swirling round me. I'm touched when Poppy brings up the horrible comments on social media. A few hours ago she was angry with me, and now she is angry at them, we all are. It's not just me, either, it's Nikki and James, which is worse because half of theirs are horribly racist. When Shelley suggests that we do a video to a pop song, it seems the perfect riposte. Though I have to be taught the dance, and I realize I probably look ridiculous, I enjoy joining in, screaming 'Shake it Off' at the top of my voice. Let the haters hate indeed.

'We've got an announcement,' Nikki's says after the dancing is finished. 'We're getting married.' And suddenly, there is no time to think of the future, we are all just excited and happy for them. Here's Nikki being mobbed by the women, here's James receiving a hug from Yan. And here's me, remembering my happy day with Richard, giving Nikki my ring. We leave the men behind so we can help the bride get ready in the clubhouse. We climb the slope giggling with excitement.

I break away from them at the top of the car park to check my phone. I watch as they run into the changing room. I have something I can wear in the car, but first, I must see if Kath has replied. Then I must talk to Hellie.

There is a message in my inbox:

Dear Margaret,

    Thanks for your message. I've lain awake all night thinking about it. And though it is too little and way too late, I do love Hellie and she is not part of our fight. And whatever has happened between us in the past, what is happening to you now is so unfair, so horrible. I am so sorry. I'm mad that we don't have time to sort out our differences but of course, you can send, me Hellie's details and I promise I will look out for her. It's what grandma would have wanted after all. Family always wins.

    As for us. You should have started this conversation a long time ago. Can't tell you how angry I am we can't finish it properly. Which I guess is my way of saying I love and miss you.

    All my love, Kath xxx

Thank God for that. I text back Hellie's address and phone number with a final message and then it is time to ring Hellie,

Miss you too.
Margaret.

'Morning, Mum.' Hellie is clearly making an effort to be bright, happy, hopeful.

'Morning. Did you sleep all right?'

'Surprisingly, yes, I was exhausted.' She pauses, 'And things do feel better today.'

'I told you they would.' I try to avoid too much emotion for the moment. Tears can wait till the last call. I tell her about Shelley's video, Nikki and James's wedding, Kath's offer. The last few hours have certainly been eventful. 'So you see, I'm going out on a high.'

'Oh, Mum.'

'And Hellie, whatever happens, I want you to know that I've had a good life, a lucky life. Your dad and I didn't have long together but we had the best time. I've had you and Toby – and I'm so proud of you both. I had an interesting career, good friends. If this is to my last day, I've spent it in good company. Life doesn't get much better than this. Sunshine, beauty, love. Never forget that . . .'

'I won't.' Hellie is working hard to keep her voice under control. 'I almost forgot – Toby started walking this morning.'

'That's marvellous!'

'He just climbed out of bed and walked into our bedroom. Now he's careering around the house like a demented puppy.'

'You'll have your work cut out from now on. Listen, love, I've got to go, but I'll call later.'

I hang up and join the others. The surf club is full of excited chatter as the young women help each other with hair and make-up. It feels a happy place, if happiness is possible, here, in this place, at this time. The words of the prayer I read earlier come back to me, 'let the luminous senses and the bright thoughts shine within us'. I look

Virginia Moffatt

around at their glowing faces and think that God has not brought me a boat, or a life jacket, but he has provided me with this. And for this brief moment, I believe it is enough.

James

I wake with a stiff neck, dry mouth and a headache. For a second I wonder where I am and then, as I open my eyes, see the deep blue sky fading into lighter blue, the stars slowly disappearing, I remember. The dread that lay dormant as I was talking to Nikki returns with the force of a tidal wave. Above me the gulls are already calling to each other, the choughs cry out in staccato. I pull myself down in sleeping bag. I do not want to wake to this day. When I went to sleep, I had my arm round Nikki but she has rolled away from me, leaving me alone with this panic and fear. What is it going to be like to drown? Will the force of the wave knock me unconscious or will I feel every moment, as water squeezes the breath out of my lungs? And after all this life, all this being, and acting, and doing, will there be anything to follow or will it just be blackness?

The roar of the sea interrupts my thoughts, reminding me of holidays in Cornwall when I was a kid. The mornings I would rise before dawn, and make my way down to the beach alone, so I could have the ocean to myself.

Sometimes I would paddle, make a sandcastle, but mainly I would sit, listening to the water crashing, the birds swooping ahead, sinking into sounds, the smell of salt air, the feel of grains of sand beneath me. Some days I would stay for a couple of hours like that, drawn into the landscape as if I was part of it. Remembering this, I feel calmer, and, as I hear a tent unzipping, I am able to raise my head, glance towards the camp to see Yan's bulky frame wandering down the beach.

It comes to me that I am alive now. For the first time in over a year I have a beautiful woman beside me. Someone who makes me feel safe, warm. I open my eyes and glance over to her. She is lying on her back, one arm on her stomach, the other flung to the left. I stare at her beautiful face, the finely shaped cheeks, smooth skin, and the strands of hair that have crept out from the top of the scarf. She will complain of sand and salt when she wakes. I prop myself up to appreciate her better. And then despite what is coming I know that right now, I am the luckiest man in the world. Nikki is wonderful and Lisa is a distant memory. I am torn between a desire to wake her to tell her how I feel and a wish not to disturb her peace. I decide the latter, watch her chest rise and fall, her breaths in concert with the waves. Time hangs suspended. There is no past to regret, or future to fear, it is just the two of us side by side. As the blue above me lightens, she wakes, looks straight back at me with her dark brown eyes.

'I was just dreaming of you,' she says and smiles.

I put my arms round her. 'Good,' and begin to kiss her. This time the kiss doesn't feel staged or awkward. She kisses me back. This time there is no hurry, there is no desperation. This time it feels right, natural, as if we fit together. We gradually undress each other, skin touching skin with electrifying caresses. As I slide into her, she is ready for me, and we move together as if our bodies have always known each other. Out of the corner of my eye, I am aware the sky is glowing red with the rising of the sun. I lose myself in the climax which I reach at the same time as her. We stay locked together until I am limp again and I roll off her.

'That was . . .' she says.

'Yes.'

'It almost makes me glad.'

'Almost,' I say and laugh, and then, because I don't want to think about that, snuggle back down with her. But Nikki doesn't seem to want to let the subject drop.

'I wonder how far away it is.'

'I don't want to talk about it.' Suddenly I feel angry. We have so little time, why must she spoil things by bringing it up? I want to pretend life is normal for as long as possible. That we have the rest of our lives to look forward to. I don't want to think about the volcano, the wave and what is to follow.

'Sorry . . .' Her face crumples. Oh God, I didn't mean to do that. But I can't bear thinking about the wave.

'No. *I'm* sorry. It's just . . .'

'I get it.' She squeezes my hand. Oh, she's lovely . . . I wish, I wish . . . I can't speak my wish out loud, so to distract myself, I check Facebook and immediately regret it.

'Fucking bastards!'

'What?' I show her comment after comment with foul abuse for me and even fouler for her, a lot of it deeply racist. 'Hold on a minute,' she says as she takes the phone off me. 'This isn't just random. These idiots are all Lisa fans. Now why would they be contacting you? Has she said anything on Facebook?' We check, but the Lisa Lusk page hasn't been updated since the beginning of the week. There's nothing on Twitter, and it is not until we hit Instagram that we find them. I read Lisa's posts in disbelief. To the uninitiated it sounds as if I was responsible for the break-up.

'How can she?' I say. Nikki laughs. 'It's NOT funny, that woman left me a mess and now she's claiming that stupid song is about ME? It's nothing to do with me. She used to play a version of it when we were together. Back then, she said it was about her first boyfriend. Her One True Love. As she never ceased to remind me.'

'I didn't mean to laugh,' says Nikki, 'It's just . . . Reading her page and the comments. She's so self-involved. It's like she has to be in this drama and rewriting your history gives her all the attention she desires.'

She's right. And, her saying it removes the last bit of feeling I have for Lisa. All this time, I've wasted my energies on someone who never gave a toss about me. I delete all the comments, take another selfie of me and Nikki and post it. Underneath I write, 'In love for the first time in my life.' Nikki grabs my phone and writes a text. *Thanks for your concern, Lisa, we're fine. If you want to do anything to help, call off the racists.* I'm about to protest, and then I think she's right, which is when I know exactly what I want to do next.

'Marry me,' I say, as I press send.

'What took you so long?'

'I had to see if there were any other options first.' She kicks me in the shins and then kisses me. 'Of course.'

'We should do it on top of the cliffs.'

'Invite the others.'

'Yes.' While we have been talking Yan has started cooking breakfast. A scent of bacon wafts up the beach.

'Mmm, that smells good,' says Nikki. 'Let's go and eat.'

Even though it is pointless, I pick up the rubbish and carry it with the sleeping bags back to the campsite.

'Morning,' says Yan. He serves up crisp and salty bacon with crusty rolls as Shelley hands us thick dark tea.

We sit down by the campfire. She seems more cheerful, almost happy. Part of me thinks it is absurd that we are exchanging pleasantries and yet it is also strangely comforting that ordinariness can prevail. Poppy and Margaret run towards us, dripping wet, and red-faced with the cold.

'Nice dip?' I say when Margaret emerges.

'Cold, but refreshing,'

The minutes are passing too fast, yet we find time for a leisurely, enjoyable breakfast, and a solution to the abusers on Facebook. If you'd told me a week ago, I'd have been dancing to "Shake it Off" with a bunch of strangers, I wouldn't have believed you. Yet here I am joining in with enthusiasm and laughing with the rest as it comes to an end. It is nearly seven o'clock, our announcement cannot wait any longer.

'We're getting married,' we say as everyone squeals with delight and begins to plan. Their warmth and enthusiasm is infectious and I'm grinning inanely with the rest. The women whisk Nikki away, leaving me behind with Yan.

'Well done, mate,' he says for the second time as we watch the women walk up to the cliffs.

'Better sort some clothes out.' I enter the tent, rifle in my bag, and find a clean white shirt and chinos, lend Yan a pair of dark-blue trousers and a blue shirt. We shave and dress and make our way to the clifftop. The day is already warm. Yan insists we pose for photos, and then we walk to the rendezvous. It is there that Yan offers his ring to me. His father's ring, given to the sister who died. I'm speechless. It's such a generous gesture, and totally unexpected. I am pleased Yan is beside me, it occurs to me that if had he not told me about the beach, Nikki and I might never have happened. We might have stayed in the car, getting angrier and angrier at our lack of options. He may be the only choice, but I cannot think of a better best man.

The Wave

'Here comes the bride,' says Yan as the women make their way along the path towards us. Nikki is dressed in a plain lilac dress. She has flowers pinned into her loose flowing hair and is carrying a posy of yellow, white and purple. She looks stunning. She smiles as she reaches me.

'We haven't really rehearsed this,' I say, 'We'll say a few words and then declare ourselves married.'

'Sounds like a plan,' says Yan.

I take Nikki's hands, gaze into her eyes and see everything I have ever needed.

'Nikki, we have known each other such a short time, and yet I know I want to be with you always,' I take the ring from Yan, 'With this ring, I promise to love you always, take care of you always, now and for the rest of our lives.'

Nikki smiles at me. 'James. When I woke up yesterday, it was to the worst news imaginable. And yet, the moment we met, I felt that everything was going to work out. I feel safe with you, loved by you. I love you.' She puts the ring on my finger and I feel whole. 'With this ring, I promise to love you always, take care of you always, now and for the rest of our lives.'

'We now declare ourselves husband and wife,' we say in unison, kissing each other to an eruption of applause and a flurry of petals the others have gathered from cliff flowers. Poppy pulls out a bottle of wine and, though it is strange to be drinking at this time of the morning, I down my glass in one as I toast my new bride. I have all I need, now and for always. Let the sea do its worst.

Nikki

The sun is shining. The sky is blue. I am walking by the seashore with James. We are holding hands, letting our toes sink into soft sand as the warm water washes over us. Dowetha Cove is at its best, inviting, safe, happy. James leans down to me and kisses me, I kiss him back. The sea crashes behind us. The gulls fly overhead. The beginning of a perfect day . . .

. . . I open my eyes, wrapped in the warmth of my dream to see James's face gazing down on me. It is still dark but the sky above is shifting from indigo to pale blue.

'I was just dreaming of you,' I say.

'Good.' He moves in to kiss me, a firm kiss, not like the dream kiss, but real and strong. Now I am happy to move towards him, to slowly undress, to let him caress me. Unlike our thwarted attempt at lovemaking in the cave, this feels like the natural way to start the day. Soon he is inside me and we move together in a way that is easy and familiar. We roll over with James on top. In the sky above, I sense a bright glow from behind the cliff. James closes his eyes but I keep mine open, so the moment of climax is accompanied by the sight of the red sun rising above our heads. Shortly after, James rolls off me.

'That was . . .'

'Yes.'

'It almost makes me glad'

'Almost.'

He sits up. The dawn is beautiful, but I cannot hide from the fact the wave is coming. As James cuddles up to me again, it seems important to acknowledge it.

'I wonder how far away it is.'

'I don't want to talk about it.' James is uncharacteristically sharp and suddenly we are at odds. How did that happen? A moment ago we were united in body and soul. It shocks me how easy that sensation can vanish. We can't let that happen, not now.

'Sorry', I say, unable to hide my hurt. Another man would have missed it, but this is James. He is immediately apologetic and I see quickly that he just doesn't want to think about the wave right now. Which is understandable really. We don't speak for a moment and then he swears at his phone. His page is filled with nasty comments about us, some of the more unpleasant ones seem to be Lisa fans. She's has been using Instagram to suggest that she is the injured party in their break-up, suggesting that she's lost the love her life. When I read through her posts, I'm staggered by how self-centred she is. It's laughable really, even if it has created this tirade of abuse. The racism is foul –

though, to be honest, most of it is pretty unimaginative, and a lot of it no worse than I had at school – but the idea that he is cheating on her, when she left him ages ago, is simply hilarious. It is satisfying to get rid of the comments together and I particularly enjoy telling Lisa where to stick it.

'Marry me,' he says after we send the text. I gaze at his face, his beautiful face. I feel I have always known this face. The last twelve hours have been the most intense of my life, the most awful and the most wonderful. Even though everything is about to end, I love him and want to be with him.

'What took you so long?' I quip, enjoying his teasing me back. We kiss and kiss and laugh and laugh. I realize I have rarely felt this at ease with anyone.

I enjoy getting dressed with him, holding his hand as we walk to the campsite and join the others for breakfast and chat. I enjoy being a couple amidst these new friends who love and cherish us. And I enjoy dancing with him to 'Shake it Off' as we collectively tell the trolls what we think. Best of all I enjoy announcing the news that we want to get married, seeing the astonishment on people's faces, and then receiving their joyful congratulations. It occurs to me that we're not just doing this for ourselves. We all have something else to think of in this last hour.

There isn't much time, I grab my bag as the women sweep me up to the clubhouse. I find a lilac dress that has miraculously not creased and a red one for Shelley. She helps me comb through my hair, shaking out the sand as we sing, 'Shake it off, Shake it off!' at the top of our voices. She massages the roots with oil and does a great job too.

'How come you know how to do this?' I ask.

'Saturday job in a salon in Streatham. Good training for a white girl.'

'Thanks. You're better than my hairdresser.' Shelley doesn't say anything, but beams with pride. It is good to see her realising her talents. Even if . . . I don't follow that thought to its end, I want to keep this happy for as long as I can.

Margaret disappears to phone her daughter and find flowers. Poppy, meanwhile, has taken out her iPad and films us, so my parents will have a record of me applying make-up, trying different hair styles and putting on my dress. My hair has frizzed in the night, but I decide not to straighten it. I like my curls. Working in the chippie has meant keeping them up all summer. It feels liberating to let my hair down.

'You look gorgeous,' says Shelley.

'Thanks. I should have asked before, but will you be my bridesmaid? I have a little sister, but obviously she can't be here in person, so . . .'

Shelley looks like she is about to cry. 'I'd love to. I always said I'd do it for Alison. I feel awful that I can't. Thank you so much.'

We hug, just as Margaret returns with a bunch of yellow, white and lilac flowers. She slides some of the lilac ones in side combs which I put in my hair and makes two neat posies of the rest. I stare at myself in the mirror and am pleased with the result. I am ready to Skype my family. The four of them are sitting on the end of the double bed in the hotel, all wearing their smartest clothes.

'You look beautiful,' says Mum.

'So do you,' I say

'I wish we could be there,' says Dad.

'You are here, Dad.' He looks away to avoid me seeing his tears. I can see Mum squeezing his hand.

'How did you persuade this stupid man to marry you?' grins Ifechi.

'Through my charming and delightful personality,' I reply.

'Riiiiiight,' he says.

'Sod off,' I reply, but I appreciate his joshing. It helps keep the emotions at bay and knowing Ifechi, that's exactly why he's doing it.

'Is he good-looking?' says Ginika.

'Definitely. But he's also good, and kind, and thoughtful. Which counts for more. You'll be able to see for yourself in a minute.' Ginika smiles.

This is not how I imagined my wedding day to be, and yet I can't help feeling that this is the wedding day I've been preparing for all my life. Though I still wish I had left for Manchester in time, if I had, I would never have met James. And I know I'm glad that we did meet, glad that this is happening now, even in these circumstances.

It is time to go. I pass the iPad to Poppy who films Margaret giving us our bouquets as we form a bridal procession. The sun is shining and the sky is the brightest of blues. Joking and laughing we walk to the spot where James and I sat last night. Only a few hours ago I was so angry at him, at God, at the Universe I was almost prepared to walk in the water to escape him. And yet now, as I reach him and see his soft and funny face, I cannot imagine him not being in my life ever again.

'Here comes the bride,' says Yan, passing Margaret's ring to Shelley

James takes my hands, gazes into my eyes and I see everything I have ever needed.

'Nikki, we have known each other such a short time, and yet I know I want to be with you always,' He takes the ring from Yan, 'With this ring, I promise to love you always, take care of you always, now and for the rest of our lives.'

I smile at him, 'James. When I woke up yesterday, it was to the worst news imaginable. And yet, the moment we met, I felt that everything was going to work out. I feel safe with you, loved by you. I thank God for you. I love you, too.' I take the ring from Shelley and put it on his finger, 'With this ring, in front of God, our family and friends, I promise to love you always, take care of you always, now and for the rest of our lives.'

We kiss. The others shout in celebration. They throw petals over us. I can hear my family clapping in the background. We raise glasses to them and switch Skype off, so Poppy can quickly send the film to them and James's family.

'Congratulations, Mrs Davies,' says James, giving me another kiss.

'Congratulations, Mr Akinwe,' I say, laughing, kissing him back.

'How about Davies-Akinwe?'

'Or Akinwe-Davies?'

'Davkins?'

'Akinavies?'

'Vieskin?'

'Inweda?'

'This could go on a bit . . .'

'Stick to our own names?' He smiles. I think, but don't say, *what about the children*? It is too sad to acknowledge that children will never be part of us and I want to be happy now. Instead, I draw him to me, sinking into another long and satisfying kiss. The perfect start to an almost perfect day.

Harry

When I wake up, the first thing I notice is that my neck is stiff, my arms are aching. The second is that I have dribbled all over the steering wheel. Fuck. I fumble for a tissue, so I can clean it and then realize the third thing. Dawn is approaching. The sky is no longer dark but pure blue and getting lighter all the time. Fuck, I have slept too long. I check the time. It is past five o'clock. The wave is on its way and I have to get to the beach. Sorry Shells, but I won't be able to come and get you after all.

I sit up, swig water, rev the engine and put my foot down on the accelerator. Normally I'd be taking these corners at ninety miles an hour, but with the burden of the trailer swinging behind me, I manage sixty at most. I swing into St Ives. The town is deserted. I drive towards the wharf, the trailer rattling behind me. The sea is still a way out. I'll have to drive down the slipway and onto the beach. It's going to ruin the chassis, but since the car's going to be destroyed anyway, needs must.

The sand is soft and I have to keep moving to avoid the

wheels sinking. I drive to the edge of the sea, turn the car round so the trailer is fully in the water. My hands are shaking as I unhook it. I have time, I know I have time, and yet part of me is afraid that I have left it too late. I push the trailer but it is more of an effort than I could have imagined. I am tired and it dawns on me that I don't have the strength to do this alone. Fuck. Why didn't Shelley come with me? Why couldn't I persuade her? Just as I'm thinking I could really do with her help, I receive a text from her. *How dare you tell people about Margaret? What a foul thing to do. Unforgivable. Fuck you.* Well, fuck you, Shelley, I'm glad I've run out of time to get you. I check my watch again, five forty-five. I have just over two hours. The sun will be up soon but I can still make it. All I have to do is get this boat in the water. Simple enough outcome, but how? How?

Of course . . . The car. The bloody car. I can use it to push the trailer further into the water and if I untie the chains the boat will just float off. Pleased with my ingenuity, I get back into the driver's seat and start the motor. It works like a charm. The boat floats out, just as I'd hoped. I put the brakes on, jump out, grabbing the tow rope just in time before it drifts away and takes my only hope of escape. I tie it down to the inside handle of the front door, the water splashing my calves. I walk over to the boot to collect my suitcase. Shelley's bags are still in there too. Seeing them, I almost relent of my decision not to go back for her, but I know deep down I've run out of time. I wonder whether I should take the case with me, in some vain hope that she might escape by some other means. I think of her face when we meet up again and I've left her best clothes behind. It is not worth the aggro, so I pick up both and throw them on board. I make one more trip back to the car to get the food and drink and my wallet. I can't be without my wallet. I check my watch again. Six o'clock. I have time; I must leave now, but I have time. I have survived so many things in my life; know I will survive this.

I pull myself onto the boat and am about to start the engine when I spot my mistake. I roll my trousers up, jump into the sea and wade back the car to untie the rope. The boat is bobbing in the water and it is hard to hold it steady but I manage to clamber back on board, sweating and out of breath. I am wet and tired but ready to move out. I text Shelley, just in case she's thinking I might come for her. *Only just got in the water. I'm sorry. I can't get to you in time.* I am. I truly am. I wish I could save her but I can't. Haven't I always told her it's a dog-eat-dog world, survival of the fittest? She is not the first person I have had to leave behind. Though I expect she's the one I'll regret. If she'd only believed in me, she would've been here with me now. If only . . .

I turn the ignition. I have never driven a boat before. I'd hoped it would be like driving a car, but it is not as easy as I thought it would be. It takes a while to locate the manufacturer's instructions of how to work the outboard motor. And then, when I do, it takes longer than I'd imagined to steady it over the waves that are stronger as I begin to move away from the slope. It takes me a full ten minutes to navigate to the end of quay, past the wall. A further twenty to get out of the bay and on to open water where I am faced with a new challenge. The waves are so high, water is splashing in. I try to remember if I have read anything about driving a motorboat. Wasn't there something in GQ once? I stop the motor for a minute and consult my phone. Sure enough, I locate the article which advises riding at an angle. It takes a few miles before I have mastered the rhythm of the rise and fall of the waves: up, and down, up and down, each up seeming steeper than the last, each descent a lurch in body and stomach. I am conscious of the sun creeping up through the sky. I have no desire for it to rise any higher. If it rises much higher I will know that I have failed and I am sure I have time to succeed. I will win as I always do. I must stop thinking about the sun and focus on this one single thought: every mile is taking me further north to safety.

There is no map on the boat and it's too old for GPS. I have no idea how far I have travelled, and it is just my luck the speedometer is broken. I have no idea how fast I am going. Only that I have been in the water for an hour, the sun is rising in the sky and there is an hour to go. I have the engine at full throttle, but the waves are choppy in the middle of the sea, so I move closer to the coast. I pass villages and bays. I have a feeling that once I am around that big headland, I may be nearly in Devon and safety, but I am not sure. It is just crossing my mind that I might not be sure until eight o'clock when the wave is due, when there is a bump, a shudder, a scream of metal, and the boat comes to an abrupt halt. The engine is still running but when I try to move forward nothing happens. I turn it into reverse, and push backwards; still nothing. It is then that I spot water on the bottom of the boat, the rock pushing through the whole in the floor. Fuck. I've run aground. I look around for a bucket, a container, anything, but there is nothing. I try to empty the water with my bare hands, but it is no good. The sea is forcing its way through the cracks and the boat is sinking. I am a few hundred yards off land. I grab the lifebelt and throw myself into the water. Even with the lifebelt, it is a struggle to get to the shore, but I make it eventually, throwing myself against the rocks. I look at my watch again. I have half an hour left. The cliffs above me are smooth – there is no way to climb up them and there is sea to the right and left. This is my final destination. I have run as far as I can, and it is not far enough. The wave is coming for me after all. I cannot escape its path. I scream and bang the stones in fury. After all my efforts, I might as well have stayed on that damned beach.

I stop shouting eventually, because, really what's the point? There is nothing I can do. I have nothing left to do except say goodbye to the only two people I really care about. I cannot face ringing Val and, anyway, she'll be at her cleaning job, where she's not allowed a phone. I send her a text telling her what's happened, that I love her. I wish I could hear her voice one more time but she won't see this till it's too late. It's probably better that way.

My second text is for Shelley. *I've crashed. I'm in the same boat as you. Ha Ha. Love and miss you. Hx*. I still think I was right to try, but part of me wishes I was back there with her. It would be a damned sight more comfortable than this clifftop. My phone beeps. It is Shelley. *Shit. Sorry to hear that. I recorded a song. Download it and think of me, won't you? Take care x.* She hasn't said she loves me, but perhaps she doesn't anymore. It doesn't matter now. I'll never see her again not in person. All I have is the video. There she is, with a guitar, standing on a cliff, looking every inch a singer. And then she sings and her voice is high and clear and beautiful. The song is sad, and true. The water *is* too wide, I cannot get over it, nor can she. We are lost to each other, and I am lost to the world. And yet, when the song comes to an end, I want to play it again. I sit with my back to the cliff, gazing to sea, listening to her over and over again. I wish I had wings to fly, but that is impossible. The words offer no comfort, and yet the song is soothing in a way. I close my eyes, let the sun warm me, try to pretend I am safe, rescued . . . Miles from here.

Shelley

I was so caught up in making the video and seeing Dad and Alison's reaction that I missed Harry's text. I only noticed it when I checked my phone at breakfast. And even then I was still so happy they were proud of me and so pleased that they thought it was a good idea that I didn't let it bother me at first. I told myself I'd blown my bridges when I decided to stay here, and made it certain with my angry text about Margaret. But when I sat down with my bacon buttie, it dawned on me that this was my last meal. The anxiety I'd been pushing aside rushed back, because after this there was nothing much else to do today but drown. What made it worse was the realisation that I could have got away if I'd done things differently. If I'd not rowed with Harry, if I'd held it together for just that little bit longer, I would be with him, wherever he was, on the open water. Much as I have grown to love my new friends in the last twelve hours, I have given up my one chance of escape for a bit of personal growth that I could have achieved when I was safely back in London.

I try my best to join in the chat about previous camping trips we've taken. I even dredge up a story of a rainy trip to the Lake District with Dad and Alison. I make them laugh with my account of the mud in the campsite, how our tent nearly collapsed and how, in the end, we left at three in the morning, driving all night to get home to our warm beds. Throughout it all, I can feel the panic and dismay bubbling just underneath the surface. Fear at what is about to come, and despair that I have made such a mess of my life; I am dying needlessly because I chose the wrong moment to face up to leaving my boyfriend. I don't know how the others can be so calm; perhaps it's because they know there's nothing they could have done about their situation, or maybe they're just better at hiding it. Though I have a secret hope that perhaps Harry was kidding or trying not to raise my expectations and is actually on his way here right now, I know this is just wishful thinking. I know he means what he says. I can picture him now, standing proud at the wheel of the boat, speeding to safety, without a care in the world, leaving me behind to die. I can imagine this becoming one of Harry's stories of survival, how he regretted he couldn't persuade me, but short of kidnapping me and putting me in the boot he couldn't make me come, could he? And once he'd discovered he didn't have time to come back to me, he had no choice, did he? He'll make quite a tale of it, I'm sure, and my part will become more stupid and stubborn, his more heroic. He'll pull a few women on that one, I'm sure. Meanwhile, I'm about to die.

The terror is so overwhelming that I lose the thread of the conversation. It is only when Poppy mentions trolls that I sit up and pay attention. I knew about Margaret, but now it appears James and Nikki have been victims of it too.

'What do you suggest?' says James.

'A statement and a joke.'

'How about we all sing "Shake it Off"?' says Nikki.

'"Shake it Off"?' Margaret asks.

I show her the video and soon we are filming each other each other in stupid poses as we scream the words to the sound of Taylor's sick beat. When the song finishes we laugh hysterically. It's a welcome relief.

Even better, Nikki and James announce they are getting married, and now we have something good and lovely to think about. Now I am up with the women at the surfer's hut, helping Nikki with her make-up, nails and hair. Margaret has gone in search of flowers, while Poppy is filming everything for Nikki's parents.

'I've never helped a bride out before,' I say as I take the comb gently through Nikki's hair, untangling the knots, and then massaging it.

'How come you know how to do this?'

'Saturday job in a salon in Streatham. Good training for a white girl.'

'Thanks. You're better than my hairdresser.' I blush. It's nice of her to say so. I don't think I've ever been with people who've been so nice to me outside my family. I wish I'd found people like this to hang around with sooner.

'You look gorgeous,' I say, as I finish coming out her hair. She has decided to let it be natural and it suits her.

'Thanks.' Nikki smiles. 'I should have asked before, but will you be my bridesmaid? I have a little sister, but obviously she can't be here in person, so . . .'

That is so lovely, I almost burst into tears. 'I'd love to. I always said I'd do it for Alison. I feel awful that I can't. Thank you so much.' I give her a hug. Poor Alison, if she ever gets married, she'll have to do this alone. It doesn't seem right.

Margaret returns, her hands full of flowers. She puts some in side combs for Nikki and then makes the others into posies for the pair of us. All of a sudden, I am taken back to a rainy afternoon in childhood, sometime before Mum died, when Alison and I were playing 'Here comes the bride'. We made paper bouquets and she dressed herself in her communion dress and veil. I walked behind throwing tissue paper as pretend confetti. We got into trouble later for the mess, but at the time it was so much fun. We always talked about being there for each other on our wedding days. It seems so wrong that I won't be. I have to call her to let her know I'm thinking of her.

'How are you doing?' she says, her voice is a little teary

'Getting ready for a wedding.'

'Really?'

'Really. Nikki and James. They met yesterday.'

'A bit quick, isn't it?'

'Nothing to lose.'

'I suppose not.'

'Listen, don't get Dad, I'll call you both again later. I just wanted to say that I'm sorry I won't be here to do this for you. At your wedding.'

'Oh, Shells . . .'

'Sorry, too, that I've been such an awful little sister. Pretending I didn't know you at school, refusing to do my homework, winding you and Dad up.'

'Takes two, hon. Sorry I was so uptight. It was just hard moving south, after Mum died. Like I had to be the responsible one all the time. I think I overdid it, sometimes.'

'You did,' I say and laugh. 'Sometimes . . . Anyway, just wanted to say, pax?'

It is Alison's turn to laugh, the old signal for making up after a fight, 'Pax.'

'I'll send you some photos of the wedding preparations and the service. When it's your turn, you can photoshop me into your pictures.'

'You're a daft mare.'

'I know. Speak later.'

I hang up, take the red dress Nikki has lent me, and pull it over my head. I pull the belt tight and brush my hair. I leave it loose and flowing; like Nikki I don't want to be hampered with a fussy hairstyle.

The others are ready, and we make our way out of the car park towards the men standing on the cliffs. James's face breaks into a smile as he sees Nikki coming towards him. What it must be to feel loved like that? Harry never looked at me that way. Although part of me envies the two of them for being able to get married like this, watching them together makes me sure I was right to leave him. I never loved him the way I can see Nikki does James. And he never loved me that way either. We were just two people sharing a flat who fancied each other for a while. I should have stayed with him long enough to get out of here alive, but there's no point having regrets now. I have made my choice and right now it is good to be here.

James and Nikki make their vows under a blazing sun. It is already warm, even though it only 7.30. We cheer, shower them with petals we plucked from the cliff, and raise glasses to life and happiness. Wine early in the morning is a bit rancid, but it seems important to go the full hog, and watching Nikki and James smiling, kissing, touching each other, I raise my glass with pleasure.

My phone buzzes. It's a message from Harry. It is not the good news I expected. *I've crashed. I'm in the same boat as you. Ha Ha. Love and miss you. Hx.* God, poor Harry. After all that effort, he deserved to get away. Fuck. I've made the right choice after all. While he is stuck on his own, I am, surrounded by friends celebrating. Poor Harry. All my anger disappears, No-one should die alone like that. I send him the video of my song. It's not his kind of music, but maybe he'll find it comforting now. Even though we have broken up, I still feel for him. I don't want him to suffer. He's all alone and here I am, surrounded by love. I raise a glass to him silently, hoping he's not feeling too awful.

Yan wanders up to me.

'You know it's tradition for the best man to get off with the bridesmaid, don't you?'

'You wish.'

'You know I'm kidding, right.'

'Of course.' I smile, 'I like that you can kid with me.' He beams.

There isn't long to go now. Our lives are hanging on a thread, and yet, as I stare from face to face, seeing the way Nikki and James have let their happiness infect us, it feels good to be here. We are alive for such a short period, and my life has turned out to be shorter than most, but it hasn't been a total waste. I wish I'd done more – travelled, studied, had a decent relationship, been kinder to my family. I wish I'd done less – wasting time with Harry, all those years trying to be more grown up than I was, worried about stupid things like how popular I was at school. But I can't do anything about it now. I am terrified of what is about to happen. I do not want to leave this world, with all its beauty and its pain, but I know I cannot do anything about it now. And since I do have to leave before my time, I am glad that I have had this small consolation, to go out in style, in splendour and, in love.

Instagram

Image of a heart and two fingers in the peace sign.

LisaLuskOfficial *Hey guys. Some of you have been a little overzealous on my behalf. It's not cool, guys. Leave James and his girlfriend alone. Things don't always work the way you want. That's life. And they're about to die. So respect that. Love and Peace. Always*

WonderWoman 2018 *Lisa you're so good. Always thinking of others.*

AllieSmith4 *Yeah, Lisa. Love you*

Jenny5001 *I wouldn't forgive them. That's what makes you special Lisa!*

LisaLuskOfficial *Oh, you guys.*

Facebook
Dowetha Live

A message from us all.

Thank you for all the kind thoughts expressed on this

page tonight. We've appreciated the love. Sadly, we've had to disable comments due to the uninformed opinions of a few idiots. For the record. None of us blame Margaret for what happened. Nor should you.

Nikki and James getting together is the best thing that has happened to all of us. We know most of you agree and we're glad to announce they have just got married. We'll post pictures below. We're happy. They're happy. So should you be.

And for anyone who doesn't love love, and anyone who's wasted their venom on us, here's a message for you. (link to video 'Shake it Off')

Love, peace and heartfelt thanks,

Poppy, Yan, Margaret, James, Nikki and Shelley xxx

PS Please look out for Shelley's video 'The Water is Wide' and support the campaign to raise funds for the clear up after we are gone. xxx

PRAYERS FOR THE DEAD

Poppy

The wedding is over. The happy couple are using my iPad to talk to their parents, the others have separated, each going to speak to their loved ones for one final time. I envy them. All of them. I have spoken to my friends during the night, of course I have. But there is nobody now that is desperate for my call, and though my friends will be sorry, none of them will be as devastated as Margaret's daughter, or Shelley's family. It occurs to me that, right at this moment, the five people on the clifftop are the closest friends I have in the world. I don't know whether to be sad or happy that this is the case, but as Seren would say if she was here, I only have myself to blame.

Seren. Will she give me a second thought after tomorrow? Will she speak about me her to friends as the person who committed the unforgivable crime? Or the person who had good in her, despite her failings? I will never know. Perhaps I don't deserve to either. There's no use brooding, though. What's done is done, and I can't be sure, even knowing what I do now, that faced with the same choice, I wouldn't do the same thing again. And now I am so close to the end, I can admit to myself the truth that I could never share, even when I was trying to be honest with her. It wasn't just lack of money, my parents' dying that motivated me, though that was part of it. Sitting here, with only myself to answer to, I have to admit that I enjoyed it. The secrecy, the power it gave me over people, the way my employers valued my work. I regret it, not because it was wrong, but because I lost Seren. I have to admit it: I enjoyed it while it was happening, whatever I said to her. I enjoyed it. I *would* probably do it again.

The wind ruffles my hair and I am reminded of the moment I came to the beach yesterday, wondering if anyone would come. At least I can say I made this happen. At least, I did this good thing too.

James and Nikki have finished their Skype call; they hand me back the iPad and leave me to compose one final post. I scroll through the messages, too many to respond to, and then, seeing the time, begin to type as fast as I can. I'm not even sure why, really, just that I need to leave something of myself in the world before I leave it. And that every moment I type can stop me thinking about the terror that is to come.

I am so absorbed in my typing, the others have to shout three times to get my attention. When I look up, the water is looming, a huge moving blue wall topped with frothing white foam. I jump up, and seeing the fear in everyone's faces, throw my arms out, 'Group hug.' It's silly but it works. We all laugh, and then gradually peel away, holding hands in the face of the oncoming water. 'If you exist God, make it quick,' I think. 'For all our sakes, let this be over quickly. If you exist, at least, God, give us that.'

Yan

Everyone has broken apart. No one has said it, but we have less than twenty minutes. Instinctively, we are reaching for phones for one last conversation. I wander down the path so that I am out of earshot, and take my phone from out of my pocket. I stare at the screen; should I or shouldn't I? What have I got left to say to her? Or her to me? And then, an image of Karo flashes into my mind. Karo in happier times, running along a cliff like this, stretching out her arms, declaring she wanted to live for ever. It was just before the end of the summer holidays. She was about to return to Oxford, to her golden life of academic success, rich with possibility, and I remember how I envied her the chances she would have. But then I remember too, how later that day, in the pub, she became more serious.

'If this is the last time I see you,' she'd said, 'I'm glad we've had such a lovely time. I'm glad I've got such a lovely brother.' I'd laughed it off at the time, and forgotten about it until the morning she died, when I understood that it

343

was the last day she seemed truly happy, truly free. I'd needed that picture of her to blot out the bad pictures that followed: Karo ringing at midnight sobbing because no one liked her; Karo refusing to believe she was any good because she hadn't got a first in her end of term exams. And near the end, monosyllabic on the phone and unwilling to see anything positive about her life. It occurs to me that I don't want to leave Mum with an image like that. I owe her this phone call.

'Mum, it's me. Yan.'

'I've been to church. Father Piotr and I prayed. We prayed so hard for you Yan.'

'Thank you. I just wanted to ring to say . . .' I stop. To say what? 'That I'm fine. I'm scared. But I'm with good people. And my friends have just got married.'

'Where?'

'On the clifftop.'

'Without a priest?'

'Not many to hand, Mum . . . I'm sure God won't mind.'

She mutters something incomprehensible, and then, 'Better marry than burn.' I smile wryly, that's an endorsement of sorts . . .

'I haven't got long.'

'It is kind of you to call. You've always been a good son to me.'

I hadn't expected that. Tears prick my eyes. I gaze at the horizon. The water has retreated, the seabed exposed for miles. I turn back towards the clifftop, where I can see

Margaret walking towards the newlyweds. 'I have to go, Mum. Take care. And . . . I love you.'

'Yes, of course.' She sounds like she might be crying. 'Tell Karo for me . . . tell her I'm sorry. She was a good girl.'

Now I am crying too, I don't care that anyone can see or that she can hear it. 'I will, Mum. Goodbye.'

'We'll meet in heaven.' I doubt it but I won't argue now.

'Goodbye.' I hang up, and join the others. After we have hugged, I grab Margaret's hand on one side and Poppy's on the other. Funny how, yesterday the thought of Poppy had filled me with so much desire. Now, I am just glad to have a friend to hold on to. Margaret is praying the Our Father. Whether it is the habit of childhood, or some need to reach out beyond me, I find that I am joining in, and for the first time in years, the words comfort. Margaret's hand is strong like a mother's and when I see the wave rushing towards across the sea, the squeeze reassures me. I close my eyes. I am on a beach, a long, long time ago. And I feel arms around me. The arms of my mother, lifting me to safety.

Margaret

The exuberance of the wedding lasts long enough for everyone to toast the happy couple with the remains of the white wine, warm from sitting in the sun. There are photographs of Nikki and James, Nikki and Shelley, James and Yan, then a kerfuffle with cameras as we pose on benches to take an automatic picture so everyone can get in. There are jokes about not standing too close to the edge. Laughter when a seagull flies into Poppy

And then, gradually, the laughter quietens and we begin to separate as, instinctively, we sense the time has come to make final goodbyes. I ask Poppy to send a couple of pictures which I text to Hellie, saying, 'Look at us!' Then it is time to pick up the phone. I put the number in slowly, as if by doing so I can stop time altogether.

'Hi, Hellie.'

'Hi, Mum. I've got someone for you . . .' She shuffles with the phone. 'Gramma,' Toby says. Margaret smiles. 'Hello, Toby.' He says nothing for a minute, then 'Bye, Gramma' and he is gone. Hellie returns.

'Give him a hug for me and tell him thank you.'

'I don't know what to say.'

'Listen, then. I love you. I'm proud of you. You're a great teacher, a good friend, wife, mother. Enjoy the life you have. Remember to be kind. Remember I've had a good life. It's ended sooner than I hoped, but it has been a good life. Kath has your details. She'll be in touch.'

'I'm glad you've made up.'

"We've done as best as we could. Tell her I'm so sorry, that I always missed her . . .' I pause, as I notice the beach; the sea has withdrawn exposing mudflats and rocks for miles. 'I have to go.'

'Mum!' Hellie cannot stop crying. This is too much.

'I love you.'

'I love you too, Mum.' In the background I can hear Toby calling, 'Mummy!'

'I think someone needs you.'

'I can't . . .'

'Then I will.' With a final goodbye, I cut the call off. Shelley calls out to me and when Poppy joins us we gather together for one final hug. We break apart. Poppy takes Yan's hand, I take the other one and Shelley's, who grabs James whose other arm is round Nikki. We stand hand in hand, gazing out to sea. Twenty years ago, I stood on a cliff near here, watching the shadow of the eclipse race across the ocean towards me, feeling like I was watching the end of the world. This time, as the water froths and rises rushing towards us, it really is.

Death is coming. I am lucky I can look it in the eye. And now I know there is really nothing I can do, a calmness spreads over me. I squeeze Shelley and Yan's hands and begin to pray. 'Our Father, who art in heaven, hallowed be thy name . . .'

This then, is to be the hour of my death. Let it come. I am ready.

James

After the service and the pictures are done, we take Poppy's iPad and sit on a bench setting up a joint Skype call with our parents. Nikki's family answer first. The four of them are sitting on the bed. Achebe, Nikki's mum, speaks while we are waiting for my parents to pick up in Lusaka. Nikki introduces me and they all smile. 'Welcome to the family,' Issa says a with carefully controlled calmness. 'We are very happy for you,' agrees Achebe. 'Rather you than me,' says Ifechi, while Ginika manages a shy 'Hello.' Behind their smiles I can see their eyes are afraid so I am glad that my parents pick up. They are huddled together at their kitchen table, forced grins on their faces. We introduce everyone and there is a flurry of congratulations followed by an awkward silence.

'It was a lovely ceremony,' says Achebe presently.

'Lovely,' says Jill. The others nod and then fall silent again. This is disastrous. I am about to hang up when, somehow, Nikki manages to salvage it.

'Mum and Dad, did you know Jill and Stu live in Lusaka?'

'Do you? We honeymooned at Victoria Falls,' says Achebe

'We met in Lagos!' cries Jill excitedly. And soon they are off, discussing the differences between East and South African cooking, why Nigeria has more renowned novelists than Zambia, and how post-colonial politics has shaped Africa. I grin at Nikki. 'Look what you've started.' And then my smile falters, because this is a conversation we should be part of, but once the call ends, we never will. It is hard to accept that I will never bring Nikki to sit in my parents' kitchen, never meet Achebe and Issa in the flesh, or befriend her siblings. That our parents will go on living without us, that we will not produce grandchildren or care for them as they get older. It isn't right. Or fair. When it comes to say goodbye, I grab Nikki's hand and squeeze it tight, turning my face away so as not to see the tears in everybody's eyes. We hand the iPad back to Poppy who sits down on the bench and begins to type furiously.

'Dance with me,' I say to Nikki, my wife, my beautiful wife, as we walk a little distance away from the others, to the cliff edge.

I pull her towards me, surprised to find my legs are shaking. Holding her calms me. I sing to her softly, closing my eyes, trying to enjoy the warm sun, the breeze, the murmur of the sea below. When the dance ends, I sigh. She says nothing, but I know she feels it too.

'I've had a thought,' she says. 'I don't want to be apart from you. We should link ourselves together.'

'Good idea.' She takes the sash from her dress and loops it through my belt hooks, tying it tight with a reef not.

'There,' she says, 'you can't get rid of me now. And then, in a softer voice, 'Look.' Below us the sea is rushing back down the beach, beyond the low tide mark and off into the distance. 'I suppose it was too much to ask.' I nod and hold her closer. The others join us for one last hug, taking each other by the hand. I hold onto Shelley on one side and put my arm round Nikki. She leans into me. The wave is coming for us, and I am terrified. Yet still I am glad to be here, by her side.

Nikki

It is James's idea to speak to our famiiles after the wedding. I think it is a good one, but when we connect with my side, all of us making an effort to be light, all I can think of is the distance between us. The gulf between life and death separates us: there is no way we can cross. When James's parents join the call, it feels even worse; every attempt to speak is drowned out by the unspoken sorrow that is too hard for any of us to express. After Jill's comment about the flowers, no one speaks for several minutes, we can hardly bear to look at each other, but nor can we bear to hang up. *Come on, somebody speak . . .* I avoid Jill and Stu's eyes, and gaze at the wall behind them, taking in the pictures, and wall hangings, trying to gain a sense of who they are. In the far corner, I spot a tapestry of elephants and giraffes, laid out in red, black, brown and white. It reminds me of a similar picture in my grandparents' home, and I realise that both couples have more in common than we do. To my relief, when I mention that Jill and Stu live in Zambia, Mum and Dad are quick to respond. Soon they are chatting about books and politics and, for a brief moment, no one has a care in the world.

James squeezes my hand in appreciation, gripping it tighter as the call comes to its inevitable end. Our faces are wet as we hand the iPad back to Poppy and walk towards the edge of the cliff.

'Dance with me,' he says, our first, our only dance, as a married couple. I lean into him, as he softly sings about forgetting the world. If only I could, if only we could . . . The dance is over, and I have railed against the unfairness of it all, I know I don't want to be parted from him, so I tie myself to him with my sash. When I am done, I see the sea retreating and I know there is nothing I can do. I shout to the others. Margaret responds first, she points out the horizon where we can see the water rising, rising, rising, into a large blue mass topped with foam white breakers. Yan follows, then Shelley, who is clutching her phone and seems to be talking to someone. Poppy is still typing, but at last she puts it down and races towards Yan. 'Group hug!' she yells, and though it is cheesy it breaks the terror as we come together before breaking apart and standing hand in hand facing the sea. No one speaks. What is there left to say? James puts his arm around me and I half turn to him. My chest is pounding, my hands sweaty. Shelley takes his other hand, while Margaret on her other side begins to say the 'Our Father'. I join in, finding the familiar prayer calming. There is nothing I can do to stop it, nothing

I can do to survive. I am glad to be with James, but in the end, we are all alone here, as we stand together waiting for the wave to break.

Harry

Ilisten to Shelley sing over and over again. I always used
to take the mick out of her dad's folk singing, we both
did. I thought she agreed with me that it was lame. I'd no
idea she had it in her. It isn't my kind of music but I'm
surprised how much it affects me. It makes me feel sad,
lonely, lost and loved all at once. I had no idea she could
do that. Nor that it would make her so happy. I can't
remember when I last saw her smile the way she is smiling
in the video. Why had she never told me she wanted to
sing? It almost makes me feel sorry that she never told me.
I'd have done anything for her. If she'd only said she wanted
to sing, I'd have made it happen, hired studios, found a
producer, got her an agent. But it's too bloody late now.
Besides, why should I feel sorry for her, when she refused
to come with me? If she'd been with me, none of this would
have happened. She'd have reminded me about the petrol,
made sure I didn't fall asleep, shouted at me before I got
to the rocks. It was her idea to stay on in Cornwall in the
first place. If she hadn't done that, I'd have finished my

meetings and we'd have been home by now, far away from all of this.

I switch off the phone and sit back against the rocks. The damp ground seeps into my trousers and the stones are sharp and dig into my skin – but so what? Very soon I'm hardly going to care about that. I hope when the wave comes, the force will be so strong it will knock me out straight away. Since I can't change what's about to happen, I will settle for over quickly. After what I've been through, I don't need my agony prolonged.

The water is wide . . .

Fuck it! Shelley's song has really got under my skin.

I cannot get o'er . . .

The words and music wash through me; suddenly I am drowning in memories of her. The night I first saw her in the club, entranced by her heady mix of innocence and worldliness. First thing in the morning, her hair tumbling over the pillow, before she'd tamed the curls into perfect straightness. Laughing at shared a joke in the pub. Making love early in the morning. I can't leave it like this. I send her a text. Nothing too heavy, but enough to prompt a response, I hope.

*Thanks for the music. It's brilliant. **You're** brilliant.*

She doesn't reply. I pull my knees up, bury my head in them and grip them tightly. Last time I felt this alone, I was ten years old, hiding in my cupboard, trying to make sure Dad didn't come anywhere near me. That time Val had come to my rescue; she can't save me now. No one can.

The Wave

The phone rings; it is Shelley. She doesn't say much, but it is enough to make me sob. Her voice is soothing and I am comforted by her suggestion to stay on the line. In the distance, I can see a column of water coming towards me. I stand up, clutching the phone to my ear. 'I love you,' I say. Her goodbye comes from a long way away. 'Goodbye,' I reply – and then the wave begins to break.

Shelley

After the 'I love you' from me to Dad, to Alison, and back again, there is nothing left to say. The silence hangs between us until there is no point keeping the line open. I hang up.

A seagull sweeps above my head – *awk, awk, awk* – and moves on out to sea. My stomach tightens. I take a deep breath, inhaling the fresh, salty air. The sky is the clearest I have ever seen it, a dazzling blue promise of the day to come. Even this early, I can feel the comforting warmth of the sun on my back, luring me into a false sense of hope that all will somehow, miraculously, be well.

My phone buzzes, a text from Harry, thanking me for the video; he thinks the song is brilliant. All my fury at him disappears. Poor Harry. Stuck on a rock with no one by his side. All he was trying to do was to survive, and it's admirable, in a way, that he refused to give up. It seems so unfair that it should all go to waste. That he will be swept away by the same wave that is coming for me, and that unlike me, he will be alone. I dial his number, after all our time together, I owe him this.

'Shells?' For once, I have managed to surprise him.

'I wanted to say . . . I don't know . . . that I'm sorry how things have turned out?'

'You should have come with me . . . it's been a hell of a ride.'

'I bet. Listen. You shouldn't be doing this by yourself. Keep your phone on, we'll do this together.' Harry doesn't reply. For a moment, I think he has hung up, but then I can hear that he is crying. My eyes fill with tears. If only I had had the courage to leave him before. We would have never come to Cornwall; instead, we would both be carrying on with our lives, watching on TV like the rest of the world. If only . . . if only . . . if only . . .

'We had some good times, didn't we, Shells?' Harry's voice sounds muffled, as if he's already underwater.

'Yes . . . Yes we did.' I switch on the loudspeaker and tuck the phone under my bra strap as Poppy pulls us in for a final hug. Ahead of us I can see the wall of water coming closer; it is racingup the beach. We all join hands and I grip onto Margaret and James tightly.

'I love you,' says Harry. I wonder if there is really a life after this as Margaret thinks. And if there is, whether I'll see him, or Mum there. Or if this is it, our final moment.

'Goodbye' I say. His response is drowned out as the wave hurtles towards us, hits the cliff edge and....

FACEBOOK
Poppy Armstrong.

30 August 7.50 a.m.

I thought I would have a lot to say in this final post, but now I am here, the words disappear as soon as they form in my mind. I used to think that my Facebook page was a way of making a permanent mark on the world, that if anything happened to me, at least my words and images would be here. A reminder to people of the person I was. But now I am less sure. Now I think it will fade and disappear, as I will, as everything does eventually. After all, aren't we just imprints in the sand?

I must go, but I find myself unable to move. I used to do this on the last day of the holidays, standing at the top of the beach, not daring to go down. Because once I put my first foot in the sand, it was an admission that everything was coming to an end. Today, I know that once I turn off my iPad, there is no going

365

back. I am not quite ready to make that walk yet.

So I remain here, trying not to imagine the wave that is coming, trying not to fall into the delusion that somehow, even now, we might escape it. Instead, I will try and make these last words count. I will try to be honest as I leave this world.

I did something terrible once, to someone I loved and then I ran away. There were circumstances that led to my deceit (mitigating ones if you're inclined to be nice, no excuse if you are not). But I did a wicked thing, and then I was ashamed, and I didn't know how to put it right. I thought one day I would find a way to repair the damage. But I left it till there was no time left, and though I have apologized, I left it too little, too late.

I did something terrible, but . . . I hope people will remember me for who I am now rather than the person I was a decade ago. It will be up to you all, of course. I'll have no say and I suppose it won't matter much to me.

Margaret and Nikki are sure, afterwards, we will all go to Heaven and be with their God. Though they cannot describe where that is, or what it would be like. I can't quite believe that, any more than I believe James' idea that once we are gone we will become as one with the air and linger on in spirit. I have never been much of a believer in anything, but I find myself, as I come to the end, having one last wish. Many of

The Wave

you have asked what you can do to help, and I have
said, nothing, your presence and thoughts are enough.
But now, as I steady myself to walk over to the others
I find myself wanting you to do one thing for me, for
us. For the next few minutes, for the next few days,
can you do this, one small thing, please?

Pray for us.

Acknowledgements

I am hugely grateful to the many people who have helped me bring *The Wave* to life.

There are three groups who have been particularly important:

For several years, I was a regular participant in #fridayflash an online writing community. Each week we would post short fiction on our blogs providing each other with valuable critique. *The Wave* was one such story. As usual, community members were supportive and encouraging in their responses and it was enough to make me think I had the beginnings of my next novel. Thanks to all of you who commented on this and other stories, you really helped me progress as a writer.

In November 2013, I signed up for National Novel Writing Month, in the hope that it would help get me going. To my surprise I ended the month with 50,000 (very bad) words in the bag. I highly recommend #nanowrimo as a way to kick-start a writing project (my third novel has begun life that way too) and am grateful to all those who make it happen.

I have been a member of the Cowley Consonants since 2006 during which time we have read and enjoyed many novels together. Thanks to all of you for reading mine and being such enthusiastic cheerleaders.

The following individuals have also been enormously helpful:

In 2015 I entered the opening chapter of *The Wave* in a Retreat West competition. Thank you, Amanda Saint, for putting me on the shortlist at a time when I was despairing of ever being published. Thanks also to Jo Unwin, the judge of that competition, who provided me with encouraging feedback which helped convince me the book was worth pursuing.

My twin sister, Julia Williams, is my first reader and always provides excellent insights. Thanks so much for your enthusiasm about *The Wave* and for being such a powerful advocate for the book.

Anne Booth is the friend every writer needs. Thank you so much for always being there for me and your constant support for me during the writing of this novel.

I am grateful also to Scott Pack for invaluable advice, and for generally being brilliant and to Xander Cansell and John Mitchinson for your kindness and understanding.

A book cannot come into being without a great editorial team. I am so lucky to have Kate Bradley as my editor for this book. Thank you so much for your warm and percep-

The Wave

tive appraisal, helpful challenge and for telling me when to stop. Thanks also to Charlotte Ledger for championing the novel, to Kati Nicholl for copyediting and the design team for the fabulous front cover.

Finally, an author is only able to be an author with the help of their family. I am so lucky with mine. To my children, Beth, Claire and Jonathan, thank you for putting up with me spending November 2013 glued to the computer and for frequent disappearances in the years that followed. And most of all to my husband, Chris, whose unfailing love, support and tolerance make it all possible.

ONE
MORE
CHAPTER

YOUR NEXT GOOD READ IS
JUST A PAGE AWAY...

JOIN THE BOOK CLUB &
FOLLOW US ON SOCIAL MEDIA!

@ONEMORECHAPTER
@ONEMORECHAPTER_
@ONEMORECHAPTERHC